Jeremy Fink and the Meaning of Life

Jeremy Fink and the Meaning of Life

wendy mass

LITTLE, BROWN AND COMPANY

New York ⋅ Boston

Also by Wendy Mass:
A Mango-Shaped Space
Leap Day

Little, Brown and Company

Hachette Book Group USA
1271 Avenue of the Americas, New York, NY 10020
Visit our Web site at www.lb-kids.com

First Edition: November 2006
The characters and events portrayed in this book are fictitious.
Any similarity to real persons, living or dead, is coincidental
and not intended by the author.

Library of Congress Cataloging-in-Publication Data

Mass, Wendy.
    Jeremy Fink and the meaning of life / by Wendy Mass. — 1st ed.
        p. cm.
        Summary: Just before his thirteenth birthday, Jeremy Fink receives a keyless locked box — set aside by
his father before his death five years earlier — that purportedly contains the meaning of life.
    ISBN-13: 978-0-316-05829-2 (hardcover)
    ISBN-10: 0-316-05829-7 (hardcover)
    [1. Conduct of life — Fiction.   2. Self-realization — Fiction.   3. Fathers and sons — Fiction.]   I. Title.
PZ7.M42355Jer 2007
[Fic] — dc22   2005037291

10   9   8   7   6   5   4   3   2   1

Q-FF

Printed in the United States of America

The text was set in Sabon.

Apple quote on page 157 by Ken Kesey
Universe quote on page 186 by JBS Haldene
Music quote on page 288 by Mickey Hart
A section in Chapter 12 originally appeared in similar form as "The Invisible Boy," Girls' Life, *Volume 8*
#5, April/May 2002.

The American Museum of Natural History as described in Chapter 13 is a fictionalized version. Scientific
material in that chapter is adapted from Bill Bryson's *A Short History of Nearly Everything* (New York:
Broadway, 2003).

*For Griffin and Chloe, who we've loved
from the second they entered the world screaming.*

*And for my family and friends who so generously shared their
insights on the meaning of life and helped me find my own.*

*A special thank you to Stu Levine, Hayley Haugen,
and Karen Parker for reading the pages
as fast as I could write them and for making
them better, and to my editor Amy Hsu,
for believing from the start.*

The creature has a purpose, and his eyes are bright with it.
—*John Keats*

Preface

July 22

My sweat smells like peanut butter.

Since I'm such a picky eater, my mother feeds me peanut butter sandwiches at every meal, including breakfast and midnight snacks. I have a lot of midnight snacks because I like to be awake when the rest of the world is asleep (except for the people in other time zones who might still be awake, but you couldn't prove it by me). So now when I sweat, it smells like peanut butter instead of B.O., which I don't think is such a bad thing. I'd rather smell like a school cafeteria than a school gym.

Right now my best friend, Lizzy, is sitting next to me, holding her nose. Not because of the peanut butter, which doesn't bother her anymore. The offending odor belongs to that special combination of soggy marshland and rotting fish that Mosley Lake in northwest New Jersey is famous for.

It is the middle of a long, hot summer, and I, Jeremy Fink, a city kid born and bred, am sitting on a big rock in the middle of the lake, which, while certainly smelly, is also very serene. The sky is a clear blue, a light breeze blows from the west, and pale green water sloshes against the side of the rickety old rowboat that brought us here.

On my lap I am balancing a smooth box made of light-colored wood, the size of a toaster. The box has the words THE MEANING OF LIFE carefully engraved across the top. Underneath, in smaller letters, it says, FOR JEREMY FINK TO OPEN ON HIS 13TH BIRTHDAY.

Today is my thirteenth birthday. I never would have guessed, when I was given the box a month ago, that those instructions would be so impossible to follow.

Lizzy keeps poking me on the arm, urging me to hurry up and do what we've come here to do. Yes, my best friend is a girl, and no, I don't secretly have a crush on her. Lizzy and her dad moved to the apartment next door when she and I were one year old. Her mother had left the family and moved to one of the Dakotas with some guy who worked on a cattle ranch (which explains why Lizzy became a vegetarian as soon as she was old enough to re-alize what a cattle ranch was). So Lizzy stayed with us during the day while her father went to work at the post office. My mom used to change our diapers next to each other. You can't get romantic with someone after that.

Also, Lizzy is a notorious troublemaker. She has a lot of opinions, usually negative. For example, she thinks my col-lection of mutant candy is gross. I think she's jealous because she didn't think of it first. Some of the best are a square Good & Plenty, a candy corn with an extra layer of white, and my pride and joy — a peanut M&M the size of my pinky finger. I bet I could get a fortune for that one on eBay.

Our journey to this rock started a long time ago — before I was even born. If my father had been allowed to spend *his* thirteenth birthday playing Little League with his friends instead of being dragged by his parents to Atlantic City, I wouldn't be sitting here, and the box wouldn't exist. Who ever would have imagined those two events would be linked?

All those years ago, while my grandmother was in a shop buying saltwater taffy, my father wandered down the boardwalk and wound up in front of an old palm reader. She picked up his clammy hand and held it up to her face. Then she let his arm fall onto the velvet-covered table and said, "You vil die ven you are forty years old." My grandmother arrived in time to hear the fortune-teller's declaration, and she yanked my dad away, refusing to pay. Whenever my father told the story, he laughed, so we laughed, too.

It turned out that the fortune-teller's prediction was wrong. My dad didn't die when he was forty. He was only thirty-nine. I had just turned eight. Dad must have taken the prophecy more seriously than he let on, because he prepared for his death, and this box proves it.

"What are you waiting for?" Lizzy yells into my ear.

Lizzy has her own way of talking. Usually she shouts. This is partly because her father is deaf in one ear from going to too many rock concerts when he was younger, and partly because she is on the shortish side and over-compensates.

I don't answer, and she sighs. Even her sighs are loud. The edges of the box are digging into my bare legs, so I move it to the towel that Lizzy has spread out on the rock between us. This box has come to symbolize all my hopes, all my failures. Before I do anything else, I need to go back over everything that has happened this summer: the Big Mistake, the old man, the book, the lamp, the telescope, and this box, which started it all.

Chapter 1: The Box

June 22

"Did you ever notice how the colors seem brighter the first day of summer vacation?" I ask Lizzy. "The birds sing louder? The air is alive with possibility?"

"Huh?" Lizzy mutters, fingering through the comic books on the wall of my Uncle Arthur's store, Fink's Comics and Magic. "Yeah, sure. Brighter, louder, alive."

It would bother some people if their best friend only half-listened to them, but I figure talking to Lizzy is one step better than talking to myself. At least this way people on the street don't stare at me.

Over the next two months I plan on learning a new magic trick or two, borrowing the eighth grade textbooks from the library to get a jump on my assignments (but not telling Lizzy, who would make fun of me), and sleeping as late as I want. This is going to be a summer of leisure, and smack in the middle, the state fair and my long-awaited thirteenth birthday. Usually I love going to the fair, but this year I actually have to enter one of the competitions, and I'm dreading it. At least my birthday comes the same week. I am so tired of being considered a "kid" and am eager to officially become a teenager. I will finally learn the secret code of Teendom.

I hope there's a handshake. I've always wanted to belong to a club with a secret handshake.

"Run!" Lizzy whispers sharply in my ear. Lizzy saying *run* in my ear can mean only one thing — she has stolen something. She is lucky my uncle and cousin Mitch are in the back room and didn't see her. They do not look kindly upon shoplifters.

By the time I manage to thrust my comic back on the shelf, she is halfway out the door. In her rush, she's knocked over my backpack, which I had propped up carefully on the floor between us. All the stuff flies out the unzipped top for the other shoppers to see. I grab the bag and quickly toss back in my dog-eared copy of *Time Travel for Dummies,* a half-eaten peanut butter sandwich, a pack of Starburst, two bite-sized Peppermint Patties, assorted magic tricks that I've collected over the years, the bottle of water that I always have on me because one can never be too hydrated, the astronaut pen that allows me to write in all conditions (including underwater and while lying on my back), and finally my wallet, which always has at least eight dollars in it because my dad once told me that if a man has eight dollars on him, he can always get home. Then I take back out one of the Peppermint Patties, quickly unwrap it, and stick in my mouth. I blame my dad for my sweet tooth. His motto was *Life is short; eat dessert first.* How can I argue with that?

Slinging the backpack over my shoulder, I slip out the door and look up and down the street for Lizzy. Her red hair makes her easy to spot. She's leaning against the window of Larry's Locks and Clocks, admiring her newest treasure — an orange flyer advertising the debut of a *Betty and Veronica* double issue. Only moments ago it had been taped up to the wall in the store.

"Can't you use your talents for good instead of evil?" I ask, swallowing the last of my Peppermint Pattie.

She doesn't answer, just folds the paper haphazardly and tucks it in her back pocket.

"Why, Lizzy?" I ask as we start walking down the block toward home. "Why?"

"Why what?" she asks, popping a piece of grape Bazooka in her mouth. She offers me one, but I shake my head. Grape and peppermint just don't mix.

"Why steal something that has no monetary value?"

"Would you rather I'd stolen something that *does* have monetary value?"

"Of course not."

"Well stop complaining then," she says. "You know I can't explain the reasons for the things I take. I don't choose them, they choose me."

"What about all the customers who won't learn about the new *Betty and Veronica* because of you?"

She shrugs. "Nobody reads Archie comics anymore."

It's true that the Archie comics are always the last ones left at the end of the month. Archie was my dad's favorite when he was a boy, so he always made sure to stock them. Uncle Arthur doesn't know enough about comics to tell the difference between *Mutant X-Men from Outer Space* and *Richie Rich*, so he keeps ordering all of them.

"That's not really the point," I tell her.

"It's not like you'll cry over your uncle losing a sale or two. You can't stand him, remember?"

"It's not that I can't stand him," I insist, crossing my arms. "You try having an uncle who ignores you and who is the identical twin of your dead father and see how you like it."

Lizzy is quiet now and entirely focused on picking the scab on her elbow. I shouldn't have said that, about my dad. When he died, Lizzy was almost as upset as I was. He was like her second parent. As upset as she was, though, she still slept on the floor of my room in her sleeping bag for three straight weeks until I could sleep through the night again.

We manage to reach our apartment building in Murray Hill without either of us further depressing the other and without Lizzy stealing anything else. One of our neighbors, Mr. Zoder, is slowly heading up the steps. It's Friday, so he's wearing yellow. My parents always said that New York City is full of characters, and that's why they wouldn't want to live anywhere else. We're about to follow him inside when our mailman, Nick, shows up wheeling his huge blue cart.

"Howdy, Nick," Lizzy says, saluting him.

"Well if it isn't Lizzy Muldoun and Jeremy Fink," he replies, tipping his hat. All the mailmen in the neighborhood know us because Lizzy's dad works at the post office.

"Let's see what I've got for you guys today." Nick reaches into his cart and lifts out a big cardboard box. To my surprise, it's addressed to Elaine Fink, with our address on it! I can't imagine what it could be, since Mom never buys anything through the mail. In fact, except for food and my clothes (which I insist have to be new, after a kid in my class told me I was wearing a sweater his mom had thrown out the week before), we don't own much of anything that wasn't from a flea market or found on the street on bulk trash day. It's not that we can't afford new things. Mom has a good job at the library. But she believes retail is for suckers and that recycling other people's belongings saves the environment somehow.

SO WHAT IS IN THAT BOX?

Nick is about to hand it to me when he hesitates and then sets it back in the cart. Instead, he hands me our regular assortment of bills and junk mail.

"Wait," I say after he hands Lizzy her mail. "What about that box? Isn't that for my mom?"

"Sure is," Nick replies. "But it's registered mail. That means it's gotta be signed for by an adult."

"But my mom's at work all day. I'm sure she won't mind if I sign for it."

"Jeremy is as tall as some adults," Lizzy states. "That should count for something."

Nick shakes his head. "Your mom can pick it up at the post office on her way to work tomorrow."

Not one to give up, Lizzy says, "That box looks heavy. You don't want to have to lug it around on the rest of your route, do you?"

Nick laughs. "It's not that heavy. I think I can manage." He starts to wheel his cart to the next building, and we keep pace with him.

"But Nick," I plead, "tomorrow's Saturday and our branch of the post office is closed. My mom wouldn't be able to get the box until Monday. If it's special delivery, maybe that means it's really important —"

"Like *medicine* or something!" Lizzy adds.

"Right," I say eagerly. "Something that can't wait a whole weekend."

"I thought I heard Mrs. Fink coughing this morning," Lizzy says. "She could have that bird flu thing, or German measles, or —"

Nick holds up his hand. "Enough, enough. Soon you'll have her quarantined for the plague." He reaches over for the box, and Lizzy and I flash each other a quick grin.

I sign my name as neatly as possible on the slip and hand it back to him.

"Just make sure you leave it for her to open," he instructs, laying the box in my waiting arms.

"Yeah, yeah," Lizzy says. "Opening other people's mail is a federal offense, we know the drill."

"Bye, Nick," I say, eager to get the package upstairs. It isn't heavy, but it's awkward to carry.

"Stay outta trouble," he says in parting.

"Who, us?" Lizzy calls after him. We climb up the short flight of stairs to the first floor where we both live. Mom told me last week that a new family would soon be moving into the empty apartment at the end of the hall. I'm very curious to see who they will turn out to be. Circus performers? A minor league baseball player? Most kids would probably hope for more kids his age, but I don't care about that. Why would anyone need more than one good friend?

Since my arms are full, Lizzy uses her copy of my apartment key and opens the door. I head straight into the kitchen and rest the box on the three-legged kitchen table, which is a big improvement over the two-legged one that my parents had to glue to the wall to keep it from tipping over.

"So?" Lizzy asks, that familiar let's-do-something-bad gleam in her eye. "Are we gonna open it?" At the same time we both lean closer to read the return address label. It's scuffed up and hard to make out. "Folgard and Levine, Esquires," she reads. "What does 'esquires' mean?"

"'Esquires' means lawyers," I explain. I pride myself on knowing many obscure facts. It's all those midnight hours of reading.

"Why would a bunch of lawyers send something to your mom?"

"I don't know."

"Maybe she robbed a bank," Lizzy suggests. "And the evidence against her is in this box!"

"Come on," I say. "As you can tell by our apartment, Mom isn't interested in having fancy things."

I watch Lizzy's eyes take in the curtains made from strings of beads, the tie-dyed sheet on the wall that hides a long crack, the collection of old black-and-white postcards all showing some breed of dog dressed in a tutu, the three-legged table. "Okay," she says, "so she didn't rob a bank. But hey, maybe she won something! Does she still enter all those crazy contests?"

"I'm not sure," I answer hesitantly. Mom and I don't see each other that much anymore. She has her job at the library during the day, and then she takes art classes three nights a week at the school where my Aunt Judi — Mom's twin sister — teaches. My mother is also an identical twin, but unlike my dad and Uncle Arthur, she and Aunt Judi actually like each other.

Lizzy asks, "Remember when your mom had to come up with a ten-word description for apple pie and she won a different pie every month for a year?"

Ah yes. I recall the Year of the Pies fondly. Pies are not as good as candy, but they are still better than anything else Mom has tried over the years to get me to eat. We made that final pie — rutabaga, as I recall — last for weeks, taking only a bite at a time.

This box doesn't look like it holds pies, though. Or vacuum bags, or Florida oranges, or packets of Jell-O, or any of the other things Mom has won over the years by writing jingles or collecting box tops or labels from cans. I examine the box itself. Thick cardboard, with a single layer of clear packing tape running down the center.

"You know what this means?" Lizzy asks, pointing to the tape.

"That we can lift off the tape without ruining the box, and then we can press the tape back down and my mother won't know the difference?"

"Yup!"

"Not gonna happen," I say, plopping down onto the one kitchen chair that Mom hasn't managed to turn into an art project yet. The others are either covered in a scratchy fake leopard fur, or have bottle caps (the actual caps of bottles, not the candy) running up and down the legs and across the back.

"If you're afraid of that federal offense thing," Lizzy says, "that's only if it's a stranger's mail. I think."

"We will wait till my mom gets home," I say firmly. I expect her to continue the argument, but instead she just stands by the box, looking a bit too innocent.

Gravely, I ask, "Lizzy, did you do something?"

In a rush she blurts, "It's not my fault! The end of the tape just lifted right up!"

I jump from the chair to see that she has peeled away a few inches of the tape from the side of the box facing her. I have to admit, it really *had* come up very smoothly, not ripping or taking any of the cardboard with it. "Okay," I say quickly. "Let's do it before I change my mind."

Lizzy claps her hands and we set to work gently lifting the tape up from both ends. We eventually meet in the middle and lift the whole piece straight off. Lizzy drapes it over the top of a kitchen chair. I open the four flaps, and we look in.

At first all we can see is a bunch of crumpled pieces of newspaper. For a brief moment I think there's nothing else inside. I'm afraid to touch anything, but Lizzy apparently has no such qualms because she digs right in and pulls out balls of newspaper with both hands. She tosses them onto the table and is about to reach back in for the next layer when I stop her.

"Wait," I say, gathering the balls into a neat pile. "We'll have to pack this back up later exactly how we found it." I'm about to lay a wad of newspaper onto the pile when a headline catches my eye. I smooth the crumpled page out on the table. My heart quickening, I hold the page out to Lizzy and say, "Look at this article."

She shakes her head. "You know I don't believe in reading the newspaper. Too depressing. Why would I start reading it now?"

"Just read it," I persist. "It's from the science section."

She rolls her eyes and grabs the paper from me. " 'Scientists Believe Black Holes Might Be Key to Time Travel.' So what?" she asks. "Just add this to your time travel file. Your mom won't notice one piece of newspaper missing."

"I don't *need* to add it to my file," I tell her, taking the paper back and rolling it back up into a ball. "I already have it."

"Huh?"

"This newspaper is five years old!"

She grabs more pieces out of the box until she finds one with a date on it. With a sharp intake of breath she says, "You're right! This page is from the week after . . . after . . ." Lizzy's words trail off and she busies herself pulling more paper out of the box. I know what she was going to say. The paper is from the week after my father died.

Silently we pull out the rest of the newspaper until only two things are left in the box — a typed letter on business letterhead and a rectangular object the size of a shoe box, wrapped in tissue paper. We stare at each other, wide-eyed. Lizzy starts to reach for the letter and then pulls back. "Maybe you should do it."

"But what if it's something my mom wouldn't want us to see?"

"We've come this far," she says, then quickly adds, "but it's up to you."

I wipe my sweating hands on my shorts. As much as I don't want to admit it, I'm drawn in by the mysterious package, and I can't help myself. I square my shoulders and carefully lift out the letter, trying not to wrinkle it. The address on the top is the same as the one on the return label. The letter, at least, is not five years old because it has yesterday's date on it. I read it out loud, trying to keep my voice steady:

Dear Laney,

I hope this finds you well. I know I wasn't supposed to send it until later this summer, but we have shut down the Manhattan branch, and I didn't want to take the chance of misplacing it in the move to our Long Island office. Another reason to send it early — and you won't like this, I'm afraid — is that I seem to have misplaced the keys. I am fairly certain that you sent them along with the box to my office, and I have a vague recollection of hiding them somewhere quite clever. Alas, too clever, I'm sorry to say.

The locksmith I visited explained that the locking mechanism on the box is an intricate system of levers and pulleys. Each of the four keyholes needs a different type of key, and an internal latch will prevent the box from being pried open. Figures Jack wouldn't settle for a normal box with one keyhole like everyone else. I am certain you and Jeremy will figure it out before the time comes.

I have nothing but fond memories of Jack from our college days, and I was honored to do him the favor of holding onto this all these years. All my best wishes to you.
Yours truly,
Harold

Lizzy takes the letter from my hand and reads it over to herself. "What does this mean?" she says quietly. Lizzy rarely says anything quietly, so I know she's as surprised as I am. I don't trust myself to speak, so I just shake my head. I can't recall my father mentioning a college buddy named Harold, although admittedly I tuned out whenever my parents started reminiscing about the old college days. But this Harold person must have known them pretty well since he called Mom *Laney,* which only her close friends do. So my mother sent this package to him and told him to send it back five years later? Why would she do that? And what does he mean about doing a favor for my dad?

Before I can stop myself, I reach in and lift the wrapped object out of the box. The tissue paper slides off and falls to the floor. I am left holding a smooth wooden box with keyholes on four sides. A clear varnish makes the wood seem almost alive. The first thought that strikes me is how pretty it is. I had never thought that a wooden box could be pretty. Heck, I don't think I've ever even *used* the word "pretty" before, and if Lizzy ever asked, I'd deny using it now.

Lizzy bends down to pick up the piece of tissue paper at my feet. She stands up slowly and says, "Um, Jeremy?"

"Hmmm?" I'm unable to take my eyes from the box in my hands. I shake it gently and hear some muffled objects shift and knock against each other. It can't weigh more than two pounds.

"Um, you might want to turn that over," Lizzy says. I just keep shaking the box back and forth, mesmerized. She finally grabs it from my hands, flips it over, and hands it back. Staring up at me are the engraved words THE MEANING OF LIFE: FOR JEREMY FINK TO OPEN ON HIS 13TH BIRTHDAY.

I'd recognize my dad's handiwork anywhere.

Chapter 2: The Explanation

"Looks like the package wasn't for your mom after all," Lizzy says after a few minutes.

I don't answer. My hands are shaking, and I set the wooden box down on the kitchen table. We back away about two feet and stare at it.

"So this is a birthday gift from your dad?" Lizzy asks.

I nod. My heart is beating so fast that I actually hear it pulsing in my ears.

We stare some more and the words float in front of me. *The Meaning of Life. For Jeremy Fink. 13th Birthday.* Mom has obviously known about this for at least five years. Why did she keep it from me? I don't have any secrets from anyone. Well, I guess I haven't told anyone about kissing Rachel Schwartz at her bat mitzvah last April, but that's mostly because it wasn't so much a kiss as it was our lips accidentally occupying the same space as we reached for the last Shirley Temple on the waiter's tray.

"So what do you think is inside?" Lizzy asks.

I finally speak. "No idea."

"Can the meaning of life be in a box?"

"Wouldn't have thought so," I say.

"And you never saw this box before?"

I shake my head.

"Your mom never mentioned it?"

I shake my head again and try to recall what I'm supposed to do to avoid having a panic attack. I've only had one, the time Mom and I flew to Florida to visit my grandparents last year. No matter what they say about how safe flying is, I think only birds and superheroes should be in the clouds. Deep breath in, hold it for four counts, deep breath out. I had never considered the meaning of life before. Why hadn't I considered it? What is wrong with me? Has everyone else thought about this except for me? Maybe I was too busy trying to learn about time travel so I could keep Dad from taking the car out on that fateful day. My time travel research is important though, if not *vital*, to all of mankind. How was I supposed to put that aside to ponder the meaning of life?

"Are you all right?" Lizzy asks, looking up at me. "You look a little green."

I do feel a little light-headed from all the deep breathing. "I should probably sit down." We head to the living room and sink down into the tan corduroy couch. I lean back and close my eyes. When I was three, I named this couch Mongo. It was one of the first pieces of furniture that my parents found during the height of their old collecting days, before I was born. Dad told me that objects people left on the street were called *mongo*. I think he must have told me this while we were sitting on the couch because somehow I thought he was saying the *couch* was called Mongo. The couch was old when they found it, and older still now. As the years went by, Mom kept covering up the holes with other pieces of fabric. At this point, the couch is almost ALL other pieces of fabric, but she won't get rid of it because I named it. She's sentimental that way. Apparently not sentimental enough to tell me about the box though!

"You're starting to look semi-normal again," Lizzy observes. "Not so green anymore. A little sweaty, maybe."

Nothing like the appearance of this box has ever happened to me. Or to anyone I know. Or to anyone I have read about. I need to sort this out, to make a plan. I open my eyes and say, "Let's recap."

"Okay," Lizzy says, sitting forward eagerly. Lizzy loves a good recap. We saw a detective do it on TV once, and ever since then we've occasionally recapped our day.

I stand up and begin to circle the coffee table. "Okay," I say. "We were about to go into the building when Nick came by. We convinced him to give us the big package with my mother's name on it. We promised to leave it for her, and then somehow, without realizing it, we opened it."

"That's one way to put it," Lizzy says encouragingly. "Go on."

"Inside the box we found a letter from a lawyer who was an old friend of my father's. He said he lost the keys to a wooden box that my dad left for him to give to me when I turned thirteen." I pause here to take a deep breath. "I will turn thirteen in a month with no way to open the box."

"Maybe your mom has a spare set," Lizzy suggests.

"I doubt it. Harold sounded awfully sorry about losing them, so he must have been pretty sure they were the only ones."

"Or what if your dad built the box himself? Then

for Cat, the loner. All my fish are named after other animals because Mom won't let me have real pets due to the fact that she is still mourning her childhood rabbit. Cat is a striped tiger fish who keeps to himself. Dog is brown with white spots and not that bright. He spends most of his day banging his nose into the side of the tank. Hamster is a hyper, orange goldfish who swims back and forth all day like he's in an Olympic relay race. My newest fish, Ferret, is long and silver and sometimes hard to find because he blends in with the gray rocks on the bottom of the tank. I sprinkle in some food, and they quickly swim to the surface to gobble it down.

These fish and I are a lot alike. They swim around the same four walls, safe and secure in their familiar environment. That's how I am, too. Honestly, I don't see any reason to leave my neighborhood. Everything I could ever want or need is within a few blocks in any direction: Dad's store (I still think of it as his), movies, school, the doctor, grocery store, dentist, clothes, shoes, the park, the library, the post office, everything. I don't like change.

I grab the feather duster from under the sink and run around the apartment, swishing it over every possible dust-collecting surface. I swish the mirrors, Aunt Judi's many sculptures, the tabletops, bookshelves, and the spines of the books (almost all of which were discarded from the library or bought at flea markets). I dust the television screen and the beaded curtains that Mom made the summer she was pregnant with me and stuck in bed. I am tempted to dust myself even!

Running into my bedroom, I quickly throw my blanket

over the bed, not bothering to straighten the sheets first. The stuffed alligator that Dad won for me by knocking over old milk jars at the state fair is trapped underneath the blanket. Now it looks like I'm hiding something because of the lumps and bumps. I'm about to fix it when I hear the double knock on the wall that indicates a new note is waiting for me. I lift up the poster of the solar system that covers the hole and grab the end of the rolled-up notebook page. Our walls are about six inches apart, so when we first tried to stick notes through on small pieces of paper, they would fall into the hollow space between. One day, years from now, maybe someone will find them and wonder who we were. Now we only use notebook paper, folded the long way, so it reaches all the way through.

Inside the note are two jelly beans. Watermelon, my favorite. I pop them in my mouth and read the note:

Good luck! If you get punished, there are more where these came from.

Lizzy and I look out for each other that way.

I scribble a big *THANKS* on the bottom of the note, stick it back through the hole until I see it reach the edge of her wall, and knock twice. It soon disappears from the other end.

I am straightening the books and papers on my desk when I hear the front door open. I had planned on being in the kitchen next to the box when Mom got home, but now that it's time, I can't move. I sit on the edge of my bed and wait. I hear her key ring jingle as she hangs it on the hook by the door. *Thud* goes her heavy briefcase onto floor. Now she's walking into the kitchen to get a glass iced tea. I know her patterns very well. Three more steps until she'll see the box. Two more steps. One. Now she'll be examining the package, wondering why it's open. Now she's reaching in past the newspaper and pulling out the letter and the wooden box. And now she'll call my name. Okay . . . now!

Now?

Why don't I hear anything? I expected, "Jeremy Fink! Get in here immediately!" Instead . . . silence. What does this mean? Another minute passes, and still nothing. Is she trying to make me squirm by dragging out the inevitable? Or what if she slipped and fell and is lying unconscious on the floor?

When I reach the kitchen I see that Mom isn't, thankfully, knocked out on the floor. Instead, she's standing by the table, staring down at Dad's box. I am familiar with that position, having been in it myself for quite a while. The letter is in her hand, hanging down at her side. Her face is pale. I can see some gray hair poking through the black, and for some reason it makes me sad. I have the urge to take her hand. Instead I just ask, "Um, Mom? Are you okay?"

She gives an unconvincing nod and sits down in the bottle cap–covered chair. "You should have this," she says, and hands me the letter. She runs her fingers over the words Dad engraved on the top of the box. "It was only a week after the accident when I mailed this box to Harold for safekeeping," she says, not taking her eyes off of it.

"Your thirteenth birthday seemed like a million years away back then."

She looks so sad that I wish she were angry at me instead. Not that she has a bad temper or anything, but she's big on boundaries. I know if the package had *my* name on it, she never would have opened it.

"Even though your dad insisted he would be here to give you the box himself, I knew that deep down he didn't believe it. The instructions to send it to Harold were in his will."

My throat feels like a snake is wound around it, but I manage to ask, "He believed that palm reader on the boardwalk, didn't he?"

She lets out a big sigh. "I don't know. I think some people have a greater sense of their mortality than others. He knew the number of years that were allotted to him."

Neither of us speaks for a minute. Then I whisper, "I'm sorry I opened the package." If I were a little bit younger, I would have blamed it on Lizzy.

Surprisingly, she smiles. "Your dad would have opened it, too. He was curious about everything. That's why he loved flea markets and collecting so much. He was fascinated by what objects people kept, and what they threw away. Remember those stories he used to make up about each thing he found?"

I sit down across from her and nod. I do remember, but the memories are very foggy. After Dad died, it was like all the furniture was talking to me (but in Dad's voice), and I had to make a conscious effort to remember that the hall table was just a table, not the very table on which the Declaration of Independence was signed. Which of course it wasn't really.

She runs her hand over the scratches that burrow deep into the kitchen table. "Remember what he said about this broken table when we found it?"

I shake my head.

"When we found this at a tag sale, your dad said it belonged to an old woman who was very overweight. She was sitting at the table when she saw in the newspaper that her lottery numbers had come in. In her excitement she fainted and fell forward onto the table, breaking one of the legs underneath her weight." Mom gestures to the box and says, "He was so excited the day he got this box. He said it was the most unique one he'd ever seen, with all those keyholes. You were six at the time, and he starting filling it for you that very night. He didn't engrave it until a few months later."

My eyes begin to sting with the onset of tears, but I blink them away. "So you know what's in it?"

She shakes her head. "He was very secretive about it. He kept it at the comic store in the vault."

So that's why I never saw it around the apartment! "Do you have an extra set of keys?" I hold my breath until she answers.

She shakes her head. "There was only one set. It takes four different keys to open it, and I mailed them to Harold. I can't imagine what he did with them."

"Maybe Dad made an extra set and kept them at the store. I can ask Uncle Arthur if —"

She just shakes her head. "I'm sorry, Jeremy. I cleaned

out all your father's things from the store. There's no other set."

I pull hard on the top of the box, not really expecting anything to happen. It is sealed up tight. "How am I going to open it, then?" I ask.

"I honestly don't know." She stands up and takes the pitcher of iced tea out of the fridge. As she reaches for two glasses she says, "Lizzy's dad has some tools. We can ask him to saw through it if you haven't found a way to open it before your birthday comes."

I jump out of my chair, nearly knocking it over. Snatching the box from the table, I hug it to my chest.

"I'll take that as a no, then?" she says, sounding slightly amused.

"Yes, that's a no," I say firmly, tightening my grip. I can't let Dad's box get sawed in half after hearing how much he loved it. After five years, he has sent me a message with one instruction, to open this box on my thirteenth birthday. Somehow, no matter how impossible it might seem, I am going to do exactly that.

Chapter 3: The Keys

I send Lizzy a note telling her that Mom doesn't have the keys and that, miraculously, I'm not being punished. Hours later, as the grandfather clock strikes eleven, I finally get a response.

> I have a plan. Come over at 10 am. Bring the letter and the box. Sorry it took so long to get back to you, what with the whole Friday Night Is Family Movie Night thing. Field of Dreams again: AGAIN!!
> Don't be late!
> Lizzy

Lizzy's plans always make me nervous, but in this case I have nothing to lose. Between dinnertime and now, I exhausted my own methods for opening the box. To see if extreme temperatures might loosen the locks, I put the box in the freezer for an hour. No change. Then I put it in the microwave. But before I hit start, I took it out, because what if the meaning of life is actually some tiny alien baby that my father rescued from certain persecution? I didn't want to microwave the little guy to death.

My final attempt was to wedge a butter knife under the lid, but instead of sliding inside the box, it only hit another layer of wood and wouldn't budge.

I do not like surprises. I won't watch scary movies. I

won't answer the phone unless I can see who is calling on caller ID. I don't even like it when someone says "Guess what?" and then waits for you to guess. Surprises make me nervous. Once you've had a real surprise, one that knocks the wind out of you and changes your life, all the little surprises remind you of that big one.

This box is a little like that.

It is now sitting on the center of my desk, mocking me. Only the size of a shoe box, it somehow overshadows everything else in my room, including the life-sized cardboard cutouts of the hobbits from *The Lord of the Rings*. And they're not easy to overshadow.

I write Lizzy back and ask for details of her plan, but she doesn't take the note from the wall. After a few minutes I pull it back out and stick my ear to the hole. The poster covering her end of the hole blocks any light from coming through, but I can still hear her cat, Zilla, purring loudly. Actually, he roars rather than purrs. Zilla (short for Godzilla, since he destroys everything in his path) is fiercely protective of Lizzy and will lunge at anyone who goes near her room. I haven't been more than one foot inside her bedroom in two years. I think Zilla believes he's a pit bull. I knock a few times on the wall, but not too loudly.

Mom taps on the door and brings me a peanut butter sandwich on a napkin. She gives the box on my desk a long look and starts closing the door behind her. Then she stops and says, "Oh, wait, I have something for you." A few seconds later she's back.

"In all the excitement, I forgot to give you this." She holds out what looks like an ordinary yellow Starburst candy. But as I examine it more closely, I realize the bottom half is actually orange. It's a mutant Starburst!

"Thanks, Mom!" I jump up from the bed and deposit the Starburst in the airtight Tupperware dish along with the other candy in my collection. It's been a few months since I've added anything new. Airtight or no, the peanut M&M is starting to look a little green in spots. It was yellow to begin with.

"You've had a big day," Mom says. "Make sure you don't go to sleep too late." She makes a move like she's going to kiss me on the forehead like she used to when I was little. But then she just tousles my hair and gives the box one more glance before closing the door for good. I have named the hour between eleven and midnight the Hour of Jeremy (H.O.J. for short). The city is so quiet and peaceful except for the police and ambulance sirens, the beeping of the car alarms, and the rushing of the water in the pipes. But when you grow up in the city, that stuff feels like background noise, and you don't notice it. I feel like I'm the only person alive on the earth.

Because of all my H.O.J. reading, I know a little about a lot. I always win when I play Trivial Pursuit. I would make an excellent *Jeopardy* contestant. Last night I learned that for everyone alive on earth today, there are thirty ghosts lined up behind them. Not literally lined up, of course, but that's how many dead people there are compared to living people. In all, around a hundred billion people have walked on this planet, which, interestingly enough, is the same number of stars in our Milky Way galaxy. Science is my favorite class in school. I have a healthy fascination with the Milky Way, and not just because it has the same name as a chocolate bar.

Usually my H.O.J reading is a mix of any of the books on my shelf (along with at least fifteen minutes on time travel). But tonight's H.O.J. will be spent only learning about keys. This is what the Internet tells me:

1. The first keys were used four thousand years ago by the ancient Egyptians to protect their caves.
2. Locks were initially made of interlocking wooden pegs, with a wooden key that raised one section of pegs out of their grooves so the lock slid open.
3. The Romans later began making keys and locks out of metal, mostly bronze and iron, and began using springs inside the locks. The keys were called *warders,* and most had an oval shape at the top and a long straight middle section, with one or two square portions sticking out near the end.
4. Next came the pin tumbler locks from England and America, followed by time-release locks. These have a clock inside that turns a wheel with a ridge in it, and when that ridge lines up with the keyhole, the box springs open. (As soon as I read this I put the box up next to my ear. No ticking. I knew that was too good to be true.)
5. They now make bendable keys so that no one can pick the lock with a regular hard piece of metal, like a hairpin.
6. I do not know what a hairpin is.

The Hour of Jeremy is almost up. I have time for one more quick search. I type in the words "the meaning of life" and hold my breath.

Two seconds later I receive 2,560,000 hits. TWO MILLION FIVE HUNDRED SIXTY THOUSAND HITS. I click on what seems like the most obvious place to start, a definition of the word *life*.

life: *noun 1. a state that is not death*

That's it. The definition of life is not death.

I shut down my computer, climb into bed, and throw the covers over my head.

I wish I could say things look clearer in the fresh light of a new day, but so far a new day means only that I have one less day to figure out how to open the box. Lizzy opens her apartment door with one hand while shoving a blueberry Vitamuffin down her throat with the other. Her dad makes her eat all this healthy food, and she actually *eats* it! My theory is that he doesn't want Lizzy to take after him in the girth department. A small man he is not.

I follow her into the kitchen, where she hands me my daily chocolate Vitamuffin, the only flavor I will eat. I put the box and the letter on the counter and try to ignore the high vitamin and mineral content while concentrating on the chocolaty goodness of my muffin. Nothing like chocolate (even healthy, non-fat, good-for-you chocolate) to start the day off right.

"So what's your plan?" I ask, reaching into the fridge for the container of milk. "And will it get us arrested?"

"Have we *ever* gotten arrested?" Lizzy replies, giving me a dirty look as I guzzle the milk straight from the carton.

"We've come close," I remind her. "There was the time you convinced me to sneak into the pool at the Senior Center, and the guard chased us for seven blocks. Or the time you made me be the lookout while you stole a menu from that outdoor restaurant, and the waiter threw water on us. I'd say those were pretty close calls."

"For the record," Lizzy says, "it was over a hundred degrees when we snuck into that pool. It was totally worth it." Under her breath she mumbles, "And it was iced tea he threw at us, not water."

Lizzy leaves the kitchen to get her chart. Every plan has a chart. Some are even color-coded. I place the box on the table and sit down to wait. Lizzy must have been going through her playing cards collection before I arrived, because they're spread out on the table. I have my mutant candy collection, and Lizzy has her playing cards. But while I'll happily accept a mutant piece of candy from anyone who finds it, she will only add a playing card to her collection if she finds it herself, in a public place. No duplicates either, and she won't look anywhere obvious, like the sidewalk outside the 33rd Street Bridge Club. She prefers to find her cards on subways or park benches, or sticking out of sewer grates. She is only missing three now — the two of clubs, the eight of hearts, and the jack of diamonds.

I remember how proud my dad was when Lizzy started her collection. He thought it was very creative. I mean, sure, putting together a full deck of cards by finding them one by one is certainly *different*, but it's not like you can eat it afterward, like *my* collection. In fact, some of her cards are so dirty you can barely read the number and suit. As much as he encouraged us to have a collection, Dad could never land on one himself. He collected baseball cards for a while, but only of players who played for just one year. Then he was big on finding foreign stamps from countries that no longer existed. One stamp became his holy grail, and he would look for it everywhere he went. It was printed in Hawaii in 1851, over a hundred years before Hawaii became a state. The stamp came in denominations of two cents, five cents, and thirteen cents. Dad drew pictures of it so Mom and I would recognize it if we were out on our own. I still look for that stamp, but I'm beginning to think he made it up. Before he died, he had moved on to fast food restaurant giveaways, which was great for me because he needed a kid in order to get the toys. Now I can't go into a fast food place without feeling sad.

Lizzy returns with a piece of construction paper rolled up under her arm. Zilla follows behind her and growls up at me. Always one for the dramatics, Lizzy unfurls the paper with a snap of her wrist and lays it out in front of us, right on top of the playing cards. The first things I notice are the two pencil drawings of the box. She didn't get all the keyholes positioned exactly right, but it's a pretty good rendering.

"Sorry for the rough sketch," she says modestly. "As you can see, I have numbered our options. The list goes from easiest to most difficult. Plan A —"

"You can cross that one off," I instruct after reading it ahead of her. "I already tried that."

"You stuck the box in the freezer?" she asks, surprised.

I nod. "And the microwave."

She gives me a long look, and then crosses off Plans A and B.

"You can cross off Plan C while you're at it. I already tried sticking a knife under the lid and it won't budge."

With a loud sigh, she draws a line through the next entry.

"May I continue?" she asks.

"By all means."

"Plan D: We take the box to Larry's Locks and Clocks to see if he can do anything."

I nod in agreement. "That's a good one."

She continues, "And if that doesn't work, Plan E is take the subway to the 26th Street Flea Market this afternoon. We might get lucky there. Some of those vendors have got to have old keys for sale."

I squirm a little at that one. "I've never seen keys there."

"That's because you've never had a reason to look."

"Maybe. But still . . . it's all the way across town."

"You just don't want to take the subway without an adult," she says accusingly.

As my mother says, we all grow at our own pace. Crossing my arms in front of my chest defiantly, I say, "You *know* I don't take the subway alone."

"You wouldn't *be* alone." Two red blotches appear on

Lizzy's cheeks whenever she gets irritated. I can see them beginning to creep across her face. "Come on," she says. "We're almost thirteen. It's about time we got around the city on our own. Maybe you didn't have a good reason to do it before, but what better reason is there than to get this box open?"

She has a point. Resistance is clearly futile. "Okay," I say flatly. "If the locksmith can't help us, and we have to go to the flea market, I'll go."

"Good!" she says.

"As long as my mother says it's all right," I add. "I have to stay on her good side after yesterday."

Lizzy rolls her eyes. "Fine, whatever, let's just get going." She turns the paper over so I can't read the last item on the list and grabs the box.

"Wait," I say as she heads toward the front door. "Aren't you going to tell me what Plan F is in case the locksmith and the flea market don't work out?"

She pauses for a second, and then shakes her head. "Let's hope you never need to know."

I don't like the sound of that. We stop at my apartment to grab my backpack. While I'm stuffing the box inside, Lizzy grabs a handful of subway tokens from the dish on the kitchen counter.

"You might as well call your mom now, just in case Larry can't help us."

I grumble, but I do it anyway. Mom says it's fine to take the subway as long as we're careful. Is it wrong of me that I had sort of been hoping she would say no?

In all of my nearly thirteen years of living two blocks

away, I have only been inside Larry's Locks and Clocks once. When my dad found our grandfather clock, he was obsessed with making it work. He dragged it straight to this store from its previous home in some stranger's bulk garbage pile. When Dad was alive, Mom always threatened to break the clock again because the chimes drove her crazy. But after he died, she stopped complaining about it.

The sign on the window says the store is open only until noon on Saturdays, so we made it just in time. Lizzy pushes open the door, and a little bell rings above our heads. No one else is in the shop. Shelves of clocks in various states of repair surround us. Other than my dad, I hadn't thought anyone repaired clocks anymore instead of buying new ones. I look closer and see a thick coating of dust on most of them, like people dropped them off a decade ago and couldn't be bothered to come get them. My nose tickles, so I quickly move away from the shelf before I sneeze on everything. When I sneeze, I sneeze big. It runs in the family. Dad once sneezed so hard on the guy in front of us at the movies that the guy turned around and dumped his popcorn on Dad's lap.

Lizzy and I approach the narrow counter that runs along the back of the store. Keys of all kinds hang from hooks behind it. A thin man in overalls wanders in from the back room, wiping his hands on a napkin.

"What can I do for you today?" he asks, flicking a crumpled McDonald's wrapper off the counter. It lands directly in the garbage can to the left of him.

"You Larry?" Lizzy asks.

The man shakes his head. "Larry Junior."

Lizzy looks at me, and I shrug. I can't see that it matters which Larry helps us. She turns me around and unzips my backpack, pulling out the box.

"I could have done that," I whisper.

She plops the box on the counter. "Can you open this?"

"What a pretty box!" the man declares, turning it around in his hands.

Aha! I feel vindicated. He thinks it's pretty, too.

"The meaning of life is in this box, eh?" The corners of his mouth twitch upward.

I pretend not to hear him. If my dad says the meaning of life is in that box, then darn it, it's in there. "I've lost the keys," I explain in as patient a tone as I can muster. "Do you have ones that might fit?"

He examines the box closely and furrows his brows. "Hmm. Let me see. No markings on the box indicating where it came from or who made it. That would have been helpful. These keyholes are very specific — made for this box alone. Maybe there's some other way to get in it." He slides the box under a lamp and switches on the light.

"The meaning of life in a box," he mutters as he bends down to scrutinize it. "Who woulda thunk it."

An older man in identical overalls comes out from the back room. "What's this I hear about the meaning of life in a box?" he asks.

Larry Junior points to us. "These kids brought this box. Don't have the keys."

"No keys, eh?" he asks, looking at us closely. "I'll take over," he says, stepping behind the counter.

"That's okay, Pop," Larry Junior says. "I got it."

The old man — who I assume is Larry himself — shakes his head. "We just got a call that Mrs. Chang locked herself out again. I need you to go help her."

Larry Junior shrugs and grabs a toolbox from the shelf. "Good luck," he says, and heads out. The bells tinkle behind him.

We turn back to Larry Senior. He is resting his hands on the box, eyes closed. Lizzy and I raise our eyebrows and exchange a look.

"Um," I say tentatively, "so do you think you can open it for us?"

Larry's eyes snap open. "Nope."

My shoulders sag a bit.

He continues. "This is no ordinary box. It has an elaborate locking mechanism inside with levers and pulleys and —"

"We know," Lizzy interrupts, and then recites Harold's letter, "and each keyhole needs a different type of key. And an internal latch will prevent the box from being pried open."

"Not just *that*," Larry says, "but under the wood is a layer of metal. That means no one is getting through this without destroying the contents. A saw or an axe would crush the whole thing. You can see the edge of the metal layer if you look closely in the gap."

We lean into the counter and peer under the light. He's right. I hadn't noticed the thin sliver of metal visible along the opening. Why couldn't my dad have bought a normal box like anyone else would have? With only *one* keyhole?

He switches off the lamp and pushes the box across to us. "Sorry to disappoint you, but the only way anyone is getting into this box is with the keys."

Lizzy points to the rows of keys behind the man. "What about those? Will any of those fit?"

Larry doesn't even turn around. "Nope. Those are blank keys that we use to make copies of existing ones. But I do have a box of spares that I've collected over the years. You're welcome to 'em."

He bends down and fishes around under the counter for a minute. Lizzy and I stand on our toes, eagerly peering over. He finally stands up and hands me a cigar box. It doesn't even feel full. I try not to show my disappointment. I had pictured a huge box with hundreds of keys.

"Thanks," Lizzy says gamely. "And if none of these fit, what do you think our chances are of finding keys that will? I mean, somewhere else in the city?"

"I'd say slim to nil, but slim ain't left town yet, if you know what I mean."

We stare at him blankly.

He chuckles. "That means it's doubtful, but anything's possible. After all, you've got a mighty good cause. Trying to find out the meaning of life, and all."

"Thanks," I say with more enthusiasm than I feel. "We'll bring these right back."

"No rush," he says, waving his hand in the air. "How long you got till your thirteenth birthday anyway? I'm assuming you're the Jeremy Fink on the box?"

"A little under a month," I reply as we head toward the door. It's hard to keep the disappointment out of my voice.

"A lot can happen in a month," he calls after us. "Keep the faith."

"You bet," Lizzy says. "Amen."

When we make it outside I tell her, "I don't think you're supposed to say 'Amen' when someone says 'Keep the faith.'"

She shrugs. "How am I supposed to know? All I know about religion is that *dog* spelled backwards is *god,* and I learned that on a Saturday morning cartoon. Let's go sit in the park and try the keys."

We head around the corner to the park where we've played since we were little. It has a different feel to it now that we're on a mission. I wonder if the men reading the newspaper on the benches, or the women watching their kids in the sandbox, can sense that we're up to something important. We settle under a tree near the playground where the grass has been worn smooth. I dump the keys onto the ground in a pile. It's not a very big pile. Thirty keys, at most. We agree to try each key in each keyhole, and then if it doesn't fit, return it to the cigar box. That way we won't try the same key twice by mistake.

Lizzy takes the first one and, before she puts it in a hole, covers it with both hands and whispers something to it.

"What are you doing?" I ask.

"I'm saying a little prayer for good luck," she answers. "I might not know anything about religion, but that doesn't mean we can't pray. You know, to the powers of the universe or something. Come on, do it with me."

"What am I supposed to say?"

She thinks for a minute and says, "How about: O Master of All Things Locked, please allow this key to open Jeremy Fink's box." After a short pause she adds, "Amen."

I glance around to make sure no one sitting nearby heard that. "Why don't just *you* say it? We don't want to confuse the Master of All Things Locked with two different voices."

"Suit yourself," she says, and prays to the key louder than I would have liked. She then tries it in all four holes, to no avail. We go through each key that way. None fit. Most of them won't even enter the keyholes at all. About a handful of them actually slide in a notch, but don't go any farther. By the time we're down to our last key, Lizzy's prayer has become a mumble of *Masterkeyboxamen*. This time I add my own little silent *Amen,* but it does no good. Larry's box is now full again, and I have to go on the subway. Ugh.

Chapter 4: The Flea Market

Lizzy goes in to return the keys while I wait outside, gathering my nerve. I'm not proud of the fact that I've never taken public transportation without an adult, but everything I need is usually within walking distance.

The bells jingle as Lizzy comes back out and begins marching down the street toward the subway. The closest stop is a few blocks away, and I find myself trailing behind. I have a lot on my mind. I can't be expected to walk so quickly. She waits for me at the next corner, tapping her foot impatiently.

"I have an idea," I tell her, trying to sound enthusiastic. "We can go to some garage sales right here in the neighborhood."

"You know our best bet is the flea market," she says firmly, taking off again. "We'd have a much better chance there than at some little garage sale."

I know she's right. The 26th Street Market in Chelsea is the biggest in the city. My parents and I spent many weekends there. After Dad died, Mom and I went on our own, but it wasn't the same. In the last year or two, we haven't gone at all.

"How do you know which train we should take?" I ask as we descend into the muggy darkness of the subway station.

"There's a map right here on the wall." Two older

boys are standing in front of it, arguing about which way to go. One of them bets the other that he can't eat fifteen Nathan's hot dogs in under five minutes when they get to Coney Island.

I whisper to Lizzy, "I once stuffed twenty-seven candy corns in my mouth at once and then ate them all. And I didn't even need anyone to bet me."

"That's gross," she says, tapping her foot at the boys, who ignore her. Finally they move on, and we move closer to the map.

She traces her finger along one of the subway lines. "It looks like this one will take us right to Sixth Avenue, and then we just need to walk two blocks. And it's only five stops, so don't be a baby."

"If it's only five stops, maybe we should walk," I suggest. "You know, save our money."

"We're not using our money," she says, digging into her shorts pocket. "We have your mom's tokens, remember?"

"Tokens are still money," I mutter under my breath as she forces one into my hand.

We approach the turnstile, tokens held at the ready. But when we get there, neither of us can find a place to stick them in. It's been a few months since Mom took me on the subway, and I guess I didn't pay enough attention because I can't remember what to do. I feel a tap on my shoulder. A man wearing a Yankees cap and T-shirt points to a sign that says: NO MORE TOKENS. METRO CARDS ONLY. I tap Lizzy, who is frantically trying to stick the token in anything that remotely looks like an opening. She whirls around, and I point to the sign. We sheepishly step out of line and watch the Yankees fan swipe his card through a groove. He pushes through the turnstile and turns around to face us when he gets to the other side. "Come on," he says, holding his card out. "I can use the good karma. The Yanks are playing the Red Sox today."

"Thanks!" I say, taking the card from his outstretched hand. I swipe it, walk through, and pass it back to Lizzy. After she comes through, she returns it to the man and mumbles an embarrassed thank you. Lizzy doesn't like to admit there's something she can't do. I don't have that problem. I know I can't do most things.

As we carefully dodge the used gum and unidentifiable puddles, I say to Lizzy, "I wonder why my mother kept those tokens in the kitchen if they can't be used anymore?"

"Half the things in your house don't have a purpose," she points out.

Actually, I'd say more than half.

We wait for the train a good distance behind the yellow line and listen to a short, wide man with a crewcut play a guitar and sing about lost love. He looks like he should be on the football field, not singing in a subway station. I don't turn away until the high-pitched squeal of the arriving train drowns out his singing. Lizzy takes hold of my arm, and we push our way through the doors.

Grasping onto a pole with a tighter grip than is probably necessary, I try to keep my brain occupied by staring at the nearest advertisement. GET RID OF ADULT ACNE. Adults have acne? I glance at Lizzy and wonder if she's thinking about the same thing I am — the appearance last

Christmas of Lizzy's first pimple, better known as The Pimple That Ate Manhattan. She looks at me, looks at the poster, then scowls. But when she thinks I'm not looking, I see her reach up and rub her cheek. In the right light one can still see a faint red mark from where she savagely attacked the pimple with a pair of nose-hair tweezers. After that, Mom made Lizzy promise to come to her with any beauty emergencies. Lizzy's dad is useless when it comes to girl stuff. He's the one who gave her the tweezers!

"Are we there yet?" I ask her as the train slows to a halt.

"This is only the second stop," she says.

"It feels like the fourth."

"Well it isn't."

"Are you —"

"Yes! I'm sure! Stop being such a baby!"

"I'm not being a baby," I mumble.

Lizzy digs into her pocket. "Here," she says, thrusting a Milk Dud into my palm. "This should make you feel better." The half-melted Milk Dud is covered in a light film of pocket lint. I pop it in my mouth anyway. The chocolate-caramel goodness does indeed make me feel better.

A tall, middle-aged man standing nearby chuckles, and I turn to look at him. He nods his head toward Lizzy and says, "You and your sister remind me of the way my sister and I used to be. Oh, the fights we would have! But there's nothing we wouldn't do for each other."

"She's not my sister," I quickly reply. My eyes dart over to Lizzy, but she seems oblivious to the conversation. She's staring at the adult acne poster with a pained expression.

The man raises his brow in surprise, then nudges me with his elbow and says knowingly, "Ohh, she's your girl-friend!"

"No, she's not!" I exclaim, this time getting not only Lizzy's attention, but the attention of everyone nearby. I feel my cheeks begin to burn. It's not like it's the first time I've heard that. Kids make fun of us at school all the time. But still! From a stranger! On the subway!

"*Now* we're here," Lizzy says, grabbing my arm and pushing me toward the door. I glance back at the man, and he gives me a little wink.

ARGH!

"That wasn't so bad, was it?" Lizzy asks as we climb the long stairs back into the bright sunshine.

"I guess not," I mumble. I swing my backpack around to the front to make sure no one unzipped a zipper when I wasn't looking. That guy might have been trying to dis-tract me while his accomplice went into my bag. I check all the pockets, but everything is safe and sound (includ-ing the pack of Razzles I forgot was in there, which is al-ways a nice surprise).

The flea market is basically two big parking lots that get taken over every weekend by all types of vendors. It's very crowded and smells like a combination of boiled hot dogs and sweat. And not the good, peanut butter kind of sweat. Even though this used to be a home away from home for me, I stick close to Lizzy.

It takes a while for us to wind our way past the section of artists selling their crafts so we can get to the second-hand section. It's so strange being here without either of my parents or Aunt Judi. Mom and Aunt Judi are equal-opportunity flea market shoppers. Not Dad. He always went straight for the second-hand stuff, also known as the junk. The junk section is where I feel at home, since after all, most of my home started out on these sidewalks. One of Dad's favorite quotes was, "One man's trash is another man's treasure." Every time he said that, Lizzy used to whisper, "One man's trash is another man's *trash*," but never loud enough for Dad to hear. Whenever Dad found something he considered a treasure, he'd do a little dance right there on the sidewalk. People would laugh, and I would be embarrassed. I don't see anyone dancing today.

We walk past vendors selling used clothing, children's toys, old *Life* and *National Geographic* magazines, and rare comics in slipcovers. My legs slow of their own accord when we pass the comics, and Lizzy has to push me forward. I don't see anyone with stamps, but there's a table of old postcards that my mom would love. There aren't any of dogs in tutus, so we choose one with a lady sitting in a museum staring at a painting, except it's not a painting, it's a mirror. It's just strange enough that Mom will love it and will hopefully forgive my recent transgressions. Plus, it costs only a dime.

As the woman slips the card into a small bag for me, I turn to Lizzy and ask, "Did you know when you look in the mirror, you're actually seeing a slightly younger version of yourself?"

"Is that so?" she mumbles, her eyes darting to the next table, which is piled high with cheap makeup that looks half-used.

"Yes. It has to do with the time it takes light to travel between the mirror and the person standing in front of it."

"Uh huh," she says.

I don't bother continuing my explanation about the speed of light, and ask her if she wants to stop at the makeup table. She pretends to be horrified that I'd even mention it and harumphs. Lizzy is very attached to her tomboy reputation.

We make our way up and down the rows, scanning the wares for keys. Halfway through the third row, we find a woman with blankets of stuff spread out on the ground. She also has a table with a tray full of mismatched jewelry and a bowl filled with brass doorknobs. I feel like we're getting warm. The table is crowded, and we have to wait for a rather large woman to finish haggling before we can see the rest. The haggler is trying to get the similarly large woman on the other side of the table to take a dollar for the whole tray in front of her. She's holding up the tray, and we can hear its contents clashing and jingling, but can't tell what it is. What if we're a minute too late and this woman goes home with *my* keys?

Lizzy stands on her tiptoes and tries to peer over the lady's shoulder but almost falls right on top of her instead. Patience never being her strong point, Lizzy finally has enough and pushes her way in.

"Oh," I hear her say. "It's just a bunch of broken buttons. Why would someone want a tray of broken buttons?"

The shopper in question turns to glare at her, then shoves a dollar in the seller's hand and storms away.

46

"Sheesh," Lizzy says as we step up to the table. "Some people are so sensitive."

"Don't worry about it," the vendor says, tucking the dollar bill into a small canvas bag at her waist. "She's here every week and never wants to pay more than a buck for anything."

"I know the type," Lizzy says, gesturing to me with her thumb.

"Hey," I say, offended. "There's a difference between thrifty and cheap."

Lizzy is already busy rummaging through the other trays. "No offense," she says to the woman, "but why *would* someone buy buttons or old doorknobs, or any of this stuff?"

The woman shrugs. "All different reasons. Sometimes people are looking to fix up something they already got, and are searching for a particular thing. Some folks are looking to add to a collection. You wouldn't believe the things folks collect."

"Like mutant candy?" Lizzy asks innocently.

The lady looks puzzled. "Can't say I've heard of that."

I elbow Lizzy in the ribs and say to the woman, "We're looking for some old keys. Do you have any?"

"Sure," she says, snapping her fingers. "I got some around here somewhere." She goes off to search through her stuff on the ground, and Lizzy and I high-five. The woman unearths a faded metal trashcan from behind a pile of mismatched shoes, and waves us over. We hurry around the table and kneel down onto the old threadbare blanket. Greedily, we dig our hands into the can and pull out handfuls of what we expect will be keys. We look at each other and frown.

The lady is busy giving change to a young man who just bought a pair of old tap shoes for $1.50, so we have to wait until she is free again. I tip the trashcan forward so she can see inside and say, "Um, these aren't exactly what we had in mind."

"Huh? Why not?" she asks.

"Well, for one thing," Lizzy says, "they aren't keys. They're locks."

"Is that right?" the lady asks, peering into the can. "Oops, sorry 'bout that. Keys, locks, all part of the same thing, right?" She laughs a little, and then turns away to assure a young mother that the Sing and Snore Ernie doll will still work if she puts fresh batteries in it and sews the ear back on. With a sigh we drop the locks back into the can.

After a quick detour for a slice of pizza, we find a bearded man who has a small dish of assorted keys amidst a selection of marbles and plastic combs. Even Mom wouldn't buy used combs. I can't help wondering if the man brushed his scraggly beard with those combs. Lizzy quickly reaches for the keys, but the man puts out his hand to stop her. "You break it, you bought it," he says gruffly.

"How could we break a key?" Lizzy asks, hands moving naturally to hips.

"Kids have a way of breakin' things," he replies. "You'd be surprised."

"We're not really kids," I feel compelled to announce. "We're almost teenagers, actually."

"That's even worse," he says.

"Look," says Lizzy, "we just want to see if your keys open a box that we have."

"Yeah? What box is that?"

"Show 'im, Jeremy," Lizzy says.

I'm about to unzip my bag when I realize I don't want this guy's big dirty hands all over my dad's box. I shake my head. Lizzy opens her mouth to argue, but then stops when she sees my expression.

"You want the keys?" the man asks. "You'll have to buy 'em like everyone else."

"Fine," I say, reaching into my pocket. The first rule of flea markets is that you only put a few dollars and some change into your pocket so the vendor will think that's all you have. If they see more money, they'll ask for a higher price. I pull out fifty cents. "Is this enough?"

The man shakes his head. "Two dollars," he says.

"Two dollars!" Lizzy exclaims. "There's only, like, eight keys!"

The two of them have a standoff. Lizzy glares, and the man looks bored. Then all of a sudden Lizzy darts her hand out and grabs the dish with all the keys. Before the man can register what she's doing, she takes off running down the aisle. My mouth falls open. The man starts to go after her, but soon realizes he can't leave his stand. He stands directly in front of me and holds out his hand. Hands shaking, I hurriedly place two dollars into his waiting palm.

"You can add the extra fifty cents, too," he says. "For the dish." I have no choice but to hand over the quarters.

"Your girlfriend's quite a firecracker," he says with a hint of admiration in his voice.

"She's not my girlfriend!" I tell him, already hurrying to put as much distance between him and me as possible. I move as quickly through the crowd as one can with a backpack on his back, and find Lizzy waiting on a bench near the front of the market. She is already halfway through a snow cone.

I sit down next to her and watch as the blue ice drips down her chin. "Words fail me," I say, pulling the Razzles out of my backpack. Candy never fails me. I rip open the packet and hold it up to my mouth. I shake it until all the Razzles empty into my mouth. Now I couldn't talk even if I wanted to.

"I know you don't approve," Lizzy says, tossing the empty cone into the garbage next to her. "But come on, that guy was totally obnoxious."

I continue to chew furiously and don't respond.

"Okay," she says. "You don't have to say anything. Let's just try the keys."

She pulls the box out from the bag on my lap and tries each key in each hole, just like we did before. One of them slides halfway into one of the holes, and we both give a little jump. But then it won't go any farther no matter how hard we push. When she's done, Lizzy tosses the whole bunch into the garbage bin.

"Why'd you do that?" I ask, almost choking on the huge chunk of gum. "We should have kept them."

"What for?" she asks.

"I don't know, but they cost me two-fifty!"

She laughs. "You paid the guy?"

"Of course I paid him! He was gonna beat me up!"

"He wasn't gonna beat you up," she says.

"I thought you only stole things that had no monetary value," I point out as we head back into the market.

"We were just going to borrow them," Lizzy insists. "He was the one who was so rude about it."

"No excuses," I demand. "No rationalizations."

"Fine!" she says. "Let's just keep going."

I pause to spit out my gum into a garbage can. Razzles lose their flavor pathetically quickly. We don't speak to each other as we scour the booths. We continue to find people who have small jars or dishes of keys, and if they don't let us try the keys for free, no one charges us more than a quarter. A girl with an NYU tank top and a hoop earring in her nose keeps turning up at the same booths and buying keys each time. At one point she and I reach for the same key, and I pull back my hand. I turn to Lizzy and whisper, "Are you gonna ask her, or should I?"

"I'll ask her," Lizzy says, and taps the girl on the shoulder.

The girl turns around and raises an eyebrow at us. "What?" she asks.

Lizzy points to the girl's nose ring and asks, "Does that hurt when you sneeze?"

Ugh! That wasn't the question! She was supposed to ask why the girl was buying so many keys!

The girl stares at Lizzy, and then shakes her head.

"Why? You thinking of getting one?" she asks. "It would look good on you."

"Really?" Lizzy says, clearly flattered, although I can't imagine why. Before she can get directions to the nearest piercing place, I step forward and ask, "Why are you buying so many keys?"

The girl laughs. "What are you guys, the flea market police? I'm doing an art project. I have about a hundred keys so far," she boasts. "Sometimes I make jewelry out of them, too. See?" She moves her long black hair away from one ear. A tiny silver key dangles from a hook. "It's from my diary in fifth grade!"

"Cool," Lizzy and I say, because really, what else could we say?

"Any more questions?" she asks, letting her hair fall back down over her ear.

We shake our heads, and she turns back to the table and scoops up another dishful of keys. What if the keys to my dad's box are already a part of some art project? Or hanging from some girl's ears? Whatever happened to the good old days when all people wanted keys for was to open locks? We reached the last block of the market when Lizzy stops short and grabs my arm. "Look!"

I follow her gaze to an entire table with what looks like all different types of keys and locks in clear plastic bins. We hurry over, jostling a customer or two out of the way. This is key heaven! Small keys, long keys, fat keys, short keys. Old rusted keys, shiny new keys. My eyes can't absorb all the bounty before us.

"Where do we start?" I ask Lizzy in a daze.

She just shakes her head, equally overwhelmed.

An elderly couple sits behind the table on matching rocking chairs. They look like they'd be more at home on a rustic porch than in lower Manhatten. The man chomps on a pipe and seems unmoved by all the hustle and bustle going on around him. The woman waves a paper fan to try to cool off as she rocks ever so slowly back and forth.

"You know," I can't help but tell her, "studies have shown that using a hand fan actually takes more energy than the resulting breeze generates. So really, you're just making yourself hotter."

"What's that?" she says, cocking her ear toward me.

Lizzy pushes me aside. "Never mind him," she says loudly. Turning to me, she says, "Can we show them the box? Otherwise we could be here for hours, and I *know* you don't want to take the subway home in the dark."

I scramble to slip my arms out of the straps and unzip the bag. Lizzy takes the box from me and lays it gently on the table. The couple lean forward in their chairs and peer at the box with interest.

The old man takes his pipe out of his mouth and taps it on the edge of the table so the burnt tobacco falls onto the asphalt below. "That's a might pretty box you got there," he says in a gentle voice.

"Do you think any of your keys will open it?" I ask eagerly.

"Hmmm," he says thoughtfully. "Mind if I take a closer look?"

I push the box closer to him, and he lifts it up and turns it around a few times. He doesn't ask me about the words engraved on it. He mumbles to himself something about not having seen a box like this in years, and about true craftsmanship being a dying art.

"You've seen boxes like this before?" I ask. Then I turn to Lizzy and say, "If we could find the manufacturer, I bet we could get keys from them!"

"But Larry Junior said there's no name on the box," she replies.

The old man nods in agreement. "This here's handmade. Used to know a guy and his wife who sold stuff like this. But they retired from the flea market circuit a few years ago."

"Any way to contact them?" Lizzy asks. "Maybe they'd know where it came from."

The man shakes his head. "Sorry. Haven't a clue."

Lizzy and I share a disappointed look.

"But you're welcome to go through my collection and see what you can find," he says, handing me back the box. "As you can see, we got all kinds." He points to each bin in turn. "Over here you got your railroad keys, then your jailhouse keys, keys to open luggage, wind pocket watches, then there are the Ford Model T and Edsel car keys, and these here opened the rooms at the fine Seaview Motel before they went to those plastic cards." He gives a little shudder when he mentions the plastic cards.

"And here," he says proudly, pointing to a tall board attached to the end of the table, "we got our pride and joy." The board is covered with rows of hooks with very old-looking keys hanging from them. Most are rusted, and some on the bottom row are over six inches long.

They look like big skeleton keys. The man tells us how he got them from all over the world and that some are hundreds of years old. They are actually very cool, and I can see why they are his pride and joy. Lizzy has been shifting her weight from one foot to the other impatiently. Finally she blurts out, "Don't you have any *regular* keys?"

I cringe. Lizzy really has to work on her manners. The old woman pushes herself out of her rocker and says, "Come on, George. Show the kids what they want."

"Yes, dear," the man says, winking at me. He picks up a small bin from between the watch winders and the luggage keys and hands it to Lizzy. "Give these a shot," he says. "These are the ones that don't fall neatly into any other category."

"We'll bring them right back," Lizzy promises, hugging the box close to her chest.

"You look like trustworthy kids," the woman says. "We'll be here all day."

Lizzy beams at being called trustworthy. She thanks them and quickly hurries toward the closest bench. I grab my box off the table and have to jog to keep up with her.

When I join her on the bench I notice her brow is crinkled, like she's thinking hard about something. "Something wrong?" I ask.

"I don't know," she says, gesturing to the table we just came from. "All those keys."

"What about them?"

"They were all made to open something specific, right? Like one particular lock or door or briefcase or something?"

"I guess so."

"So what if there are people all over the world — people like *us* — who have a lock but can't find the key? Don't you think that's kind of sad?"

Every once in a while, Lizzy says something that really makes me think. I can see her point. Two parts of a whole, separated and lost from each other. "Like swans," I say.

"Huh?"

"You know, how swans mate for life, and then if one of them dies, the other just swims around alone for the rest of its life. Keys are like that. My dad's box is like that. Only one key will fit. Well, in our case, four keys."

Lizzy considers this for a minute, then says, "Can we forget about the swans and just try these keys?"

"You're the one who brought it up," I point out.

"I did *not* bring up the swans!"

"You just don't like learning anything new," I argue.

"I just don't see the point of knowing a lot of useless facts."

I am *not* going to get sucked into this argument again. "Let's just try the keys," I say through clenched teeth.

We get about halfway down the bin when something happens. A key fits all the way into a hole! All the ridges line up. I keep slipping it in and out to make sure it's really happening. Lizzy grabs my arm and squeezes. "Does it turn?" she asks breathlessly.

I try to turn it in both directions, but it won't move. I shake my head and hand Lizzy the box. She tries a few times too, before giving up and slipping the key into her pocket. "Let's keep going," she says, grabbing the next key from the bin.

We don't have any more luck, but there is a new lift in our step as we walk back to the table.

"How did it go?" the man asks when we return the bin to its rightful place.

Lizzy pulls the key out of her pocket and says, "This one fit in one of the holes, but it won't turn."

The man nods. "You can keep that one, but I suspect your box was made exclusively for one set of keys. You may find a few more to fit the holes, but I doubt you'll get 'em to turn."

I look down at the box in my hand. My dad's words stare back at me and then swim a little as my eyes get watery.

"Here," the old man says, reaching up and pulling one of the big keys off the board. He hands it across to me along with a padded bag. "Take this as my gift. Anyone looking for keys as hard as you is a kindred spirit."

Surprised, I gingerly take the key from him. Some of the rust rubs off on my hand. "Thank you," I say sincerely. "What did it open?"

He shrugs. "Probably an old barn or storehouse."

"Great," Lizzy mutters. "Now we've got four locks with no keys and two keys with no locks. We're worse off than before!"

I carefully slip the key into the padded bag and put it and the box into my backpack.

"Thank you for the gift and for all your help," I say to the couple. "We really appreciate it."

"It's a shame you lost those original keys," the man says as he and his wife head back to their rockers.

I'm about to tell him that it wasn't us who lost them, but before I get a chance Lizzy says, "Don't worry, we know where they are and we're gonna find them."

I'm about ask Lizzy what the heck she's talking about, when the old man relights his pipe and says, "Good, good. Be sure to come back and tell me what the meaning of life is once you find out."

"We will," Lizzy says, already turning away. She puts one hand on my back and starts pushing me down the aisle.

When we get far enough away I ask, "Why did you tell him we know where the original keys are?"

"Because we do," Lizzy replies. "And that brings us to the next item on my chart. The one I hoped we wouldn't have to get to."

A chill literally runs down my spine. Not a good sign in eighty-degree weather. Hoping I don't sound as worried as I feel, I ask, "You wouldn't happen to have another Milk Dud in your pocket, would you?"

Chapter 5: Plan F

"You're kidding, right?"

Lizzy has just read the final item on her chart. My outburst causes Zilla to growl at me and position himself between the two of us. Lizzy lays the chart back down on the kitchen table.

"Our keys are hidden in Harold's office somewhere," she insists. "He said so himself. Maybe they're under the carpet in a forgotten corner of the supply closet. Or stuck in the back of a desk drawer. Or glued to the ceiling. We're gonna get into that office, and we're gonna find them."

"Breaking and entering? That's your big plan? That's illegal!" I slip carefully past Zilla and into the living room, where I begin to pace and think. The law office is all the way uptown. I'm sure Mom wouldn't approve of us going there, so I'd have to lie. Can this be the only answer? What if other people are already using that office? Maybe if we kept looking at flea markets and tag sales, we'd eventually find keys that would work? But would we find them in time?

I'm getting a bit dizzy from circling, so I sit down on the couch that, unlike ours, has no holes and no name. I practice my deep breathing. Architecturally our two apartments are identical, just flipped around. But they couldn't be more different inside. Practically everything in Lizzy's house is beige. Her dad says that it makes it easier to decorate. I have to admit, it's more calming than all the crazy colors of my place.

Lizzy comes in and sits next to me on the arm of the couch. She picks at a stray thread and doesn't look at me. "Sorry," she says. "The box is yours, and I've been acting like it's mine, too. Making all these plans, dragging you all over the city. I'll stop, and you can do whatever you're comfortable doing."

I'm so surprised by her words that at first I wonder if I misheard her. It *sounded* like she was apologizing for being bossy. Yes, I'm pretty sure she was! But to be honest, she doesn't have anything to apologize for.

"Um, thank you for that," I say haltingly. "But we're in this together. I asked you for help, and you've had really great ideas."

"Aw, shucks," she says, punching me lightly on the arm.

Always one to try the easiest way first, I say, "Before we go to Harold's office, let's at least call him. Maybe he's still there and will look a little harder."

"That's the spirit," Lizzy says. She jumps off the couch and puts up her hand for a high-five. I give her a weak one. She takes the letter out of my backpack and reaches for the phone. As she dials, I remind her that it's Saturday and maybe we need to wait till Monday. She shushes me and moves the phone between us so we can both hear.

It's a recording. "You have reached the law offices of Folgard and Levine. We have closed our Manhattan branch and will be reopening in Long Island in September, following a safari in Africa. Peace out."

"Peace out?" Lizzy repeats, hanging up the phone. "What a strange guy."

"Maybe Levine is the strange one," I offer.

"Who's Levine?"

"The other guy in the office. Harold might be perfectly normal."

Lizzy shakes her head. "If he was friends with your parents, he's probably not normal."

She has a point.

"We need to make a list," she says, suddenly all business. She grabs a pencil off the coffee table and looks around for something to write on. "To recap what we've learned: It will be extremely difficult, if not impossible, to find keys that will fit the box. The box cannot otherwise be broken into, at least not without destroying it and, most likely, its contents. We know Harold is no longer in his office, and might even be in the jungle." She finds a copy of an old issue of *Post Office Weekly* and rips off the back, which is blank. She begins to scribble. "We'll need gloves, a flashlight, a screwdriver, a briefcase, candy, a map of the city, and some nice clothes." She taps her forehead a few times with the pencil. "Now what am I forgetting?"

"The kitchen sink?" I volunteer.

"Why do we need the kitchen sink?"

"Why do we need a briefcase or a flashlight?" I ask. "We're not going in the middle of the night. And candy? You know I'm in favor of bringing candy anywhere we go, but why for this mission?"

"Duh," she says. "To bribe the security guard, of course."

I laugh. "You think a security guard is going to let us snoop around someone's office because you give him a Twizzler?"

"I was thinking more like a bag of Skittles," she says. "And then if he still won't let us in, a king-sized Snickers oughta do it."

She may have something there. He'd have to be a man of strong resolve to turn down a king-sized Snickers.

"And if that doesn't work," she says, pulling her hair out of its ponytail, "I'll just use my feminine wiles."

"What feminine wiles would those be?"

She shakes her hair out and does this pouty thing with her lips.

I burst out laughing. "You look like one of my fish!"

She chases me around the room, swinging her hair and hips, and puckering her lips.

"Speaking of my fish," I say, running to the door. "I have to go feed them. Cat and Dog were ganging up on Ferret last night. I better make sure they haven't eaten him."

Lizzy says, "You're just afraid of my feminine power." She closes the door behind me. I give a little shiver. I don't usually think of Lizzy as a girl at all. It's just too disturbing.

I awake on Sunday morning to the sound of one of those big trucks backing up. *Beep, beep, beep.* The brakes hiss as the truck comes to a stop. Why would a big truck park in front of my building? Unless . . .

I jump out of bed and peek through the blinds. It *is* a moving truck! Our new neighbors have arrived! A small red car pulls up behind the truck, and the four doors open. The first thing I see are four blond heads. Mother, father, boy, girl. At the same time, all four crane their necks and look up at the building. The father points first to the roof, where people sit on July fourth to watch the fireworks, and then down to the window of the apartment that will be theirs. He doesn't look like a minor league baseball player or an acrobat, or any of the other things I had been hoping for. He's actually wearing a suit, which I think is weird for a Sunday and even weirder for moving day.

Since my window is only about ten feet above their heads, I can see them very well. The boy is scowling, and the girl's face is sort of crumpled. Streaks of brown makeup run off from the sides of her eyes. She must have been crying. I want to call down that this is a nice place to live, but never having moved in my life I can't really identify with what they must be feeling. I plan on living here forever.

The parents start directing the moving men, and the kids lean against the car. The boy crosses his arms and kicks at the ground while the girl twists a strand of hair around her finger. I'm about to go get Mom to tell her the new neighbors are here when I see our upstairs neighbor, five-year-old Bobby Sanchez, run down the porch steps and up to the car. His mom hurries to catch up.

"Hi!" Bobby says to the new kids, sticking out his hand.

I can hear him clearly through my window screen, but the new boy pretends not to. The girl forces a smile and shakes his hand. "I'm Samantha," she says. "This rude kid is my brother, Rick. We're moving in today."

"Cool!" Bobby says, scratching his head with one hand and shuffling his feet. That boy is never still.

"I'm five," Bobby adds. "How old are you?"

"We're fourteen," Samantha replies. "We're twins, but I'm older by six minutes."

Rick kicks her in the shin, and she jumps. "Well it's true!" she says. A roll of thunder passes by, and everyone checks the sky. I hope it doesn't rain on them.

With both of my parents being identical twins, I would have expected to come across more twins in my lifetime, but this is the first boy-girl set I've ever seen. They don't look very much alike. She has an oval-shaped face, and his is squarer. I am starting to feel a little creepy spying on them, so I scribble a note to Lizzy and stick it through the hole. By the time I use the bathroom and throw on shorts and a T-shirt, there's a response waiting for me.

J –
Not leaving my apartment today = not meeting new neighbors. You can come over if you want. Your grandmother e-mailed me about the state fair. I'll wait till you get here to open it.
L

I write back:

L –
Why aren't you leaving your apartment?
J

She responds:

N.O.Y.B.? Why isn't it my business that she won't come downstairs? And Grandma was very sneaky to e-mail Lizzy instead of me. She knows I delete anything with "state fair" in the subject heading.

I go back to the window, but the new family is no longer outside. They must have gone up to their apartment. It has started to drizzle, and the movers are carrying bundled furniture up the stairs along with a seemingly endless number of boxes. I debate going to their apartment, but figure I should wait for Mom to do that. She'd want to bake something probably. I think that's what you do when someone new moves in. If these were just new kids at school I wouldn't even think of trying to meet them. But I feel it is my neighborly duty to be, you know, neighborly.

Since I'm dressed now, I might as well go to Lizzy's. I leave a note for Mom on the kitchen table. I am very responsible that way.

Grandma knows I'm dreading keeping my end of the bargain that we made last summer. Each summer Lizzy, Mom, and I visit her at the bed-and-breakfast she runs in New Jersey. It's basically the only time I leave the state. Last summer, as she does each year, Grandma took us to the state fair nearby. I basically ate my way through the whole thing — caramel apple, candy apple, funnel cake, cotton candy, and a root beer float. Mom said I would pay for it later, but I was fine. I have an iron stomach.

Grandma bet Lizzy and me that the woman at the Guess Your Weight booth would guess both our weights exactly right. She said if she won the bet, then Lizzy and I would agree to participate in the Young Talent Competition next summer. She'd been trying to convince us to participate for years. Apparently competition is good for the soul and builds character. She herself enters the Table-Setting Competition every year and also the Make Your Own Jam. If the woman was wrong, Grandma promised never to mention the competition again.

Lizzy may be short, but she has muscle. She weighs more than she looks. We exchanged knowing glances and agreed to take Grandma's bet. The guess-your-weight woman narrowed her eyes at us, then scribbled some numbers on her pad. She put the pad on the table and gestured for us to step on the scales. When she showed us the pad, she was exactly right.

Clearly there was some kind of scam involved, but Grandma dragged us away before we could do a thorough investigation. I bet the woman had scales buried under the ground that she could see somehow.

So now we have to be in the stupid talent show. At least we can choose our own act. We need to come up with one today that won't be too humiliating.

Lizzy's dad opens their door. He's still in his pajamas. They have ducks on them, and little clouds. As I've mentioned, Mr. Muldoun is a hefty man, so there are a lot of ducks and a lot of clouds.

"Before you say anything," he says groggily as he steps

aside to let me in, "they were left over from the last auction, and all my other pajamas are in the laundry."

At the post office they're always auctioning off packages that have been deemed undeliverable, like they don't have addresses or return addresses. Usually it's stuff like clothes, CDs, and books, but they've found snakes, a hamster, and even some poor guy's ashes in an urn! Mr. Muldoun gives my mom the heads-up on what will be available. That's how I got my computer. Mom once got a whole box of mixed beads. Just what we needed in our apartment — more beads. The law says they couldn't auction off the urn, so it sits on a top shelf in the post office, and every once and a while someone will put a flower next to it.

"Not every man can wear ducks," I say, following Mr. Muldoun into the kitchen, where he offers me a blueberry muffin. I politely decline. He gives a dramatic sigh, and hands me the chocolate one.

While I munch on it, he says, "Lizzy told me about the box from your father. I hope that's okay."

I nod.

"You must be pretty curious about what's in it," he says.

"Very," I reply, trying not to spray little pieces of muffin.

"Hey, I bet I know where you'll find those keys," he says, peeling a banana.

I look up from my muffin in surprise. Is he saying he has a set? "Where? Where will I find them?"

He grins widely. "In the last place you look."

"Huh? Where's that?"

"Don't you get it?" he asks. "You always find something the last place you look. Because once you find it, you stop looking!"

"Ah, a joke," I reply, rolling my eyes. "I should have known."

"Should have known what?" Lizzy asks, entering the room.

I'm about to tell her when I am caught off guard by the round Band-Aid in the center of her chin. "Cut yourself shaving?"

"Very funny," she says. "I don't want to talk about it." She storms into the living room. I follow with a glance back at her dad. He mouths the word *pimple*. So *that's* why she doesn't want to meet the new neighbors!

Lizzy and her dad share a computer that they keep on a desk in the living room. I plop down on the couch as she reads the e-mail from my grandma out loud:

Dear Lizzy,
Hello, darling. As you know, the fair is coming up in only a few weeks. I've tried to get in touch with Jeremy, but his e-mail must be broken. So I have taken the liberty of choosing your routine for the talent competition. Remember that lovely skit with the hula hoop? That is what you will be doing. The act must be between three and five minutes, so do time your music accordingly.
Much love, Grandma Annie

Lizzy whirls around, her hand over her mouth, eyes wide with horror.

This is exactly why I don't like surprises. Once I get over the initial shock, I jump up from the couch. "This is a nightmare. We can't perform that routine in front of hundreds of strangers!"

Lizzy's face is getting redder by the second. "She isn't talking about that thing we used to do where you throw me a football while I'm hula hooping and I throw it back? And then I eat that banana?"

I nod miserably. "That's the one. Remember we made that up the summer we went out there and it rained the whole time?"

"We were SIX!" Lizzy shouts.

Lizzy's father hurries into the room. "Everything okay?"

Lizzy fills him in on our dire situation.

Mr. Muldoun shrugs. "Doesn't sound so bad. Could be a growth experience."

We glare at him.

"Is there a prize?" he asks.

"I think it's fifty dollars if you win," I reply.

With a wink, Mr. Muldoun says, "That'd buy some kid a lot of Snickers bars."

Hmmm. He has a point.

"Fine," Lizzy says, throwing up her arms. "But if we lose out to that kid who plays the harmonica with his nose, someone's gonna pay."

"That kid won't win," I assure her. "He won last year, and you can't do the same act twice."

"It's a good thing I like your grandmother," Lizzy says. "I wouldn't hula hoop for just anyone."

"I know you wouldn't." I refrain from reminding her that when we were younger, she used to want everyone to watch her. "Are you sure you don't want to meet the neighbors now? I don't think they're too happy to be here."

She gestures wildly at the Band-Aid on her chin. The subject is closed.

Monday morning comes all too quickly. Lizzy shows up at my bedroom door dressed in a long skirt and a clean white top. Her hair is out of its ponytail and has actually been brushed. The Band-Aid is gone. I rub my eyes to make sure it's her.

"Why aren't you dressed yet?" she demands. Yup, it's her all right.

"It's only eight-thirty!" I reply, letting my head fall back on the pillow.

She walks over and tugs the pillow out from under me. "You know we have to get an early start. We have a lot to do before we go."

I groan. "Like what?"

She ticks off the list on her fingers. "First, you have to get dressed. *Nicely.* Second, you have to gather your items from the list. Third, we have to go to the store to get the candy. Luckily for you, the best way to the office is by bus so you're spared the subway for today."

I sleepily sit up and move to the edge of the bed. "You

forgot the part where I have to lie to my mom on the way out. She's off from work on Mondays so she's home now."

"Already taken care of," Lizzy says with a dismissive wave of her arm. "She saw me coming in and asked why I was dressed up. I said we're meeting my dad at the post office and he's going to give us a tour."

"But what'll happen if she sees your dad later and he doesn't know about any tour?"

"Don't worry so much." Lizzy pulls my closet door open and reaches inside. "We'll ask my dad for a real tour tomorrow just in case. Here," she says, tossing a blue button-down shirt on my bed. "Wear this with your tan pants."

I make a face. "The only time I wore that shirt was to my aunt's gallery opening. You want me to wear it on a regular day?"

"It's for a worthy cause," she says, grabbing a pair of brown dress shoes from the floor of the closet. "We have to look respectable. And didn't everyone tell you how handsome you looked in it?"

"One old lady," I grumble. "But I think she was legally blind. All right, give me ten minutes."

I drag myself to the bathroom and throw on the outfit Lizzy laid out for me. It takes a while to do up all the buttons on the shirt. Why would anyone wear this when they could pull on a T-shirt? I grab the items on Lizzy's list that are my responsibility — the flashlight, gloves, and screwdriver — and stuff them in my backpack. Lizzy has the map and one of her dad's old briefcases. We'll have to stop at the comic store for the candy.

Mom and Lizzy are in the living room when I come

out. Mom is on her knees patching up one of Mongo's legs. It's been peeling ever since Zilla the monster cat had to stay here for a night last month while Lizzy's apartment was being exterminated. Zilla spent half the night using the leg of the couch as a scratching post. Neither of us was brave enough to try to stop her.

"Don't you look nice, Jeremy," Mom says when she sees me.

"Er, thanks," I mumble, unable to look her in the eye.

"Well, we better go," Lizzy says, hurrying past Mom toward the door. "The mail stops for no man. Or something like that."

"Just a second," Mom says, scrambling to stand up without dropping her spool of thread. My heart quickens as she comes toward me. She must see it in my face. I am the *worst* liar. To my surprise, Mom passes right by me and peers at Lizzy's chin. "I just wanted to make sure the concealer is working," she says. "Looks good to me. Can't see a thing."

Lizzy blushes furiously and doesn't look at me. I want to laugh, but she'd kill me. "It's fine, thanks for your help," she mumbles and practically throws herself out the front door. I think it's nice that my mom wants to help Lizzy with girl stuff.

Mom closes the door behind us, and I see that Lizzy left the briefcase a few feet away outside our door. She picks it up, and we're about to turn down the stairs when the new kids come out of their apartment. The four of us stand there awkwardly until the girl, Samantha, says hi, and we all introduce ourselves. Rick doesn't look quite as angry today. Perhaps he is resolved to his fate.

"So where did you move from?" Lizzy asks. She unconsciously reaches up to touch the spot where her covered-up pimple is, and then quickly lowers her hand.

"From New Jersey," Samantha answers. "Our dad works in the city and was tired of the commute."

"Did you ever go to the state fair?" Lizzy asks, in an unfamiliar high-pitched voice. "We're going to be in it next month."

I've never heard her so talkative to strangers. Why would she mention the state fair of all things?

"The state fair?" Rick repeats with a laugh. "Only hicks go there. What are you going to do? Pull a tractor with your teeth? No, wait, you're going to race pigs!"

"Shut up, Rick!" Samantha says, pushing him hard into the wall. "Ignore him," she says, rolling her eyes. "He can be so obnoxious."

"No problem," I mumble, even though I don't mean it. Rick is still laughing, and Lizzy has turned mute. It looks like it's up to me. "Well, we hope you'll like it here," I tell Samantha, ignoring Rick. Then, as Mom trained me to do, I add, "Let us know if you need anything." I point out which apartments are ours, and seeing as Lizzy is still mute, I pull her down the stairs with me.

"What was that all about?" I ask once we get outside and a few yards away.

The usual spring is missing from her step, and she's walking very slowly. Could she have been nervous because of Rick? Does she think he's cute or something? Finally she says, "I feel so stupid. Samantha's gonna think I look like this every day, with this dorky skirt. And then I go on about the stupid state fair. Why did I say that? And this stupid briefcase. Did you see her earrings? And her toenails were red!"

"I won't ask why you looking at her feet. But why do you care if some girl you don't even know thinks you look like this every day? What's wrong with the way you look?"

"Oh, never mind," she says. "You don't understand girls at all." She walks faster, almost jogging, and I have to hurry to keep up. Well, at least the spring is back in her step.

Chapter 6: The Office

Mitch is just opening the locks on the front door of Fink's Comics and Magic when we arrive. I can't help noticing the large ring of keys in his hands.

"Hey, dude and dudette," he says in a kind of drawl. He's always trying to sound like he's from California, when I know he's never even been there. It is my secret hope that he'll move there for real after he graduates. Then maybe Uncle Arthur will retire, and I'll take over the store. A kid can dream, can't he?

Mitch gives Lizzy's outfit an approving glance, but she doesn't notice. She's too busy eyeing the key ring, too.

As we follow him inside, I whisper to Lizzy, "We should check his keys in case my mom is wrong and my dad *did* leave an extra set in the store. Then we wouldn't have to go uptown."

She nods in agreement. "I was thinking the same thing."

"I'll go ask Mitch for them."

"Wait," Lizzy says, pulling me back. "He's gonna want to know why you want them. Do you really want him to tell him about the box?"

She's right. I don't want him to know about it. He might try to lay claim to it somehow, or at the very least make fun of me. I know they store the keys under the counter, so all we have to do is wait until an opportune moment to grab them. We pretend to be looking through the comics while Mitch finishes opening the register. He asks me to watch the front for a minute while he gets a new cash drawer ready in the back.

"No problem," Lizzy and I reply at the same time.

"That was too easy," Lizzy whispers once he disappears into the back room. We run behind the counter, and she grabs the keys. I unzip my bag and we quickly try the keys in each keyhole. No luck. Not even a nibble. Well, at least now I'm convinced that Harold's office is our only hope. My uncle heads behind the counter just as I'm zipping up my bag. He gives me a suspicious look.

"Whatcha doing?" he asks, glancing from me to my bag to Lizzy. Besides his physical resemblance to my dad, his voice is identical to Dad's, too. This always creeps me out (when it doesn't make me want to cry, that is).

"Nothing," I answer, swinging the bag over my shoulder. "Mitch asked us to watch the front, so we were just, you know, watching the front."

"Yeah," Lizzy says, sliding past Uncle Arthur and around to the front of the counter. "And now we're going to buy some candy."

I smile weakly at my uncle and join Lizzy on the other side. She's already placed two bags of Twizzlers and a king-sized Snickers on the countertop.

"Job interview?" my uncle asks, giving my outfit the once-over.

I shake my head. "Lizzy's dad is bringing us to work with him." It's amazing how easily I can lie to my uncle. All I have to do is remember the time he was supposed to take me on the father-son campout in sixth grade and never showed up. It may not excuse the lying, but it makes me feel less guilty.

He gives Lizzy her change and puts her candy in a bag. She flashes him a bright smile and says, "Thanks!"

We wave as we go through the door. "That was a close one," she says when we're halfway down the block.

"Why?" I ask, watching as she unwraps one of the packs of Twizzlers. "It's not like we stole anything."

She hands me a Twizzler, and I remember who I'm talking to. "We didn't steal anything, right?" I ask.

"No, we didn't steal anything!" she says. "But I wouldn't be surprised if that uncle of yours thinks we did."

"I guess I can't blame him," I say. "Each year the store loses a few hundred dollars in stolen candy and comics."

"That's so like you," she says, sucking on her Twizzler. "Always trying to find the best in people, even him."

"Hey, weren't you going to buy Skittles for the security guard, not Twizzlers?"

"I panicked, all right? Just eat your Twizzler."

At that moment we catch sight of the bus rounding the corner. We run toward it, the bag thumping against my back. Two businessmen are waiting at the stop, both holding bus passes in their hands. The bus pulls up to the curb, and I ask Lizzy if she knows how much the bus costs. Mom has always taken care of this sort of thing. I've really got to start paying more attention.

"Two dollars each way," she says. "I checked this time. You have money, right?"

"You don't?"

"I just spent it on the candy!"

I pull out my wallet as a Girl Scout troop gets in line behind us, giggling and pushing each other. The two men step on, stick their bus passes in the slot, and pull them back out. They're the same MetroCards we were supposed to use on the subway. Those things carry a lot of power in this city! The driver is waiting for us. I hand him our four dollars. It's a good thing I have my usual eight, or else we wouldn't have enough to get home.

"Quarters only," the driver says, not even looking at us.

"We don't have any quarters," I say meekly.

The driver rolls his eyes and booms, "Anyone got a card?"

The Girl Scouts behind us are getting restless. I hear one of them mutter, "Dorks!" and a few others giggle. For their rudeness, I may just demand a free box of cookies this year.

"I'll do it," a middle-aged woman in the front seat says, standing up. I elbow Lizzy when I see the woman is wearing a Yankees cap and sweatshirt, just like the guy who helped us in the subway. Good thing baseball fans are so superstitious! The woman lowers her card into the slot twice, and then grabs the four dollars from my hand.

Anxious to be away from the front of the bus, we make our way to the back and take the last two seats. Lizzy immediately turns and stares out the window. I know she feels bad for messing up our second mode of public transportation.

"Hey, Lizzy, one of the Girl Scouts just made another one cry. That should make you feel better."

I can see her smile in the reflection of the glass. Lizzy gets upset easily, but it doesn't take much to cheer her up.

I take out my book, glad to have a few minutes to study the diagram on time travel and string theory. But before I can build a time machine out of strings, I need to figure out what the heck they are talking about.

I have just opened the dog-eared page when I am hit by the overpowering stench of garlic that has suddenly engulfed the bus. I look around wildly for the source, and find a man in a construction worker's outfit nibbling on what can only be a sandwich made completely out of garlic cloves. Why does no one else notice? I can't say anything to Lizzy without him hearing, and he doesn't look like the type of person I'd want to insult. With his insanely small nibbles, it takes him ten blocks to finish it off. By that time, beads of sweat are clearly visible on his forehead. He crumples the wrapper and sticks it back in his lunchbox. He may be smelly, but at least he's tidy.

"Ours is the next stop," Lizzy says, folding her small city map. I nod, afraid to open my mouth lest the smell get inside. Although the sandwich is gone, the stench has gained in strength. I would not have thought this possible. The man is superhuman. Move over Superman, here comes Garlicman, able to leap tall buildings in a single smelly breath.

I put my book away in preparation for our arrival. All I managed to learn is that string theory doesn't actually involve strings, but rather tiny bands of energy waves. Those will be harder to find than regular string.

We get out of our seats and hold onto the poles by the back door. The bus slows as it approaches the corner, but then it rolls right past. At first this registers only faintly, but as the back half of the bus fully passes the stop, I realize the driver isn't going to pull over at all.

"Wait!" Lizzy yells up to the front. "You just passed our stop!"

The driver doesn't slow down. A woman with white hair and a silver cane leans forward and says to Lizzy, "Young lady, if the driver doesn't see anyone waiting at a stop, he will not pull over. If you want the bus to stop, you have to press that yellow strip up there. You see?" We follow as she points shakily to a thick strip of what looks like yellow tape. I realize I've seen people pressing it before, but never paid much attention.

"Oh, right," Lizzy mumbles. "Thanks."

"Can I still press it now?" I ask the woman.

She nods happily. I reach up easily and push hard on the tape. A bell dings once. I guess short people just have to ride around and around the city until a taller person helps them.

"Now the driver will pull over at the next stop. You see?" the woman says. "You're only two blocks from where you wanted to be." She settles back in her seat.

Who says New Yorkers aren't helpful? Of course two more blocks means we're stuck with Garlicman for that much longer. I wonder if anyone ever died from odor assault.

It turns out the next stop is full of people waiting, so the driver would have stopped anyway. The bus pulls over, and the front door opens, but not the back. Lizzy yanks at the handle, but it doesn't budge. Garlicman reaches over and pushes a metal strip next to the door, and the door swings open. I take back my mean thoughts about him. He is obviously another caring citizen.

We hurry down the three steps before the driver can change his mind and pull away. My left foot sticks to each step as I descend, having picked up gum somewhere along the way. When we are clear of the crowd, I ask Lizzy to wait while I use the curb to scrape the gum off the bottom of my shoe.

"Holy cow!" she says, grabbing my arm tight. (When she was six, Lizzy's dad trained her to use expletives like *holy cow* and *good golly* instead of the other more colorful ones she had brought home from her first day of kindergarten.)

I almost lose my balance since I have one foot in the air and one arm being pulled nearly out of its socket. I follow her gaze. In the gutter about two feet away from us is a playing card. Face up, its bottom half is hidden under a Chinese food takeout menu. It's the eight of hearts, one of the last three missing cards in Lizzy's collection. It's been at least six months since she had found a card. I was beginning to think the final three would never turn up.

Lizzy breaks her grip on my arm and bends down over the card. Fingers shaking, she grasps it by one corner. She doesn't pull yet though, and I know she's saying one of her little prayers in hopes that the card will be intact. All too often she'll find torn cards, and she won't put those in her collection.

Finally, she gives the card a gentle tug and it slips out, fully intact. She heaves a sigh of relief and then holds it high above her head like she's the winning boxer in a prize fight. "Ta da!" she announces. "Only two more to go!"

She snaps open her briefcase and slides the card carefully in one of the pockets on the top. She takes a few steps in the direction of the office but stops when I don't move from my spot. "What's up?" she asks. "Aren't you psyched that I found my card?"

I nod, not really hearing her. If we hadn't missed our stop, if we hadn't veered away from our original plan, we wouldn't have gotten off here, and she wouldn't have found her card. But was it fate that brought us to this spot, or just good luck? What about fate and *bad* luck?

If Dad had taken a different route that day, or sat at a red light one second longer, he wouldn't have died. What if the lady who he swerved to avoid hitting had waited one more second before crossing the street? Or if she had been holding her package from underneath instead of by the handle, which had broken halfway across the intersection and caused her to stop walking?

Or what if it hadn't rained that morning so the street wasn't so slick that Dad's tires lost their grip on the road? Or what if I hadn't been sick that day and had been able to go with him? We might have stopped for ice cream first, and then —

"Are you all right?" Lizzy asks, peering into my face and interrupting my thoughts. It isn't like I'll ever get a chance to find out what would have happened if any of those other things had taken place. Unless I do manage to build a time machine. And that isn't looking too promising.

I take a deep breath. And another. "I'm fine," I reply. "Let's go."

"Me finding that card, that was a good sign," she says as we continue walking. "A good sign for sure!"

I hope she's right. Now that we're close by, I'm starting to get nervous. After a few blocks, Lizzy stops in front of a tall building. She consults the letterhead of my mom's letter from Harold and says, "This is it. The former offices of Harold Folgard, Esquire."

I have to tilt my head all the way back to see the top of it. Neither of us makes a move to go inside. "It's so . . . tall," I say, shading my eyes.

"Good thing you won't have to scale the outside and use a glass cutter to break into the offices," she says, leading me toward the revolving door. "That was my backup plan."

The lobby is marble and glass with tall ceilings and two banks of elevators. It's quiet, too, like a library. "The office is on the fourteenth floor," Lizzy says. Her voice echoes. There are only a few people in the lobby, none of them paying the slightest attention to us.

I move closer to the wall to read the signs. "It's this one," I say softly, pointing to the elevators on our right. "Floors one through sixteen."

"Look like you belong," she whispers back, flipping her hair behind her shoulders. She swings her briefcase gently back and forth as she walks toward the first elevator.

I straighten my back and lift my chin a little. I am sure

with my height I could easily pass as a businessman from behind — a very skinny, backpack-wearing businessman.

Lizzy is about to press the UP button when a voice booms out from across the lobby, "Where do you think you're going?"

We freeze. My heart starts racing. A man comes up behind us, and we slowly turn around. He is wearing a black security guard uniform. We'd already agreed that if we got stopped, Lizzy would do the talking. To be honest, I don't think I could speak anyway. I hope she doesn't try to pull out the feminine wiles.

To her credit, Lizzy is very composed. She looks the guard in the eye and says calmly, "Our uncle works on the fourteenth floor. We wanted to surprise him."

He doesn't answer right away, and I try sending Lizzy a telepathic message: *Offer him the king-sized Snickers . . . the Snickers!* But she either doesn't receive my message or is ignoring it. The guard finally says, "All visitors need to check in at the front desk. Follow me."

Our shoulders sag with relief as we follow him to the long marble desk in the corner of the lobby that we somehow managed to miss seeing when we came in. He steps behind the desk and puts out his hand. "Driver's license," he says in a tone that indicates he has asked this many times before.

Lizzy and I exchange a look of surprise. I *knew* I could pass for a businessman! "Um, we're only twelve," Lizzy says.

"Almost thirteen," I quickly add.

"School ID?" he asks.

"It's *summer*," Lizzy replies.

The guard sighs. "All right. I'll need you to sign in here." He pushes a clipboard across the counter to us. "And then one at a time I'll take your picture."

"Our picture?" I ask.

He nods. "Every visitor's pass has your picture on it now."

This isn't going as smoothly as I'd hoped.

Lizzy signs the clipboard and pushes it over to me. She signed in as *Tia Castaway,* the name of the little girl in our favorite Disney movie when we were little, *Escape to Witch Mountain.* She gives me a little kick on the shin, and since we're supposed to be brother and sister, I carefully write *Tony Castaway* and push the clipboard back to the man.

He takes our picture with a camera that is attached to the computer behind the desk. A few seconds later two visitor badges spew out of the printer. He hands them over and instructs us to peel off the back and wear them "on our person" at all times. We hurry toward the elevator, sticking the badges on our chests without even looking at them. Only when we're safely on the elevator do I notice my face staring back at me from Lizzy's shirt, one eye closed, the name *Tony Castaway* typed underneath. We quickly switch badges.

"This is a really slow elevator," I observe.

"Yeah," Lizzy says. "It's almost like we're not moving."

I look at the panel of numbers. "That's because neither of us pushed the button for our floor!" I lean over and push *14.* The elevator jumps a little and begins to ascend.

We start to laugh. Lizzy says, "You'd think we'd never been out of the house before."

I watch the floor numbers light up one at a time as we approach each one. "Did you know," I tell Lizzy, "that most buildings don't have a thirteenth floor because the number *13* is supposed to be bad luck? Of course there still *is* a thirteenth floor; they just call it the fourteenth floor."

Lizzy narrows her eyes. "So what you're saying is that since we're going to the fourteenth floor, we're gonna have bad luck?"

Maybe it's better when Lizzy doesn't listen when I share my knowledge of the world. "Um, forget I said anything."

When the doors open we get out and follow the signs toward Suite 42. Along the way we pass assorted businessmen and women, all who either ignore us or give us the forced smile that adults usually give to kids, where just the corners of their mouths turn up. We finally find the right door. It still has the FOLGARD AND LEVINE, ESQUIRES brass nameplate on it. Lizzy steps back and motions for me to try the door. I take a deep breath and turn the handle. Of course it doesn't budge.

"Turn it the other way," Lizzy advises.

"That's not gonna work," I say. "You always turn a knob to the right to open it." Nevertheless, I try it. I'm so surprised to feel it twist under my hand that I don't even push the door open for a second.

"Wow, that actually worked!" Lizzy exclaims, pushing through the door. I quickly follow and close it behind us. There is no electricity in the office, but enough light comes through the windows that we can easily see around us. It's like a ghost town of an office. Shells of desks and filing cabinets, stained carpet, empty cardboard boxes, a broken lamp.

"Let's get moving," Lizzy whispers. "You look in Harold's office, and I'll check out here in the waiting area."

I nod, and head into the office that has Harold's nameplate stuck on it. First I check the old wooden desk that sits in the center of the room. It's a nice desk. I wonder why he abandoned it. The drawers are all hanging out, which makes it easy. I feel around the insides of them, and also check the bottoms of each drawer in case the keys are taped there. All I come away with are a few splinters, three paper clips, and a business card for a moving company. I can hear Lizzy in the next room opening and closing drawers, too.

According to the plan, I crawl around on the carpet, feeling for lumps as I go along. About halfway around the room I actually feel something! It's about a foot away from one of the walls and is just the right size for a set of four keys and a key chain.

"Hey, Lizzy," I call out as loud as I dare. "I might have found something!"

She comes running in, and I point to the lump. She runs back out. When she returns, she is carrying her briefcase and my bag, which we had left by the front door. She unsnaps her briefcase and pulls out the screwdriver. She hands it to me, which I think is a nice gesture since I'm sure she'd be as capable as I in cutting the carpet. I would feel guilty doing what we're about to do, but the carpet is so old and stained and torn that there's no question the new tenants are going to replace it. In a way, we're helping them out.

Using the sharp edge, I hook the screwdriver under the edge of the carpet where it meets the wall. Then I move it back and forth like a saw. Even though the carpet is old, the fiber is strong. Lizzy holds the two edges of the rug apart as I go along, revealing the concrete floor beneath. I'm sweating by the time I slice my way to the lump. One last slice and the carpet reveals its hidden treasure.

Lizzy screams and jumps back so fast that she crashes to the floor, limbs flying. She covers her mouth to keep herself from screaming again and finally manages to scramble to her feet.

"You're such a girl," I tell her, letting the carpet fall back into place. "It's long dead." Instead of the keys to my box, we have uncovered the final resting place of a little brown mouse.

Lizzy shivers. "Lets just finish looking around. This place is giving me the creeps."

The only place I haven't searched yet is the ceiling. It's one of those drop-down types where you can push on the panels and they lift up. "Flashlight," I say, holding out my hand. Like a nurse handing a doctor a scalpel, Lizzy repeats, "Flashlight," and lays it in my hand. I stand up on the desk and can easily reach the ceiling. Pushing up on one of the panels, I move it aside so I can stick my flashlight up there. I have to clear away a cobweb before sticking my head in. Good thing I'm doing this instead of

Lizzy. For a tough girl, she is brought to her knees by things with multiple legs.

"See anything?" she asks. Her voice sounds muffled from up here.

"Pipes, dust, and wires," I call down. I shine the light slowly around, but just see more of the same. "Do you want to take a look?"

She doesn't answer. I repeat my question. She still doesn't answer. I duck my head back out of the ceiling to see Lizzy standing stiffly in the center of the room. A very round and red-faced policeman, in a full-on NYPD outfit, stands at her side. The security guard from downstairs almost completely fills the doorway.

All I can think to say as I climb off the desk is, "I *told* you we should have given him the king-sized Snickers!"

Chapter 7: The Job

"You didn't say *anything* about the Snickers!" Lizzy hisses as we are led into a mini police station right in the basement of the building.

"Well, I *thought* it!" I reply lamely.

The security guard, who must have ratted us out, exchanges a few words with the policeman and leaves without a backward glance. The policeman, whose nametag says POLANSKY, motions for us to sit on the wooden bench across from his small desk. Lack of beard aside, he would make a good department store Santa Claus. He isn't very jolly, though, so he probably wouldn't last long.

"Would you like to tell me what you were doing vandalizing that office upstairs?" he asks, leaning forward in his chair.

Lizzy and I exchange glances. I can see she's frightened, even though she's trying to pretend she's not. Before I can think it through, I say, "Um, we know him, I mean Folgard. Harold. I know we told the guard he's our uncle, but really he's a friend of my parents. I mean of my mom's. My dad, he's . . . he's not around, so —"

"What my *brother* here is trying to say," Lizzy interrupts, "is that vandalizing is totally not the right word. You see, we had passes to go up there." She gestures to the sticker on our chests. "So this has all been a big mistake."

"Not so fast," Officer Polansky says as Lizzy reaches

for her briefcase. "That office no longer belongs to Folgard and Levine. It was rented out last week to J&J Accountants. It was their office you were vandalizing."

Lizzy whispers out of the corner of her mouth, "There he goes with that *word* again."

"The guard in the lobby has a direct video feed to all the empty offices. Gotta make sure no squatters get in here. He saw you destroying private property."

I have no idea what a squatter is other than someone who squats, but I don't bother to ask. Instead I say, "Honestly, we were just looking for a set of keys that Mr. Folgard hid there a long time ago. We didn't mean to destroy anything."

"Breaking and entering is a very serious offense, you know," he says.

I glare at Lizzy. She shrinks down in her seat a little. Then she says, "But the door was unlocked, so it wasn't really breaking. Just entering. And really, what's so bad about entering?"

"The way I see it," Officer Polansky says, clearly not swayed by Lizzy's logic, "is that not only do you owe J&J Accountants the money for a new carpet, but you have to pay your debt to society for not respecting other people's property."

Neither of us speaks for a moment. I am calculating how many weeks of allowance it is going to cost to buy and install a new carpet. "Can't we just write a letter to J&J, and to, you know, *society*, apologizing for the misunderstanding?" I ask, hoping he can hear the sincerity in my voice.

He ignores my question and says, "Now Tony, Tia, those aren't your real names, are they?"

Neither of us answers at first. As Tony Castaway, I had felt shielded from the reality of the situation. But as Jeremy Fink, there is no escape. Officer Polansky makes us tell him our real names and addresses, and he types them into his computer. He is a very slow typist, so we have plenty of time for Lizzy to pinch my leg. As I flinch, I realize I'd been holding my breath, and I quickly let it out.

"What was that for?" I ask from the corner of my mouth.

"You were turning purple," Lizzy whispers.

"You *swore* we wouldn't get arrested!" I whisper back.

"We're not getting arrested!" she says, forgetting to whisper. Then in a smaller voice she asks, "Are we?"

Officer Polansky gives us a long look. We try to appear as innocent and wide-eyed as possible. Mom told me once in times of trouble to try to project sunny thoughts: butterflies, babies laughing, hot dogs in a ballpark on a sunny day. So I think of babies laughing in a ballpark surrounded by butterflies eating hot dogs. Very small, tiny hot dogs. I can't vouch for what Lizzy is thinking, but it must be something good because Officer Polansky says, "No, I'm not going to arrest you."

"You gonna send us to juvie?" she asks, narrowing her eyes at him.

I groan. Officer Polansky laughs. "No, I'm not going to send you to juvenile detention either. I was thinking of community service. You don't have any big plans this summer, right?"

Thinking of the box, I say, "Well, actually —"

"Nope," Lizzy jumps in. "Community service is fine."

"I'll see what's available," he says, pulling a clipboard from his desk drawer.

"Um, doesn't a judge have to assign community service?" I ask.

"We're streamlining the process," the policeman explains, "unless you *want* me to involve a judge. . . ."

Lizzy kicks me in the ankle, which actually hurts quite a bit.

"I didn't think so," he says. He scans the list in front of him. "I'm even gonna be a nice guy and give you some choices."

"Great," I mumble under my breath. I can't believe that in the few days since school ended, I am now sitting in a mini–police station being assigned community service for the summer. How did this happen? How am I going to open the box if I can't look for the keys because I will be too busy picking up garbage on the West Side Highway or planting flowers in some church garden?

"Let's see," Officer Polansky says, running his finger down the list. He is apparently unaware of my screaming inner voice. "Here's one. You can pick up trash in Central Park following the weekly free concerts. How's that sound?"

I do not trust myself to speak.

"It wouldn't be so bad," he says. "We'd give you poles so you wouldn't have to touch the garbage with your hands. And any cans you find, you can keep and turn in for five cents down at the recycling center."

"What else ya got?" Lizzy asks bluntly.

He consults his list again. "Well, the only other one that would take kids your age would be helping a man named Mr. Oswald with some deliveries. He's closing down his pawnshop and moving to Florida. The job could involve some lifting though, and I gotta tell you, you two aren't the strongest specimens I've seen."

"We'll take it," Lizzy and I say at the same time.

"We're stronger than we look," I add. While this is true of Lizzy, I'm probably just about as strong as I look.

The policeman pauses to consider it, then says, "All right. I'll call Mr. Oswald and find out when he wants you to start."

He pushes two small notebooks toward us. "You'll have to keep a log of the hours you spend on the job and your observations. At any time we might ask you to turn 'em in so we can make sure you're not skirting your responsibilities."

"Observations?" I ask. "Of what?"

"Community service isn't just about getting people to work for free. The citizen is supposed to learn something from the experience. They should come away from it a better person."

"A better person?" Lizzy repeats. "What's wrong with us now?"

"I don't know, *Tia*," he says.

That shuts her up.

He dials Mr. Oswald's number, and after he introduces himself as Officer Polansky, all we hear is, "One boy, one girl, 'bout thirteen. Yes. No. Yes. Say they're stronger than they look." He checks his computer screen and reads out our address. Then he says, "Okay. Yes. They'll be there. No problem. Good day to you, too, sir."

"You start tomorrow," he says, putting a notation next to the job on his clipboard.

"Um, how are we supposed to get to him?" I ask. "Because my mom works all day, and so does Lizzy's dad, so I don't see how —"

He holds up a hand to stop me. "Mr. Oswald will send his driver to pick you up and take you home."

"A *driver*?" Lizzy asks. "If this guy has a *driver*, why can't he just hire someone to help him pack up his stuff?"

Officer Polansky's face darkens a bit. "Would you rather take the first job?"

Lizzy shakes her head hard. "I was just asking."

"Mr. Oswald has done a lot for the city," he says. "So we like to help him out whenever we can."

I wonder how a pawnshop owner helps out the city, but I am not about to ask. Officer Polansky looks like he's on his last nerve. I don't like the idea that I'm going to be taken out of my neighborhood comfort zone, once again, and led who knows where.

"You two can go now," he says. "Nine a.m., sharp. And dress more . . . casually. Never seen kids on summer vacation dressed up before."

"We don't usually dress like this," I am quick to explain. Not that it really matters.

"One more thing," he says. "You do a good job, and we'll waive the cost of a new carpet. That one was pretty beat even before you two got to it."

"Thank you," we say in unison. We practically leap off the bench in our hurry to be out of there.

I'm about to sling my backpack over my arm when he says, "Oh, wait, what was I thinking? I still have to call your parents!"

"But they're at work," Lizzy says hurriedly. "We can just tell them ourselves."

He chuckles, but not in a very friendly way. "Doesn't work that way," he says. "Now what're their work numbers?"

"Actually," I say, raising my hand slightly then quickly lowering it. "My mom's home today."

He adds both numbers into the computer and then says, "Now get going. See if you can stay out of trouble for the rest of the day."

Lizzy grabs her briefcase, and we hurry from the room and back into the elevator. Neither of us speaks as we press the button for the lobby. It's just as well that he made us leave before calling them. I wouldn't have wanted to hear Mom's reaction. I'll hear it soon enough.

"What were you thinking?" she demands as I walk in the door an hour later. "How did you get home?"

"The bus," I told her. The return trip on the bus had been much smoother. We got quarters from a hot pretzel vendor, and Garlicman was nowhere in sight (or in smell, as the case may be). We sat in the front of the bus and I tried to eat my peanut butter sandwich while Lizzy ate a pretzel. It wasn't easy to choke down the sandwich after our experience, but just in case Mom punishes me by only serving something healthy for dinner, I had to eat while I could. Even still, I could only eat half.

"I'm sorry we lied about going to the post office," I reply sheepishly. "I know we should have told you where we were going. I was afraid you'd say no."

"Come sit down," she says, and leads me over to Mongo. We pass a painting on an easel that she must have been working on today. It's covered with cloth now though, so I can't tell what it is. We sit down, and she takes my hand in hers. "I know this is hard for you," she says gently. "You want to follow your dad's instructions, but we just might have to find another way."

"Lizzy and I have already tried everything else," I tell her. "The only way to get in is with the keys. Otherwise we'll ruin the box."

"I don't want that to happen either," she says. "But now you have to put that aside and deal with this community service mess you've gotten yourself into. You can't shirk your responsibilities with this man."

"What if he's some sleazy pawnbroker guy who just wants free labor?"

"He's not," she assures me. "I made Officer Polansky give me Mr. Oswald's phone number to check him out. I wasn't going to let my baby be whisked away by just anyone."

I groan. "Mom!"

"Sorry," she says. "I wasn't going to let my almost-teenaged son be whisked away by just anyone."

"That's better."

"He's a very interesting man. And I think you'll find this job —"

"It's not a job," I remind her. "A job is where you get paid."

She shakes her head. "A job is where you are assigned a task and you complete it to the best of your ability. Money or no money. Anyway, as I was saying, I think you might actually enjoy working with Mr. Oswald. You may find you have a lot in common."

"Like what?" I ask, but I'm not really interested. My stomach is growling. Now that I know Mom isn't going to punish me, my appetite has returned.

"The man has spent his life around other people's stuff. Sound like anyone you know?" Without waiting for an answer she stands up from the couch and says, "And by the way, you're grounded for a week. It would be more, but I figure you're already being punished. You'll do the community service, and then come straight home."

I sigh dramatically. "It's almost like you don't *want* me to find the keys."

"You know that's not true," Mom says. "It will all happen the only way it happens." She heads into the kitchen, and I follow.

"What does *that* mean?" I ask. Before she can answer, the phone rings. The caller ID shows it's Lizzy's dad. She picks up and she says, "Yes, he's grounded for a week.

Yes, I'll wait until the car comes tomorrow and call you at the post office. Thanks, Herb." She hangs up. "Hey, you got off easy. Lizzy's grounded for two weeks."

Poor Lizzy. She was only trying to help me. I'm sure this isn't how she planned to spend her summer, either.

"What do you want for dinner?" Mom asks, already reaching into the cabinet for the box of macaroni and cheese.

"Why do you ask if you already know?"

"I always hope you'll surprise me."

"Not tonight."

After years of trying to get me to eat normally, Mom has given up. Dinners are now a choice between four meals — macaroni and cheese, hot dogs, fish sticks, or pizza if we're going out. Mom once tried frying some chicken and pressing it into the shape of a fish stick, but I knew better.

She puts a pot on the stove and pours in the water. "You're going to drive me to drink with your finicky eating habits," she says.

Seeing as our house is an alcohol-free zone, unless I'm going to drive her to drink chocolate milk, I'm not too worried.

"You'll be thirteen in a few weeks," she says. "It's time to expand your horizons. I'm going to introduce one new thing each Monday night."

After what happened today, I don't dare argue. "Sure, Mom," I say, hoping she'll go easy on me and won't jump right to the broccoli.

"And since today's Monday," Mom says, swinging open the refrigerator door, "we might as well start tonight. But don't worry, I'll go easy on you." She pulls out a glass bowl covered in cellophane. I approach with caution and peer inside.

Broccoli!

Chapter 8: The Old Man

Mom, Lizzy, and I are sitting on the steps of our building waiting for Mr. Oswald's driver to pick us up. I didn't get any notes from Lizzy last night and I didn't write any either. I'm afraid she's mad at me. At least she's back in her ponytail and shorts again. No skirt and long hair blowing around.

"You've both got the notebooks that the policeman gave you?" Mom asks.

We shake our heads.

"I got the impression you're supposed to bring them," she replies. "Go on up and get them. I'll wait in case he comes."

As Lizzy and I climb the stairs, she asks if I'm mad at her.

Relieved, I shake my head. "I thought maybe you were mad at me. After all, you wouldn't be in this mess if it weren't for me and the box."

"And *you* wouldn't be in this mess if it weren't for me," she counters.

"Do you think we'll still be able to find the keys in time now?" I ask.

"We'll keep our eyes open," she says firmly. "We won't let this stupid community service thing ruin our plans."

We're about to shake on it when the new kids come out of their apartment. "Don't let us interrupt you," Rick says, gesturing to our imminent handshake.

We both pull our hands away quickly. "How's it going?" Lizzy asks in a high voice that's almost a squeak. She says it to both of them, but looks only at Samantha.

"Good," Samantha says. "We're almost all moved in."

"Cool," Lizzy says. Then she blurts out, "I like your earrings."

Samantha puts her hands up to her ears. "I'm not wearing any earrings."

Rick laughs. That kid is NOT getting any nicer, and I'm just about done feeling sorry for him for having to move to a new place.

Lizzy turns beet red. "I mean the ones you were wearing yesterday."

"Oh, thanks," Samantha says. "They were a gift from my grandmother."

"Cool," Lizzy says, and nods. "If you want to come over sometime, I can tell you about the neighborhood, that sort of thing."

"Sure," Samantha says. "Whenever."

"Cool," Lizzy says. I want to alert her to the many other words at her disposal besides *cool*, but I think she would punch me.

"Can we go now?" Rick asks, pulling his sister down the hall.

"Bye, guys," Samantha calls out.

"Bye," Lizzy says, waving a little.

"Since when are you so friendly?" I ask her.

"What do you mean?" she says innocently.

"You know what I mean."

"I'm just trying to be nice," she says, putting the key in

her door. "You know, neighborly, like you said. I'm allowed to make new friends, you know."

"Who said you weren't?" I reply, hurrying into my apartment before she can respond. I grab my notebook and head back outside, not bothering to wait for Lizzy. She sits down next to me on the stoop a minute later. She has taken out her ponytail. I don't know why it should bother me, but it does. I pull out my book and bury my nose in it.

"This must be him," Mom says, standing up and shading her eyes.

I look up to see Lizzy staring, her mouth hanging open. Coming down the street toward us is no less than a *limo*. It pulls up right in front of our building. A *limousine* is in front of our building! Like the kind *movie stars* take. The driver steps out and tips his hat at us. He is wearing a real chauffeur's uniform! I didn't think people did that in real life!

"Jeremy Fink and Elizabeth Muldoun?"

We nod vigorously. Usually Lizzy is quick to correct anyone who dares to use her full name, but I can tell she's too excited to bother.

"I'm James. I have come to take you to Mr. Oswald," he says. "And you are Mrs. Fink, I gather?"

Mom says yes, and asks to see some paperwork from the community service people. Exchanging wide-eyed glances, Lizzy and I scramble off the steps and wait by the car until Mom gives us the all-clear.

"You two behave," she says, stepping back onto the curb.

I'm surprised she's not more shocked by the limo. Mr.

Oswald must have told her that's how we'd be traveling. Did she somehow forget to tell me?

"Do you have your sandwiches?" she asks.

"Yes, Mom," I say, reddening as James looks on. When she steps aside, James opens the back door for us. Lizzy scrambles inside, and I follow her into the cool interior. I can't believe we're actually going to be driven around the city in a limo!

The seats are cream-colored, and I've never sat on anything as soft. Even though it's a bright, sunny day, the inside of the limo is dim because the windows are tinted. A small refrigerator is built into the wall, along with a television set and a radio. Another long seat faces us, and I immediately put my feet up on it. Lizzy can't reach that far. We pull away from the building and I wave at Mom as we go, but she probably can't see us through the windows.

Lizzy swings open the door of the fridge. "Look! Strawberries! Juice! Soda *in glass bottles*! Can you *believe* this?"

I shake my head, leaning back against the cool seat like I'm used to a life of luxury.

"Man oh man," Lizzy says. "If I had known doing community service was gonna be like *this,* I'd have gotten us in serious trouble *years* ago!"

At the first red light, the window dividing us from James slowly lowers. He turns his head to look at us. "I imagine everything is satisfactory?" he asks, a small smile on his face.

Lizzy unscrews the top of a Coke bottle and asks, "Is Mr. Oswald really really really super rich?"

James laughs. "He's pretty well off."

"I didn't realize pawnbrokers made so much money," I say.

James turns back to the road and shakes his head. "Oh, that's just a sideline. Used to be his family's business. Mr. Oswald's main job is selling antiques. He has a knack for finding antiques, restoring them, and selling them for much more than he bought them."

"Where does he find them?" I ask, interested.

"All over," James says. "Flea markets, antique fairs, auction houses. Sometimes even on the streets. People don't know what they have, and they just throw it out."

Lizzy turns to me, and I know what she's going to say before she says it. "Sounds like he and your dad would have hit it off."

I nod. "But my dad never fixed up anything to sell, only to use."

"Maybe he would have," she says.

I watch as the window divider slowly goes back up.

"Maybe," I say, closing my eyes. When Dad first died, I used to keep a list of all the things that happened to me that he wouldn't get to see. Like when I hit a home run in gym class (only happened once, but it *did* happen), or when I won an award for a short story in sixth grade about a boy who burned an ant with a magnifying glass, and that night his house burned down, and he knew it was all his fault. But the list was all about *me*. I had never considered what my dad would or wouldn't have done with his *own* life if he'd gotten the chance. Maybe he would have sold some of the stuff he found and made a fortune. Or expanded Fink's Comics into a whole chain. I might even have a brother or sister by now. I bet he had dreams I never knew about. Is *that* what's in the box? Dreams of a life he never got to live?

The car stops, and I open my eyes to see Lizzy happily munching on a strawberry. "Want one?" she asks, holding out the box.

I shake my head. Real fruit only makes me think of fruit-flavored candy like Starburst or Mentos, and the fact that I don't currently have any.

James opens the door, and we emerge onto the bright sidewalk. I had expected him to be taking us to a pawnshop in a less-than-desirable part of town. Instead, we're in front of a three-story brownstone on Riverside Drive on the Upper West Side. Before I can voice my surprise, the front door opens, and a tall old man appears wearing a brown striped suit with a matching hat. He is puffing on a pipe. For some reason his clothes don't seem to match the rest of him. With his round, ruddy face, shouldn't he be wearing overalls and a straw hat?

"You must be the little truants," he says sternly. His twinkling eyes tell me he's not really being mean.

Never one to take an insult lightly, Lizzy says, "I think to be a truant you have to be skipping school, and school's out for summer."

"How right you are, young lady," he says, cocking his pipe at her. "I shall have to be more careful with my vocabulary."

"All right, then," she says.

"Come." He steps aside so we can enter. "Let us get to know each other."

James ushers us up the stairs and into the house. A small entryway leads to a huge room crowded with large boxes and packing crates. It looks like most of the place is already packed up. A few paintings still hang on the walls, but all the furniture is gone. The wood-paneled ceiling is so high that the whole brownstone must be just this one floor, not three separate floors like I had assumed. A huge fireplace on the back wall actually has a fire going in it, even though it's almost July.

"An old man's bones need warmth," Mr. Oswald says, following my gaze. "That's why I'm moving to Florida. Let's go into my office and I'll tell you what you will be doing."

A round woman in an apron appears from the other end of the room, and he hands her his pipe. She hands him his mail in return. Mr. Oswald says fondly, "This house would stop running if it weren't for my housekeeper, Mary." Mary smiles at us, and I notice a Hershey's bar sticking out of one of the pockets in her apron. I smile back. She is clearly a kindred spirit. Lizzy is too busy peering inside a large open crate to pay any attention.

Mr. Oswald leads us carefully through the maze of boxes and into a room about half the size of the first. This one has another fireplace, but with no fire. A big oak desk sits in the middle, with big leather chairs in front of it. Shelves line two walls of the room, with objects of every size and color stacked on them. I see sports equipment like baseballs and bats and footballs and hockey sticks, but also lamps, clocks, paintings, sculptures, rows of books, a telescope, radios, jewelry boxes, piles of stamps in plastic folders, trays of old coins. Basically anything and every-thing under the sun. I imagine this would be my parents' vision of heaven. I have to make a concerted effort to close my jaw. I realize I haven't spoken a word since we arrived, so I clear my throat. "Um, Mr. Oswald?"

"Yes, Mr. Fink?" he says, sitting down behind the desk.

I don't know how to respond to that. I'd only heard my dad and Uncle called Mr. Fink. I don't know why it should surprise me that when I grow up people will be calling me by the same name as my father, but it does. "Um, Jeremy is good," I say.

"Jeremy it is, then," Mr. Oswald says.

"Um, would it be all right if I look at your stamp col-lection? It'll only take a minute."

"Be my guest," he says, waving me over to the shelf. "Are you a longtime philatelist?"

"I'm sorry, what?" I ask.

He smiles. "A stamp collector. They are called *philat-elists.*"

"Oh," I say, feeling a bit stupid. "No, my father was. There's this one stamp he was always looking for, so now I, well, you know."

He finishes my sentence for me. "Now you have taken on his quest?"

I nod.

"Wonderful. When you're done, you can both take a seat, and then we can chat."

The stamp is blue with the word "Hawaii" at the top, so it would be easy to spot. I quickly scan through the pages of stamps, but of course it's not there. I put the pile back on the shelf and have to pull on Lizzy's sleeve twice before she tears herself away from an oversized doll with huge blue eyes. I don't know which is scarier — the doll itself, which has a vacant stare and an I-might-come-alive-and-attack-you vibe, or the fact that Lizzy was entranced by a doll in the first place.

We sit down in the large chairs in front of the desk. As tall for my age as I am, I feel very small in the chair.

"So," Mr. Oswald begins, "I bet you'd like to know what you'll be doing here."

"Who cares what we'll be doing," Lizzy says. "This place *rocks*!"

Mr. Oswald laughs. It's a deep and hearty laugh. "Thank you, I think. I'm glad you like my home; I'll be sorry to leave it. But I assure you, I do intend to have you work."

My throat always tightens up when I look for my Dad's stamp. I swallow hard and say, "Officer Polansky said you needed us to, um, pack things up? These things I guess?" I gesture around the room at all the stuff.

"Close, but not quite," Mr. Oswald replies, touching the tips of his fingers together. "I need you to make deliveries for me. Nowhere too far, all here in Manhattan. James will accompany you."

I open my mouth to ask what kind of deliveries when Lizzy says, "Woo-hoo! We get to ride in the limo again!"

Mr. Oswald smiles at her like one would a cute child who has just recited the alphabet for the first time. Then he stands up and says, "I'm late for a meeting right now, but I'm going to get you started on your first delivery. We can talk more tomorrow."

I quickly get to my feet, too. "We won't see you any more today?"

He shakes his head. "Don't worry, James knows what to do."

"But aren't you supposed to sign our notebooks at the end of the day?"

He walks around the desk and lays his hand on my shoulder. "Don't worry so much. Just record your observations tonight, and we can go over them tomorrow, all right?"

I nod.

"You'll have to forgive Jeremy," Lizzy says, popping a Starburst into her mouth. "He always reminds the teachers if they forget to give out homework."

Where did she get Starburst and why didn't she offer me any? And I only reminded a teacher *once* before I came to my senses!

In between chews she adds, "He even reads books during the summer."

"It wouldn't kill you to pick up a book sometime, Lizzy," I say through gritted teeth, not wanting to argue in front of Mr. Oswald.

Mr. Oswald picks up his briefcase and straightens his tie. "What are you reading currently, Jeremy?" He glances over at my bulging backpack.

Lizzy rolls her eyes, but I open it and root around. I hand him my latest book, *Time Travel and the Movies.*

"Are you a fan of time travel films?" he asks, opening the book to the table of contents.

I nod. "I've seen them all," I say, hoping I don't sound like I'm bragging.

"What was your favorite?" he asks.

I have to think for a minute. "It depends on how realistic they are. Like if they could really happen. You know, scientifically."

He doesn't answer, so I keep rambling. "I mean, like, there's this one where all the guy does is lie down on his bed and then he concentrates really, really hard, and eventually he winds up in the past. Now *that* can't really happen."

"I would suspect not," he agrees, and hands me back the book. I pull Dad's box out for a second while I stick the book back in my bag.

"What an interesting box," Mr. Oswald says. "May I see it?"

For a second I'm torn. I'd decided not to show anyone else. But I can't be rude, so I hand it to him. I look at Lizzy, who mouths the words, *You brought it with you?*

I shrug. I couldn't leave it home alone. Mr. Oswald hands it back to me and says, "Lovely. I can give you some bubble wrap if you want to wrap this up. It will help protect it."

"Okay, sure," I say, surprised and slightly insulted that he hadn't said more about it, or about the words on it. I guess he sees so much stuff that one wooden box doesn't impress him.

"Help yourself on the way out," he says. "All the packing supplies are in the next room. But now let me give you your assignment." He turns to his left and slowly strolls along one of the walls of shelves. I can't imagine what he's going to pull off. He walks past the oversized doll, past an old metal typewriter, and then runs his fingers along the spines of the books. He pulls out one of them, opens the front cover, then sticks it back on the shelf and pulls out another. He keeps doing this until he opens a small book with a light blue cover, and an envelope slips out and onto the floor.

"I'll get it," I say, bending over to pick it up. The envelope is yellowed and thin, and there's a name written on the front in black ink. *Mabel Parsons*. Mr. Oswald takes it from my hand and sticks it back in the book. The cover is so faded that I can't see the title.

"Even a reader like you probably won't be very interested in the topic of *this* book," he says, placing it gently into a cardboard box lying open on his desk. "It's about woodland animals."

"Woodland animals?" I repeat.

He nods as he tapes up the box with a thick packing tape. "Owls, bears, rabbits. That sort of thing."

It does sound pretty boring. "Are you donating it to a library?" I ask.

"Oh, no," he says, but doesn't explain further. He pulls a yellow Post-it note off a pad and sticks it on top of the box. He writes an address neatly on it, and I can see his hand shake a bit with the effort. I wonder how old he is. He's definitely older than any of my grandparents. He presses an intercom on his desk, and I hear a low buzz a few rooms away. James appears a minute later, and Mr. Oswald hands him the package. "The address is on here," he says. "I'd like you to accompany the children to the door, but then they're on their own."

"Yessir," James says.

I'm about to follow the men out of the room when I turn to find Lizzy holding the blue-eyed doll in her arms. When she sees me looking, she quickly sticks it back on the shelf. I raise my brows, and she glares in return. We wind our way back to the front door, stopping once so I can pick up a sheet of the bubble wrap.

"Good luck," Mr. Oswald says warmly, swinging the door shut behind us.

"Wait," Lizzy says from the top stair. "Why do we need luck? What are we actually doing?"

"Don't worry, we'll talk tomorrow." With that, the thick door shuts. We turn to James.

"Don't look at me," he says. "I just work here."

Chapter 9: The Book

James opens the back door for us again, even though I tell him I can open it. He has the package in the front with him, so once again we have no idea where we are going, or what we're supposed to do when we get there. I search my backpack for any stray candy to bring me comfort, but I'm all out.

I hold out my hand to Lizzy, palm up. "Starburst, please."

"Flavor?" Lizzy asks, digging the pack out of her pocket.

"Red," I reply. I want to ask why she didn't offer earlier, but I don't. Pick your battles, Dad always said.

As the limo heads into parts unknown, we amuse ourselves by pressing the button to open and close the window partition. Then we look outside to count how many people turn their heads as the limo passes them. Once that gets old, I wrap the box in the bubble wrap, and I can't help popping the bubbles. Lizzy jumps every time. I then polish off one and a half peanut butter sandwiches while Lizzy eats a soy cheese-and-spinach wrap that her dad made for her. I can't even watch. We're about to turn on the TV when the car comes to a halt, and the window divider lowers.

"We're here," James says over his shoulder. "Are you ready?"

"What should we be ready *for*?" Lizzy asks. "I'm not getting out of the car until you tell us."

I take my hand away from the door handle and sit back in my seat.

James twists around till he is facing us. "You will be delivering a package, that's all."

I lean forward. "Why does Mr. Oswald need us to do this? Not to be rude, but why couldn't you, or someone else who already works for him do it?"

James smiles. His teeth are very white. "Because I don't have a debt to society to pay."

"Oh, please," Lizzy says with a wave of her hand. "That was a big misunderstanding."

James raises the window divider, and we hear him get out of the car. I'm about to open my door when Lizzy puts her hand on my arm. Her mouth opens to say something, but then she closes it again.

"What is it?" I ask.

"Nothing," she says as James opens her door. She turns away and steps out. I slide over the seat and follow. I know she's nervous about what we're going to find here, but she'd never admit it. I have no problem admitting it.

"You can leave your bag in the car," James instructs me. "You won't be needing it."

I hesitate. If Dad's box got stolen I would never forgive myself.

"It will be safe, I promise," James says.

Not wanting to make a big deal out of it, I shrug the bag off my shoulder and leave it on the seat. Then I quickly move it from the seat to the floor, thinking it's less likely to be seen there. I close the door tightly behind me and find Lizzy leaning against the car, tapping her finger on the tinted windows. Okay, so I guess my bag will be safe. James makes a big show of clicking on the alarm.

We follow James a few doors down and find ourselves in front of a tall apartment building, the kind with a doorman. James hands me the package. I hand it to Lizzy, who promptly hands it back to me. The doorman tips his hat at us, and we follow James into the building and up to the desk, where a security guard is reading the newspaper. James clears his throat and says, "We are here to see Mrs. Mabel Billingsly. She is expecting us."

The guard lazily lays his paper down on the counter and picks up a phone. He presses three numbers. "And you all are?"

James says, "You may tell Mrs. Billingsly that we are representatives of Mr. Oswald."

The guard mumbles, "Oh, may I?" and presses one more number. James pretends not to hear the guard's comment, but I'm sure he did. The guard relays the message and then hangs up. "Okay, you can go up."

We step into the elevator and James presses *14*.

Lizzy says, "It *would* have to be the fourteenth floor again!"

"What's wrong with the fourteenth floor?" James asks.

"You don't want to know," Lizzy says with a shiver.

I ask, "Why would anyone want an old book on woodland animals anyway?"

Lizzy shrugs. "Maybe it's an antique. James here, although a man of few words, did say Mr. Oswald sold antiques." Suddenly her eyes widen, and she adds, "*Unless* it's not really a book at all!"

"Interesting," I say, considering this theory. Mr. Oswald *did* shut the book pretty quickly, so I couldn't get a good look at it. "You're right! It could be a hollowed-out book with money or jewels or a treasure map hidden inside!"

"Yes!" Lizzy says, grabbing my arm. "That's why Mr. Oswald wants *us* to deliver it! As minors, we wouldn't get into as much trouble as an adult would. Maybe he's connected with the mob!"

We stare accusingly at James. Lizzy does her best hands-on-hips glare. James shakes his head and rolls his eyes. "It's a book," he says firmly. The elevator opens, and James steps out. Lizzy and I don't move. "It's a *book,*" he says, even more firmly. The doors start to close, and he has to stick his foot in to get them to bounce back open.

"We might as well go with him," I say to Lizzy. "Mr. Oswald doesn't really seem like the kinda guy who would set us up."

"I guess not," she admits.

We step out of the elevator, and James walks down the hushed hallway a few steps ahead of us. This sure is different from our apartment building. Air conditioning in the halls, for one. And carpet that doesn't have any stains on it. I run my hand along the patterned wallpaper. No dust. There are chairs and a little table every few feet. So neighbors can chat, I guess?

"Here we are," James says, stopping in front of 14G. "You're on your own. I'll be waiting out here."

"Sure, so we can deliver the contraband," Lizzy mumbles, "while you keep a safe distance."

"It's a BOOK," James insists, heading toward a chair a few doors down.

Neither of us makes a move to knock. Finally, I shift the package under my arm and ring the buzzer. A few seconds later, the door creaks open, and an elderly woman in a light pink dress stands before us. She is wearing a thin gold necklace with two entwined hearts hanging from it. Her watery blue eyes are almost see-through. She stands very straight.

Addressing me, she says, "I didn't expect Mr. Oswald to be so young." Then she steps aside to let us enter. She closes the door behind us, unknowingly leaving James out in the hall. We're on our own now.

The apartment is smaller than I would have thought, but has a big window with a wide view. We must be on the Upper East Side because I can see the East River. I've got to start paying more attention in the limo.

"I'm not Mr. Oswald," I tell her. "My name is Jeremy Fink, and this is Lizzy Muldoun."

"Mabel Billingsly," she says, holding out her hand.

In the sunlight that streams in through the window, she seems even older. Her skin looks paper-thin. I'm afraid to shake her hand too hard, but she has a surprisingly strong grip.

"So, what brings you to my humble abode?"

Lizzy and I exchange worried glances. "Er, don't you know?" asks Lizzy.

Mrs. Billingsly shakes her head.

I hold out the package. "Didn't you order this from Mr. Oswald? The antique dealer?"

"Antiques?" she repeats. "No. I haven't bought an antique in years." She leans in like she's going to tell us a secret. "Truth be told, they give me the creeps."

I like that she's not talking to us like we're little kids. "So you don't know what this is?" I ask, and hand her the package.

She shakes her head again and says, "Why don't we find out?" She leads us through the living room and into the small kitchen. Resting the box on the kitchen table, she pulls a knife out of the drawer. She neatly slices through the tape, then pushes back the sides of the box. The whole thing is very reminiscent of us opening the package with my dad's box in it. Except this time, I know what's inside, even if Mrs. Billingsly doesn't.

She reaches in and pulls out the small book. She turns it around in her hands, and tentatively opens the front cover. She reads something written there, then closes it again, hugging it tight to her chest. When she looks up, her eyes are full of tears. But they are shining, too.

"Where did you get this?" she whispers.

"We told you," Lizzy says. "Mr. Oswald asked us to deliver it. We sort of work for him."

She stares at us blankly, and then her eyes focus abruptly and she backs up a step. "Old Ozzy? No, that's not possible. Why, he'd have to be a hundred and twenty years old by now!"

I may not be great at figuring how old adults are, but I'm pretty sure Mr. Oswald isn't any older than seventy or seventy-five. Definitely younger than Mrs. Billingsly.

I shake my head. "I think he's only in his seventies. And I can't imagine anyone calling him *Ozzy*."

Lizzy nods in agreement.

Mrs. Billingsly looks down at the book and says in a shaky voice, "How much do I owe you for this?"

Lizzy and I look at each other, alarmed. Mr. Oswald never said anything about collecting payment.

"Um, nothing?" I reply uncertainly.

But Mrs. Billingsly no longer seems to be paying attention to us. She keeps rubbing her hand across the cover of the book. Abruptly she walks out of the kitchen and sits down on the couch in the living room. Lizzy leans close and whispers, "Should we leave now?"

"I don't know," I whisper back. "I'm not sure what's going on."

"Me either. She sure seems to like that book though."

I nod. "But why doesn't she remember ordering it?"

"She's really, really old?" Lizzy suggests.

"I don't think that's it."

"Let's go find out," Lizzy says. We slip into the living room and each take a chair opposite the woman.

"Um, Mrs. Billingsly?" Lizzy asks. "Are you okay?"

Mrs. Billingsly looks up from the book lying open on her lap. I notice the envelope that I had picked up from Mr. Oswald's office floor is on the cushion at her side. She smiles and asks, "Would you like to hear my favorite part?"

I find it hard to believe someone has a favorite part in a book on woodland animals. Without waiting for our answer, she starts to read:

Later on, when they had all said "Good-by" and "Thank-you" to Christopher Robin, Pooh and Piglet

walked home thoughtfully together in the golden eve-
ning, and for a long time they were silent.

Lizzy jumps up from her chair. "Woodland animals!" she snorts. "That's *Winnie-the-Pooh*!"

"Shh!" I tell her, pulling her back down. "Let her finish." Mrs. Billingsly continues:

"When you wake up in the morning, Pooh," said Piglet at last, "what's the first thing you say to yourself?"

"What's for breakfast?" said Pooh. "What do you say, Piglet?"

"I say, I wonder what's going to happen exciting today?" said Piglet.

Pooh nodded thoughtfully. "It's the same thing," he said.

Mrs. Billingsly stops reading, but doesn't lift her head. Why hadn't Mr. Oswald told us the book was *Winnie-the-Pooh*? This whole thing doesn't make sense. Suddenly I realize something that should have been obvious from the minute she took out the book.

"Mrs. Billingsly," I say, "did this book once *belong* to you?"

She doesn't answer at first, only runs her hand over the page. Then she says, "It was only half mine. The other half belonged to my best friend, Bitsy."

"You mean Betsy?" Lizzy suggests.

Mrs. Billingsly shakes her head. "Bitsy. Bitsy Solomon."

"People had funny names back then," Lizzy comments.

I glare at Lizzy. "Go on," I urge Mrs. Billingsly.

She sighs gently and says, "I haven't spoken to Bitsy in over sixty-five years."

"But you said she's your best friend," Lizzy says.

"I misspoke," Mrs. Billingsly replies calmly.

I notice her left hand is shaking slightly. She sees me looking, and quickly puts her other hand on top of it. Just as quickly, I look away, sorry that I saw it in the first place. Sixty-five years is like an eternity. The longest Lizzy and I ever went without speaking was a week, and that was because she said the things on *Star Trek* couldn't really happen.

"Bitsy used to be my best friend," Mrs. Billingsly explains. "Until I sold this book for a fancy dress. She confronted me, but I told her I hadn't taken it. I knew she knew I had. Best friends always know when the other's lying. For years I wanted to apologize, but I was too embarrassed."

"I don't get it," Lizzy says. "How could you buy a whole dress for the cost of that book?"

Mrs. Billingsly opens the front cover and turns it around to face us. We lean closer to read the faded handwriting.

To Bitsy and Mabel, Pooh's biggest
American fans
Best regards, A. A. Milne

"Oh," Lizzy says.
"Wow," I say.

"Old Ozzy gave me twenty dollars for it. Back then, in the thirties, that was near a fortune for a child."

I still think she must be confused about Mr. Oswald, since there's no way our Mr. Oswald could have bought this book from her. I don't have the nerve to tell her she's wrong though. Lizzy, as usual, has no problem coming up with something to say.

"Why'd you need this dress so badly?" she asks.

Mrs. Billingsly closes her eyes. For a few minutes she doesn't answer. I'm starting to squirm. Did she fall asleep? Lizzy pinches me on the arm and mouths, "What should we do?" I'm about to answer that maybe we should go, when Mrs. Billingsly opens her eyes and reaches for the old envelope. "It's all in here," she says, pushing the letter back into the envelope and holding it out to me. "Will you do me a favor and read it later? I'd like to be alone."

I stick the envelope in the back pocket of my shorts and, for the first time in my life, wish I had worn something less sloppy.

"Will your husband be home soon?" Lizzy asks. I hear something unusual in her voice — genuine concern.

She shakes her head and looks over at a faded wedding photo on the coffee table. "No, Richard isn't around anymore."

"How did you two meet?" Lizzy asks.

My first thought is that I wish Lizzy would stop pressing her to answer these questions. But I quickly realize what she's doing. She's keeping Mrs. Billingsly talking in the hopes that when we leave, it won't feel so abrupt.

"I met him the night I wore that dress," she says wistfully. "I was sixteen." She raises her hand to her throat and rubs the little hearts hanging from her necklace. It's a totally unconscious thing. I think she'd be surprised to know she was doing it. She continues, "Bitsy never even met him. She would have been my maid of honor."

"That's so sad," Lizzy says.

Her comment snaps Mrs. Billingsly out of her reverie, and she pushes herself up from the couch. "Now I'm sure you two have better things to do then spend a summer afternoon with an old lady." Without actually pushing us, she nevertheless herds us toward the door. "You tell Ozzy that I thank him from the bottom of my heart."

"But Mr. Oswald isn't —," Lizzy begins.

I interrupt her and say, "We will."

She closes the door behind us, and we're back in the fancy hallway. Neither of us says anything for a moment. James comes up behind us and asks, "So how did it go?"

I can't think of a word that would be a suitable reply. Lizzy just says, "Mr. Oswald has *a lot* of explaining to do tomorrow!" and storms off for the elevator.

"James," I say as we follow behind, "does anyone call Mr. Oswald *Ozzy*?"

He shakes his head and smiles. "Does he seem like an Ozzy to you?"

"No."

As the elevator doors close, he says, "Old Ozzy was what they called his grandfather."

Chapter 10: Oswald Oswald

Lizzy and I don't speak much on the way home. She's still fuming over the details Mr. Oswald "forgot" to tell us, so I spend the time preparing what I'm going to tell Mom. I know I can't tell her everything. At least not until I understand what had really happened and what I think about it. As I push open our front door, the smell of curry fills my nose. That means Aunt Judi is over making one of her exotic dishes. Mom and Aunt Judi pounce when they hear me.

"So?" they ask in unison, wiping their hands on matching aprons. "How was it?"

"I hear you were whisked away in a limo!" Aunt Judi says.

My rehearsed speech comes out in a flood of words. "The limo was amazing. There was soda and a TV! Mr. Oswald was really nice. James, the driver, drove us to our first delivery. It was a book to this lady on the Upper East Side. She was nice, too. That's about it. Is it okay if I go to my room?" By the time I finish my speech, I'm a bit breathless. Aunt Judi's smile is still wide, but my mother's has started to slip a bit at the edges.

"Ten minutes till dinner," she says, giving me a long look. But she lets me go.

I empty my backpack on the bed and search through the contents to find the envelope. It's not here. I feel panic rising in me until I remember I'd stuck it in my pocket. The letter is yellowed and frayed, but when I unfold it, the type is still legible. No computer made this, that's for sure. There are smudges of ink, and the letters don't always line up. It was definitely made on one of those old typewriters where you'd hit a key and a metal spring with a letter on the end would fly out and strike the paper. Grandma still has one, but whenever I try to use it, the keys jam together.

Leaning against the wall that I share with Lizzy's room, I begin to read.

```
Oswald's Pawn Emporium
Date: March 31, 1935
Name: Mabel Parsons
Age: 15 3/4
Location: Brooklyn
Item to Pawn: Winnie-the-Pooh. Signed by the
author.
Personal Statement of Seller: I need to sell
this book because I need money to buy a dress
for the cotillion because my parents can't
afford to buy me a new one and I'd have to
wear my sister Janie's old one but it is much
too large and I would swim in it and no one
will ask me to dance and if no one asks me to
dance, I may never get married and this may
be my only chance. I desperately do not want
to be an old maid like my Great Aunt Sylvia
who always says that she never married be-
cause she never had the right clothes. Please
do not tell my parents.
```

A black-and-white photo is taped below the personal statement. It is in surprisingly good condition for all this time. A girl in a polka-dotted dress and a ponytail is holding a book up in front of her. The cover has a picture of a bear on it, with his head stuck in a honey jar. I try to see if I can find Mabel in the girl's face, but I can't. Then I notice around her neck is that same necklace with the two hearts. I had assumed her husband had given it to her, but she must have had it before she met him. Young Mabel's eyes are focused slightly to the side of the camera and her expression is firm.

Under the photo it says:

Price: *$20.00 (twenty dollars)*
Signed by: *Oswald Oswald, Proprietor*

Oswald Oswald? Who would name their child Oswald Oswald? That's just insane. So it appears that my Mr. Oswald must have inherited the book from his grandfather. But why would he have us return it now? Why didn't Old Ozzy sell it? Isn't that what pawnbrokers do?

Mom knocks on my door. "Five minutes," she says, but doesn't come in. I take another long look at the letter, and then carefully roll it up and stick it in the tube for Lizzy. I can't explain why I don't want to tell my mom the details about what happened today. I feel like it would be disloyal somehow to Mrs. Billingsly — and to fifteen-year-old Mabel. I grab the dictionary off my shelf and look up the word *cotillion*. It means a formal ball, which often introduces young women to society. I smile to myself, picturing Lizzy being introduced to society.

At dinner I don't talk much. Mom and Aunt Judi discuss an exhibit of outsider art, which my aunt is hosting at her art school next week. Mom says, "I thought the whole idea of outsider art meant that these artists aren't interested in things like galleries or schools, or museums."

Scooping curried chicken and rice onto her plate, Aunt Judi says, "It's true that these artists are on the fringe of society, so to speak, but without an exhibit, they have no voice."

"Maybe they don't want a voice," Mom argues. "Maybe they just do it for their own pleasure."

I now officially tune out. This is a common argument between the two of them. Mom thinks that art is a personal thing, and Aunt Judi believes that art isn't art until it's appreciated by the public. I have no opinion. I do not understand art. Mom says I will when I'm older.

The curry smell has permeated the apartment to the degree that my dinner-sized double-decker peanut butter sandwich tastes a little odd. Not bad exactly. Just different. I think this is a positive step for me.

That night during the H.O.J., I take out the notebook that Officer Polansky gave us. I open it to the first page, and it feels like the first day of school. I admit, I like a blank notebook. It's the best part of school. By the second day, I'm over it.

A skilled recapper like myself should have no problem with this. Still, I find myself gnawing on my pencil top. The metallic, sawdusty taste isn't entirely unpleasant.

I bend over my notebook and begin to write.

COMMUNITY SERVICE DAY ONE: OBSERVATIONS

1. I could get used to riding in a limo. People think limos are only for movie stars and politicians and athletes, but they are wrong.

2. Lizzy does not always share. Case in point: Starburst.

3. Mr. Oswald didn't exactly <u>lie</u> to us about what we'd be doing, but he didn't exactly <u>not</u> lie, either. I am not sure why.

I chew on the pencil again, and glance at all the books piled on my bookshelf. I haven't had time to read ever since the box arrived. This must be a record for me. Suddenly it dawns on me that I didn't see any books in Mrs. Billingsly's apartment.

4. Did Mrs. Billingsly give up her love of books because of losing her friend?

5. She said she met her husband at that dance and she seems to miss him. I wonder if that means she was happy with her decision to sell the book.

6. There must be two types of choices. Choices you make that seem harmless but can wind up leading to someone's father dying, like deciding to have one more cup of coffee that morning so you need to go out and buy more and then you cross the street without looking and make an oncoming car swerve into a telephone pole to avoid hitting you. And the other kind, when you know what you're doing will lead to something either bad or good. Or in Mrs. Billingsly's case, both. She lost her friend, but she found her husband.

7. It's a good thing I make very few decisions in my life. What if I decided one day to eat three Butterfingers instead of two, and it led to war with Canada?

As I close the notebook I wonder if it's not too late for Mrs. Billingsly to have her friend back. What if Bitsy is missing her, too? With six minutes left to the H.O.J., I turn to the Internet and type in the words "Bitsy Solomon" and "Brooklyn." I know it's a long shot, but how many Bitsy Solomons can there be from Brooklyn?

Only one, as it turns out.

5/12/2002 Funeral services will be held for **Bitsy Solomon Shultz** *at the Brooklyn Memorial Chapel at 10 a.m. on Sunday, December 8. In lieu of flowers, please consider making a contribution to the Double Heart Literacy Foundation. Mrs. Shultz started the DHL Foundation in 1950, in honor of a childhood friend who ignited her lifelong love of reading. She served as honorary chairwoman from 1989 to 2000.*

My grand plan of showing up at Mrs. Billingsly's door with Bitsy's phone number is clearly not going to happen.

I scroll down until I see a photo. She sort of looks like my grandmother, and around her neck is the same double-heart necklace that Mrs. Billingsly was wearing.

I open my notebook again and add three more entries.

8. Some choices are forever.

9. I wonder if Mrs. Billinsgly knew that Bitsy named her com-
    pany after the matching necklaces they both wore.
10. Just because people aren't in our lives anymore, doesn't
    mean they stop thinking about us and vice versa.

I climb into bed and grab the stuffed alligator tight. Sometimes the Internet tells you more than you want to know.

Lizzy still isn't downstairs by the time James arrives to
pick us up. I toss my bag onto the seat and promise James
that I'll only be a minute. Out of breath from running up
there, I pound on Lizzy's apartment door. No answer. I
use my key to open it, and stick my head inside. "Lizzy?"

She still doesn't answer. I hear the sink running in the
hall bathroom. "Lizzy?" I call loudly through the closed
bathroom door.

"Just a second!" she calls back, sounding annoyed.
"Oh, all right, come in."

I push open the door to find her in front of the mirror
holding a dripping towel to her eye.

"What's wrong?" I ask hurriedly.

"If you must know," she says, pulling the towel away
to reveal a very red eye, "I poked myself in the eye."

"With what?" I ask, searching the room for any sharp
sticks.

She mumbles an answer, but I can't hear her. "What
did you say?"

She groans and repeats, "I poked myself with an *eyeliner*!"

"What's an eyeliner?"

"Hey," she says, noticing for the first time that I'm standing on the bath mat. "No shoes in here."

"Why not?"

She stares at me with her one good eye. "What if you stepped on a worm when you were outside, then you came in here and stood on my bath mat? Worm parts would get on it, and then I'd come out of the shower and step on worm guts in my bare feet. Is that what you want? *Is it?*"

I slowly back into the hall. It is best not to answer when she's in a mood like this. "You better hurry," I warn her. "James is waiting outside. I don't want to be late on our second day."

She sighs loudly and puts down the towel. "Does it look really bad?"

I shake my head, even though it does look pretty bad. "No one will even notice."

Lizzy looks doubtful, but follows me out of the bathroom after one last glance in the mirror. While she puts her shoes on, I hurry downstairs and tell James what happened.

"Women and their makeup!" he says knowingly, shaking his head. "Do they think men notice if their eyes are lined or their cheeks are pink?"

"Lizzy doesn't wear makeup," I inform him.

"She does now," a girl's voice says from behind me. It's Samantha, the new girl.

"How do you know?" I ask.

She is too busy pressing her face against the limo's window to answer me. I glance around but don't see any signs of her evil twin.

The front door of the building bangs open, and Lizzy runs down the stairs. She ignores me and James and quickly pulls her hair in front of her red eye as Samantha turns around.

Samantha looks from me to Lizzy and back again. "Is this car for *you guys*?" she asks incredulously. "Are you, like, rich or something?"

Lizzy opens her mouth, but I quickly answer, "Rich uncle." Without waiting for James this time, I yank open the back limo door. Lizzy hurries in ahead of me, her hair still hanging in her face. As James closes the door behind us, I hear Samantha call out, "Wait! *Whose* uncle?"

"That was a close one," Lizzy says, reaching into the fridge and grabbing a can of orange juice.

"Do you want to tell me what's going on?" I ask, unwrapping my breakfast sandwich.

"It's nothing," she says with a shrug. "Samantha came over for a little while last night, that's all."

I stop mid-bite and rest the sandwich on my lap. "Really?" I ask, trying not to sound surprised or, worse yet, jealous.

"Yes, really," she says. "Why is that so hard to believe?"

I quickly take a bite of my sandwich. Who can expect someone to answer with a mouth full of peanut butter? "So what did you guys do?" I ask when I'm done chewing.

She shrugs. "Girl stuff. You wouldn't have been interested."

We're now on uncharted grounds. I change the subject. "Did you read the letter from Mrs. Billingsly?"

She nods and asks, "Who would name their kid Oswald Oswald?"

"I know!" I exclaim, and we both laugh. The tension in the car dissolves. By the time we pull up in front of Mr. Oswald's building, everything's back to normal. I don't want to ruin the mood by telling her what I learned about Bitsy Solomon.

"How does my eye look now?" Lizzy asks as we climb out.

"You can't even tell anymore," I assure her. It is mostly true.

"Good," she says firmly. "Because I don't want anything to distract Mr. Oswald when I give him a piece of my mind." She storms past James and walks directly up to Mr. Oswald's door. Raising her fist, she is about to pound on the door when Mr. Oswald opens it. Lizzy barely stops short of hitting him.

"Whoa there, little lady," he says, backing up. "You must be anxious to get started."

Lizzy puts her hands on her hips and does her best glare. "You've got a lot of explaining to do, mister."

"Oh, my," he replies, unable to hide a smile. "Let's go to my office and discuss whatever's bothering you on this beautiful summer day."

"As if you didn't know," Lizzy snaps, storming into the house. I flash Mr. Oswald an embarrassed smile as I enter. I want answers as much as Lizzy does, but one can still be polite about it. As we pass through the box-filled living room, I inhale deeply. Someone is baking!

Mary is waiting for us in the library with orange juice and chocolate crumb cake. If Mr. Oswald is trying to win us over, he's got my vote. I happily munch away while Lizzy waits impatiently for Mr. Oswald to get settled behind his desk.

"Everything went smoothly yesterday, I trust?" Mr. Oswald asks.

"We do have some questions, like —," I begin, but Lizzy cuts me off.

"Why didn't you tell us Mrs. Billingsly didn't know why we were coming?" she demands. "Why did you tell us her book was about woodland animals? Why did your grandfather hold onto it for over sixty years? My father said that kids under eighteen aren't allowed to pawn stuff. It's illegal." She lowers her voice a bit on *illegal*.

Before he answers Lizzy, he turns to me and asks, "How about you, Jeremy? Do you have anything to add to that list?"

I am tempted to ask why someone would name their kid Oswald Oswald, but Ozzy *was* his grandfather, so it wouldn't be very respectful. I shake my head.

"Is every delivery going to be like that one?" Lizzy asks.

Mr. Oswald shakes his head. "Not exactly like that one," he says. "Nothing is ever exactly like anything else. I apologize for not having the time to prepare you fully yesterday, and I hope you will forgive me and allow me to explain. Jeremy?"

"Yes, okay," I say, surprised and kind of flattered that he would ask my forgiveness.

"Lizzy?" Mr. Oswald asks.

Lizzy sighs loudly. "Whatever."

"Good!" Mr. Oswald exclaims, pushing himself up from his leather chair. "I'll explain by showing you another item." He walks over to his nearest rows of shelves and reaches up for the only item on the top shelf — a brass telescope. Even on his tiptoes, he can't quite reach it. I suddenly have this horrible image of him falling and breaking a hip and us having to pick up trash in Central Park. I bound out of my chair and offer to help.

Hoisting myself up on the bottom shelf, I reach for the telescope. It's heavier than I would have thought, and my foot loses its grip on the shelf. Lizzy yelps as I start to tip over backward. Mr. Oswald moves faster than I would have thought possible and steadies me.

"Good thing you don't weigh much more," he says, clasping me on the shoulder.

"Sorry 'bout that," I say, reddening. I carefully hand him the telescope. Here I had been worrying about *him* falling, and instead I almost crush him!

"You okay?" Lizzy whispers.

I nod, embarrassed. Maybe I should take up weight-lifting.

Mr. Oswald places the telescope on the desk in front of us. "This," he says proudly, "is a Broadhurst. It was the most powerful telescope for backyard viewing in its day."

"Which was when?" Lizzy asks.

"The nineteen thirties," he replies. "Isn't it a beauty?

On a clear night, you could see the whole solar system with this one."

Unable to stop myself, I blurt out, "My very energetic mother just served us nine pizzas."

Lizzy gawks at me like I have two heads. "He's lost it; he's finally lost it. I knew the day would come."

Mr. Oswald chuckles. "Jeremy has just given us a mnemonic device for remembering the order of the planets."

Lizzy rolls her eyes. "See?" she says. "I told you he reads too much."

"I believe one cannot read too much," Mr. Oswald says. "Jeremy, your mnemonic device might have to change. I've been reading about Pluto perhaps losing its planethood. Astronomers think it's too small to fit the definition of a planet."

I nod. I had read about that, too.

"Figures they'd get rid of the one named after Mickey Mouse's dog," Lizzy grumbles.

I lean closer to the desk and check out the telescope. It is obviously very old, because it is made of some kind of heavy metal like brass or copper instead of plastic. I have asked for — and been denied — a telescope for my birthday ever since I was eight. Mom argues that it's impractical because there are so many lights in the city that we can barely see the stars. This kid at school used to brag that his family owned one, but instead of aiming it at the sky, it was pointed at the apartment building across the street from his. After I heard that, I decided to keep my blinds closed in case we have some nosy neighbors as well.

I reach out and run my finger down the slope of the

telescope. Who has stared through that viewfinder? What did they see?

"Where did you get it?" I ask reverently.

"In 1944 a young man named Amos Grady moved to Brooklyn from Kentucky. He brought this to my grandfather's shop. Granddad paid Amos forty-five dollars for it. That was a lot of money in those days. He should have turned it over to the government for scrap metal, but for reasons of his own, he did not."

"Let me guess," Lizzy says. "Today we're going to return this old telescope to Amos Grady, right?"

"No," Mr. Oswald replies. He turns back to the shelves and picks up an ornate stained-glass lamp with a frayed brown cord. "Today you're going to deliver this lamp to a Mr. Simon Rudolph on Avenue B."

He places the lamp into Lizzy's surprised hands. She examines it. "Does this thing even work?"

Mr. Oswald chuckles. "I never thought to try it."

"Was Amos Grady under eighteen?" Lizzy interrupts.

"Fourteen to the day," Mr. Oswald replies.

"Then what your grandfather did was illegal?" she asks. I slide down in my chair, unsure where to look.

Mr. Oswald nods. "Oh, yes, quite."

"I knew it!" Lizzy exclaims. "I knew there was something suspicious going on here. Didn't I tell you, Jeremy?"

I slide farther down in my seat. My eyes are level with the top of the desk now.

Mr. Oswald returns to his chair. He holds up his hand. "Before you get the wrong idea, allow me explain as I promised earlier."

Lizzy places the lamp on the desk next to the telescope and sits back, arms folded. When I'm sure she's not going to yell anymore, I slide back up in my chair.

Mr. Oswald clears his throat. "Everyone in New York City knew my grandfather, Old Ozzy, they called him, even before he got old. Priests and rabbis and business leaders came to him for his sensible advice. Little children would follow him in the streets. He always had a piece of taffy or a pickle to give them."

"A pickle?" I can't help interjecting. "Kids would follow him for a *pickle*?"

Mr. Oswald smiles. "For blocks and blocks. These pickles were aged to perfection in big wooden barrels down by the piers. Nothing like them back then, or since."

I shudder involuntarily.

Mr. Oswald continues. "But more than the pickles, the children knew they could come to my grandfather with their worries. And in those days — the nineteen thirties and forties — there were a lot of worries to be had. Now as Miss Muldoun here rightly pointed out, it was, shall we say, frowned upon to accept an item in a pawnshop from a child. But as I said, times were tough back then, and everyone had money problems, even children. So Ozzy, he made a deal with the children who came to see him." He pauses here and says, "With me so far?"

We nod. I'm actually on the edge of my seat. Even with the part about the pickles.

"Ozzy told the kids he would buy what they offered on one condition. He made up a special form for them to fill out explaining where the item came from, and why they needed to sell it. He would sit the kids down in front of the typewriter, and even if it took them all day, they recorded their stories. Ozzy never judged the children's reasons, and he always paid a fair price. Having to fill out the form scared away all but the most resolute."

"But why didn't Ozzy turn around and sell these things to someone else?" I ask. "Isn't that how the pawn business works?"

Mr. Oswald nods. "Indeed it is. But helping these youngsters out was never about the money. Ozzy stashed the items and the letters in a special closet in the back of his storeroom, and no one knew about them, not even my own father, who ran the store for thirty years."

"Do you think he meant to give them back to the kids?" I inquire.

"I wish I knew," Mr. Oswald replies, glancing over at an old black-and-white photograph on his desk.

I hadn't paid attention to the photo before, but now I lean in to examine it. It shows a middle-aged man holding up a fish and a pole, posing next to a wooden sign that reads YOU SHOULD SEE THE ONE THAT GOT AWAY!

"Old Ozzy?" I ask.

Mr. Oswald nods. "A big fisherman in his youth."

"But how did you find these people after so many years?" Lizzy asks.

"I hired a good detective. With so much information on the Internet, it wasn't very difficult to find out more than we even wanted to know."

"Tell me about it," I mutter.

They both turn to look at me. I pick up the lamp and say, "So what's *this* guy's story?"

Mr. Oswald checks his watch. "I didn't plan to spend so much time here this morning. I don't have time to pack up the lamp. You can carry it, right?"

Without waiting for an answer, he reaches into his top drawer and pulls out an envelope. He holds it out to me. I am not surprised to see Simon Rudolph's name printed on it in the same neat handwriting as the other. I slide it into my back pocket.

Before I can remind him that he still hasn't told us anything about Simon or his lamp, James appears and hands Mr. Oswald his pipe and a newspaper.

"I have the car ready for the children out front, sir," James says.

"Teenagers," Lizzy mutters under her breath. "Practically," she adds.

"Good, good," Mr. Oswald says to James. He lifts a Post-it note off the top of his desk, and hands it to him. "There is no house number outside Mr. Rudolph's door," he warns us all. "Mr. Rudolph's a bit, shall we say, eccentric. Bring your notebooks to our next visit. I'll be out of town for the next two days, so I will see you on Friday. Thank you in advance for a job well done." Mr. Oswald leaves the room, and James follows.

Lizzy and I are alone. Neither of us makes a move to take the lamp. "Um, I guess we should go, too?" I suggest.

"This is just like last time," she grumbles, but she picks up the lamp. "We don't know anything about this guy. We don't know what to expect."

As we head toward the front door I whisper, "This isn't *exactly* like last time."

"I know, I know," Lizzy replies, and then poorly mimics Mr. Oswald's voice. "Because nothing is ever exactly like anything else."

"No. I mean *this* time we know what the envelope is for."

Lizzy stops walking and stares at me. "Did I just hear what I think I heard? Is the honorable Jeremy Fink suggesting we open the envelope before we get there?"

"He might be," I say with a proud smile.

"There's hope for you yet," she says approvingly.

I'm glad she's pleased by my willingness to break the rules, even though Mr. Oswald didn't specifically tell us *not* to read it. But honestly, I'm motivated less by curiosity and more by fear. I don't like being unprepared for anything. And if Mr. Rudolph is as "eccentric" as Mr. Oswald said, I want to know exactly what we're walking into.

Chapter 11: The Lamp

"You can open it," I whisper, pushing the envelope across the seat to Lizzy.

"No, you," she says, pushing it back.

"You!" I toss it onto her lap, and she tosses it right back.

"Oh, for goodness' sake," James says from the front seat. "I'll open it."

Guiltily, I pass the envelope through the partially open window divider. I hear a ripping sound, which makes me cringe a little, and the letter appears a few seconds later. This one isn't as yellowed as the other one. I unfold it slowly.

```
Oswald's Pawn Emporium
Date: August 11, 1958
Name: Simon Rudolph
Age: 14 (today)
Location: Manhattan
Item to Pawn: Multicolored glass lamp
Personal Statement of Seller: I need the
money to buy a silver watch. All my friends
have nice watches, but my mother is too busy
spending money on herself at Bergdorf's and
Bloomingdale's to buy me anything. She has
twenty of these lamps. She won't notice one
```

missing. She does not notice anything. I
once stood on my head for twenty whole minutes till my face was purple. Mother went on
gabbing to her friend on the telephone about
what to wear to dinner at the club. EVERYONE
knows the telephone is not supposed to be
used for such everyday things. Dad claims
that I need to learn the value of money, but
I KNOW the value of money. Some day I am going to be even richer than him and then I
won't NEED to pawn anything. I'll have FIFTY
silver watches!

When I finish reading it, Lizzy says, "Wow. What a
spoiled brat."

I hand her the letter. "It says here he got twenty dollars for the lamp. Silver watches must have cost a lot less
back then."

"He looks so . . . intense," Lizzy says, staring at the
photo clipped to the bottom of the letter. "I wonder what
he was thinking at that moment." She tilts the paper so I
can see it.

"Maybe he's thinking about the meaning of life," I
suggest.

"You think so?"

"Why not?"

Lizzy leans forward and pushes the letter through the
half-open window to James. "What do you think, James?"

Without taking his eyes from the road, James holds
the letter in front of him and gives it a quick glance. "I

think he's wondering if he should have eaten that last pickle."

Lizzy and I laugh as James tosses the letter back to us and then raises the window divider the rest of the way.

Rain begins to plop down on the car. I'm very glad to be right here, in this car, at this moment. Still, finding the keys for the box is never far from my mind. Every minute we're doing something else is making me a little antsy. Lizzy turns away from watching the rain slide down the back window and opens a soda.

I clear my throat. Asking Lizzy serious questions usually doesn't go over well, but I have to try. "Um, Lizzy?"

"Hmm?" she asks, guzzling the soda so fast I'm afraid it's going to come out her nose. She's not allowed soda in her house.

"Do you ever . . . I mean, have you ever . . . I mean . . ."

She glances at her watch theatrically. "Spit it out, I'm getting old here."

"Fine. Do you ever think about the meaning of life? Like, do you think you know what it is?"

She shakes her head. "I try not to think about anything too deeply. It hurts my brain." With that, she turns to the window and stares out at the rain again.

There is no parking without a special permit on Mr. Rudolph's street, so James has to park in a lot two blocks away. It costs twenty dollars for one hour! He mutters something about highway robbery and the Better Business Bureau, and reluctantly hands the attendant the keys. The guy eyes the car hungrily as we get out. I bet it's not every day he gets to park a limo like this. As we walk toward the street, I whisper to James that he should check the odometer to make sure the guy doesn't take it for a joyride.

"You've seen too many movies," James says, but he runs back to the car, claiming he forgot something.

Luckily the brief storm ends as quickly as it began, so I don't have to be annoyed at myself for being unprepared. I make a mental note to keep an umbrella in my backpack from now on.

A slight mist rises off the hot sidewalk as we head down the block. It gives the neighborhood an eerie glow. Lizzy has passed the lamp-holding duties to me, and I notice it gets admiring glances from passersby. It really is a beautiful lamp, and I've never paid any attention to lamps before. Even though the sun isn't out, the lamp appears to be lit from within. If this lamp had been mine, I wouldn't have wanted to pawn it.

James reads out the street address. Not only does Mr. Rudolph not have a number on his door, neither do most of his neighbors. We get no answer at the first door we try. The second is opened by a little kid in a soccer uniform, who sneers and says, "I don't talk to strangers!" before slamming the door in our faces. James mutters something about this being the reason he never had children and then pushes the intercom outside the next door.

"Good morning!" a man's voice rings out. "How can I help you today?"

James leans closer to the intercom and says, "We are looking for a Mr. Simon Rudolph. Mr. Oswald sent us."

"Ah, yes," the voice cackles through the metal box.

"The mysterious Mr. Oswald who would not re~
nature of his business with me. No matter. I am alv.
happy to welcome guests to my home." A few secono.
later the door buzzes, and James pushes it open.

Lizzy and I don't move.

"What's wrong this time?" James says.

"I don't think this is the right guy," I reply.

Lizzy nods in agreement, pulling the letter out of her
pocket.

"What makes you say that?" James asks.

"He doesn't sound anything like this letter," Lizzy
says. "This guy sounds like he's been taking happy pills.
Our guy was spoiled and obnoxious."

"People change," James says with exasperation. "That
was nearly fifty years ago, for goodness' sake. This is the
right guy. He's expecting us."

"Oh, all right," Lizzy says, pushing her way past him
and into the building. "But if we get kidnapped into some
cult, my father will be *very* angry with you."

We trudge up three flights of stairs until we reach the
right door. It's open a crack. James whispers, "I'll be
standing right out here."

"Are you sure?" I whisper back, glancing nervously at
the door.

"You'll be fine," he insists, and moves a few feet away.

"We better be," Lizzy mumbles.

Tentatively I push the door open a few more inches.
"Mr. Rudolph?" A few seconds go by, and I don't hear any
noise inside. I glance at Lizzy, and she looks uneasy, too.
Then she reaches past me and pushes the door the rest of

...e way open. We find ourselves staring into a big, nearly empty room with white walls and wood floors. There is one window, one table, one small plastic lamp, one hardback wooden chair, one large framed photograph (a sunset over a beach), and one bowl with one piece of fruit (an apple). The smell of flowers hangs in the air, but I don't see any.

As we're taking in the strangeness of it, a spry, wiry man walks through an archway at the end of the room. He is deeply tanned, wearing sandals, brown shorts, and a white T-shirt with the cryptic message: THE ONE WHO DIES WITH THE MOST TOYS WINS. Based on the letter from Mr. Oswald, he must be over sixty, but he looks at least ten years younger.

"Er, are you Simon Rudolph?" I ask, searching his face in vain for a resemblance to that intense boy in the faded photo.

"At your service," he replies with a small bow. "And you two are?"

"I'm Jeremy Fink, and this is Lizzy Muldoun." Lizzy gives the man a small nod. Her red hair and freckles are the brightest things in the room, next to the lamp that I'm holding and the sunset picture.

"I've heard of traveling with a flashlight," Mr. Rudolph says with a grin. "But a whole lamp? And such an ornate one, at that."

I quickly hold the lamp out to him. "This is yours. You pawned it to Ozzy Oswald in 1958."

Mr. Rudolph's eyes widen until I'm afraid they'll pop right out of his head. He steps forward and takes the lamp from me. Running his hand over the glass, he says

over and over, "Mother's old lamp! I can't believ
simply can't believe it." Finally he asks, "How did y
get this?"

"We, er, *work,* sort of, for Ozzy's grandson," I explain. "He wanted you to have it back." I'm sort of making that up since I really don't know *why* Mr. Oswald is
returning these items, but it sounded good.

He places the lamp on the table and turns to us. "It is
a thing of beauty, is it not?"

"Yes," I say eagerly. I glance at Lizzy, expecting to see
her nodding, too. Instead she's looking around and biting
her lower lip. I realize she hasn't said a word since we
stepped foot inside the apartment. She looks a bit pale,
too. "You okay?" I whisper while Mr. Rudolph walks in
circles around the lamp, admiring it from every angle.

She whispers back, "There's nothing here. It's so
empty. There's nothing to take."

"What do you mean there's nothing to take?"

"My hands are itching. That means I'm supposed to
take something, but there's *nothing to take!*"

I quickly look over to make sure Mr. Rudolph didn't
hear that, but he's still entranced by the lamp. "We'll talk
about this later," I hiss, grabbing the envelope out of her
hand. I walk over to Mr. Rudolph and hold it out to him.
"This is yours, too. It sort of, ah, got opened a little."

He takes it from me, shaking his head in amazement.
"Why didn't Ozzy sell this? I told him it was a genuine
Tiffany. He could have made a pretty penny."

"I don't know," I tell him honestly. "He didn't sell any
of the things kids brought to his shop."

"Is that right?" he asks, shaking his head again. "Good ol' Ozzy."

Suddenly Lizzy springs to life and blurts out, "Where's the watch?"

Mr. Rudolph looks confused for a minute, and then he smiles. "Ah, the silver watch. I haven't thought about that watch in decades. I wore it every day of my working life. All those long years on the stock exchange. Every tick of the watch marked another drop of life force that I'll never get back. I gave it to a homeless man on the street the day I walked out with my first million."

A hush falls over the room. Then Lizzy yells, "You have a MILLION DOLLARS? And there's only ONE of each thing in this room?"

Mr. Rudolph laughs, and says, "I don't have a million dollars anymore. I gave most of it away. Look, I grew up with money. Then I made more than I knew what to do with. And you know what? I'm much happier this way. All of life's problems come from attachment. When you let go of being attached to things, or needing things, a sense of peace comes over you like I can't describe."

Lizzy looks doubtful. "So how do you pay your bills?"

He laughs again. "I didn't say I gave it *all* away."

"Don't you get tired of looking at the same things?" she asks. I was wondering that, too. "Like that picture. It's nice and all, but it's, like, the only thing to look at."

He shakes his head. "I don't get tired of looking at it. When each object is framed in space, when there are big blank areas around it, it changes, subtly, every day. When you have twenty of something, the individual object can't shine. Plus, I believe that once you find something you love, something that works, why keep looking for more? People always think there is something better around the corner. I decided a long time ago I'd stop wasting my time looking for something better and enjoy what I had."

"Is that what your shirt means?" I ask. "It's a joke, right? Or, like, sarcasm?"

He looks down at the words on his shirt and smiles. "Yes. This is one of my favorite sayings. The sad thing is, I used to believe it was true. But you can't take things with you when you go, so what is the point of accumulating them? I don't expect you children to embrace this way of life at your age. It's something one has to come to on one's own, if the time is right."

I am glad he said that, since I don't want to start feeling guilty over all my books, or my mutant candy collection, or my comics, or any of the rest of my stuff. Still, I can sort of understand what he means.

"You've heard the expression 'Go with the flow,' right?" We nod.

"Well, that's how I've decided to live my life. If you go along with the flow of life, without trying to change others, or change situations that are beyond you, life is much more peaceful." He suddenly picks up the lamp and hands it to Lizzy. "Here," he says, "why don't you take this."

Her mouth literally falls open. "Me? Why?"

"I already have a lamp."

We all turn to look at the small blue plastic lamp on the table. It looks like one of those lamps you could buy at a drugstore for five dollars.

"Wouldn't you rather have this one?" she asks. "It's so much nicer."

He shakes his head. "Mine is perfectly fine. It sheds light. That's what a lamp is made for. Everything is at its best when it is doing exactly what it was created for. A lamp gives light. An apple gives sustenance and refreshment. A chair is perfect in being exactly what it is — a chair."

"I have no idea what that means," Lizzy says, looking down at the lamp in awe. "But thanks for the lamp!"

"Can I ask you something?" I blurt out.

He nods with a smile. "Anything for such special guests."

"Is that the meaning of life? What you just said?"

"Jeremy!" Lizzy exclaims. I knew she'd be shocked that I asked, but I couldn't help it. If we never find those keys, I still want to know what's inside the box. This man clearly knows a lot about life, and no adult has ever said these kinds of things to me before. I can't leave until I know more of what he knows.

Mr. Rudolph cocks his head and looks at me sideways. Then he laughs and gestures for us to follow him through the archway into the next room. "This visit is just full of surprises! I think we'll need to sit down for this."

I glance back at the still partially open front door and hope James won't mind waiting a little longer. The room he leads us into is similar to the one we left, only this one is much smaller with big, colorful pillows in the middle. A vase with the largest white-and-purple flower I've ever seen rests in the middle of the circle.

"I meditate here," he explains. "And if I have guests, this is where we visit. Pick a pillow and make yourself comfortable."

Lizzy carefully places the lamp behind her and plops down on a red pillow. I choose a yellow one, and Mr. Rudolph takes the white. "Look at the flower," he instructs us. "What do you see?"

"Um, a flower?" Lizzy says, then quickly adds, "A big white-and-purple one that smells good?"

He turns to me. "Jeremy? What about you?"

I stare at the flower, inexplicably wondering if it's going to suddenly turn into something else, like a cat or a matchbook. When it doesn't, I say quickly, "Same as what Lizzy said."

"Exactly right!" he exclaims, surprising me. "It is a large white-and-purple, sweet-smelling flower. An orchid, to be precise. Now wait here." He unfolds his legs and strides out of the room.

Lizzy leans forward and whispers, "What are we *doing*?"

"This is the next plan on our list," I explain, hoping she'll understand. "We might never open my dad's box. If I can figure out the meaning of life before my birthday, then at least it won't be so awful if I can't open it."

She doesn't answer, only nods thoughtfully. "Okay, I get it. But what if this guy doesn't know the answer?"

"Then we'll ask everyone we can."

At that moment, Mr. Rudolph returns. Surprisingly, he is carrying the photograph of the sunset under his arm. He leans it up against the wall and sits back on his pillow.

"Now, what does this picture mean to you? Lizzy, you first again."

Lizzy fills her cheeks with air, and slowly lets it out. "What does it mean?" she repeats. "I guess it means that whoever took it is a good photographer. It's pretty."

"How about you, Jeremy?"

"I really don't understand art," I admit. "It's nice? It brightens up the room?"

"How does it make you feel?" Mr. Rudolph prods.

"Er, kind of sad, I guess? Like it's the end of something, but it's kind of relaxing, too?"

"Lizzy?"

"Um, it makes me want to go to the beach?"

Mr. Rudolph smiles. "Okay, great answers. To me, this photograph reminds me to treasure each moment, because they are fleeting. A minute later, and the sky would be dark. It also reminds me of the day I took the picture, and whom I was with. I can carry the beauty of this sunset with me, inside me, so that when I do not see much beauty around me, I can use some of what is stored inside. So we see that already, this one photograph of a sunset means different things to all three of us. But here's my real question: what do you think it means to the flower?"

At the same time, Lizzy and I ask, "Huh?"

"Exactly!"

"Huh?" we repeat.

Mr. Rudolph reaches out and lifts the flower out of its vase. "To a flower, this photograph means nothing. So when you ask what is the meaning of life, there can be no answer that will apply to everyone and everything. What is a photograph, or a sunset, to a flower? We all bring our own perceptions, needs, and experiences to everything we do. We will all interpret an event, or a sunset, differently."

He pauses, and I am trying to keep up with him. "Basically," I say slowly, concentrating on my words. "What you're saying is that it's all relative. The meaning of the sunset, or of life itself, is different for everyone?"

"Exactly," he says.

"Nah!" Lizzy exclaims, getting to her feet. "I'm not buying it. I think there has to be some meaning that means the same thing to everyone. Otherwise, nothing makes sense."

Mr. Rudolph smiles and stands up. "Fortunately, you have a long time to find out."

"Not as long as you'd think," Lizzy mutters.

As we head slowly into the big room, I turn to him and ask, "But even if the sunset has different meanings for everyone, it still has meaning, right?"

"That's a tricky question to answer," Mr. Rudolph says, stopping to replace the frame back on the wall. "That sunset will still shine just as surely, just as colorfully, whether it is shining on a wedding or a war. So it would seem that the sunset itself doesn't have inherent meaning; it is just doing its job. If the sunset doesn't have meaning apart from what we give it, does a rock? Or a fish? Or life itself? But just because a park bench, for instance, doesn't have meaning, that doesn't mean it doesn't have *worth*."

"I'm starting to get a headache," Lizzy mutters.

We have reached the door now, and I'm not sure I'm

any closer to understanding what's in the box. My shoulders sag.

"Maybe this will help clear things up," Mr. Rudolph says. "You need to be sure of the question you are asking. Sometimes people think they are looking for the meaning of life, when really they are looking for an understanding of why they are here. What their *purpose* is, the purpose of life in general. And that's a much easier question to answer than the meaning of life."

Lizzy is already halfway out the door. "It is?" I ask, pulling her back in by her sleeve. I'm not certain, but I think I see the tip of a white flower petal sticking out of her pocket.

"You are the same as the lamp, the chair, the flower," Mr. Rudolph explains. "All you have to do is be the most authentic *you* that you can be. Find out who you really are, find out *why you are here,* and you will find your purpose. And with it, the meaning of life."

Why I am here? I have no idea why I'm here. Am I supposed to know that? Does everybody know that but me? What's wrong with me? I always knew something was wrong with me.

"Shhh," Lizzy whispers. "You're sounding crazy."

Had I said that *out loud*?

"You shouldn't leave empty-handed, Jeremy," Mr. Rudolph says, kindly ignoring my ramblings. "That wouldn't be fair." He walks over the bowl and swoops up the apple. He tosses it to me, and I reach up just in time to catch it. To some people for whom such things matter, they might be jealous that their friend got a stained-glass Tiffany lamp while he only got an apple. Luckily for me, I am not one of them. Now if Lizzy had been given a chocolate bar and all I got was an apple, *then* there'd be a problem.

Lizzy slips through the door and takes off down the hall. I know I need to thank Mr. Rudolph for trying to help us, but my brain can't get past the idea that I don't know why I'm here on this planet. Why do I exist? "Um, thank you for everything, your time, and all, but I'm still a little confused, I guess."

He smiles and pats me on the shoulder. He points to the apple in my hand and says, "A wise man once remarked that we can count how many seeds are in the apple, but not how many apples are in the seed. Do you know what he meant by that?"

I shake my head.

"Before an apple seed is planted, no one will know how many apples will one day sprout from it. It's all about potential, and potential is hidden from all of us until we embrace it, find our purpose, plant ourselves so we can grow. I am certain you will find what you are looking for, Jeremy. Many blessings upon your head."

With that, he closes the door, leaving me clutching my apple so tightly that my fingernails have punctured the skin.

Chapter 12: The Existential Crisis

Lizzy yanks on the blinds, and light floods into my bedroom. I groan. It feels like an elephant is sitting on my chest. I just want to be invisible. If I can't figure out why I'm here, then I'm just taking up space.

"Come on," she says, tugging at my blanket. "It's eleven o'clock already."

I shake my head and strengthen my grip on the top of the blanket. "I'm not getting up." If I were invisible, maybe I could see what other people were here for, and it would help. But since the only people I know who are invisible are comic book characters or have an invisibility cloak like Harry Potter, I probably don't have much hope in that department.

"I have a chocolate Vitamuffin for you," Lizzy sings, waving the muffin in front of my nose.

"Don't want it."

Lizzy looks over at my desk, and then back at the bed. "Is that lump next to you your dad's box?"

I don't answer.

She reaches over and feels around it. "It IS the box! So you're sleeping with it now?"

How do I explain that I was tracing the words with my fingers and fell asleep? I know the curves of those letters so well by now I could copy them perfectly.

"I'm going to call your mother at work," she threatens. "You're not acting like yourself."

"Go ahead."

"Fine, I will." She storms out of the room, and returns a minute later with the cordless phone held to her ear.

"He just won't get out of bed, Mrs. Fink," she says. "No, I don't know why. He won't tell me." She holds out the phone to me. "She wants to talk to you."

I shake my head and throw the stuffed alligator over my face.

"He won't take the phone. Okay, I'll ask him. Jeremy, your mom wants to know if you're sick."

I shake my head.

"No, he's not sick," she says. Then she lifts up the alligator and yells into my ear, "Your mom insists you tell us why you won't get out of bed or she's gonna come home and drag you out herself!"

I look at her doubtfully.

"Okay, so maybe she didn't say that last part, but you better tell me."

So softly that Lizzy has to lean over to hear me, I say, "I can't face the world until I know why I'm here."

"You're kidding me."

I shake my head vehemently. "No. I need to figure out my purpose. Until I do, what's the use of getting up?"

Lizzy repeats my words into the phone, and after a long pause says, "Okay, I'll tell him. Bye." She puts the phone on my desk and says, "Your mother told me to tell you you can have your existential crisis — whatever that means — once you're out of bed. I'm pretty sure you won't find your purpose lying there with an alligator over your face. Get up!"

"Fine!" I tell her, pushing the blanket off of me and sitting up. I'm wearing the same clothes I wore yesterday. When I'm depressed, little things like changing into my pajamas seem to slip away. "But will you promise to leave me alone today? I want to be by myself."

"Sorry," Lizzy says, placing the muffin on my lap. "We have to be down the hall in ten minutes."

"Huh? Where are we going?"

"Samantha's apartment. Now get up!" She drags me off the bed, giving me barely enough time to grab my muffin before it falls to the floor.

"I'm not going to Samantha's apartment!" I inform her. "I'm spending the day trying to figure out why I'm here on this planet. You might want to do the same."

"I already know why I'm here," Lizzy says, standing in the doorway.

"Really? You do?" That doesn't seem fair. Everything comes more easily to Lizzy than it does to me.

"I'm here to get you because Samantha and Rick are waiting for us!"

I push her out into the hall and turn the lock. She knocks hard on the door. "Come on, Jeremy, just hear me out."

I put my hands over my ears, but it doesn't help. Now I'm trapped in here, and I really have to use the bathroom. I might as well eat the muffin, too.

Her voice is only slightly muffled by the door. "This morning when you wouldn't answer any of the notes I sent, I went downstairs to sit on the stoop."

I glance over and see that my solar system poster is in fact pushed a few inches from the wall. I must not have heard her knocking on the wall to announce the notes.

She continues. "The twins were outside, too, so we started talking. One thing led to another, and I told them about your box and how we can't find the keys."

At that, I yank open the door and glare at her. Pieces of muffin fly out of my mouth as I yell, "You did WHAT?"

Lizzy backs up a step to avoid being hit by half-chewed muffin morsels. "I didn't think you'd mind," she argues. "Well, I actually didn't think about how you'd feel till after I had already told them, but I'm glad I did because Samantha had a really great idea."

Before I could respond, she says, "Samantha said if we need to know where the keys are, we should go directly to the source and ask your dad!"

My stomach twists a little. "What are you talking about? Didn't you tell her about the accident?"

"Of course I told her," she says hurriedly. "Samantha said we can hold a séance, and then we can ask him. She has a Ouija board and everything."

"You're kidding, right?"

Lizzy shakes her head. "It's worth a shot, isn't it? We've tried everything else."

"But Rick is so obnoxious. Do you really want to hang out with him?"

"Maybe he just acts like a jerk because he's lonely. Mr. Rudolph turned out a lot different than we thought he'd be. Maybe Rick will, too. Let's go, okay?"

I lean against the hallway wall. What if Samantha was

right? What if I really could talk to Dad again? That would be worth having to hang out with the twins. And to be honest, I hadn't done so well with the whole why-I'm-here enigma. After contemplating the question ever since James dropped us off yesterday, I came up with only three possible answers. I'm here to be my mother's son, to be Lizzy's best friend, and to eat a lot of candy. Somehow, that doesn't inspire greatness. "Okay, I'll meet you on the stoop in five minutes and we'll go in together."

"Cool," she says, hurrying away. "You won't regret it."

Why do I doubt that?

I find Lizzy on the top step, her face tilted up to the sun. Little Bobby and his mother are there, too, sitting in the shady part.

"Jeremy," Lizzy says, "why don't you ask Mrs. Sanchez the question you've decided to ask everyone?"

Now that we're back in our regular non-limo-riding, non-returning pawned-items lives, asking people the meaning of life seems kind of embarrassing.

"Go on," Lizzy urges. "And then we have to leave."

Mrs. Sanchez looks up from combing a squirming Bobby's hair. Instead of asking what the meaning of life is, I ask, "Why are we here? You know, here, on this planet. Not like, here, on this stoop."

She smiles, apparently not surprised at my question. "You don't know this?" she asks. I shake my head.

"It is simple," she replies. "We are here to help others."

Bobby looks up. "Then what are the others here for?"

"Hush, child," she says, playfully tapping him on the

head with the comb. "The things that come out of your mouth!"

Lizzy laughs, but I actually thought it was a valid question. Could it really be that simple? If everyone helped everyone, there would be world peace. Maybe it *is* that simple. Somehow though, I don't think that's quite right. I'm all for people helping each other, but that seems more like a *good idea*, rather than the reason we're here in the first place.

Even though it's not that hot out today, I'm feeling sweaty and sticky. When was the last time I showered?

I thank Mrs. Sanchez and follow Lizzy up to the twins' apartment. Samantha opens the door, dressed in black from head to toe. "To get in the right mood," she explains when she sees us checking out her outfit. Even her eyes are rimmed in black.

Suddenly a lightbulb goes off in my brain. "Hey, eyeliner! That's what eyeliner is!"

Samantha gives me a strange look, and Lizzy kicks me in the shin. I'm trying to figure out the most important questions in all of humanity, and my biggest breakthrough is about girls' makeup? I am truly pathetic.

"Come on," Samantha says, leading us down the hall. "We have the Ouija board set up in the living room." Without turning around, she says, "Why do I smell peanut butter?"

I do a quick underarm check. Yup, it's me. I really ought to keep up with my showering schedule better.

Rick is waiting for us. He is not in black. He is, however, wearing a cape. "Don't ask," he says. "Samantha made me. She said if I didn't wear it and we couldn't contact your father, it would be all my fault. Too much pressure, so I'm wearing it. It's from an old Halloween costume. It's not like I just *happened* to have a cape handy."

This is the longest speech Rick has ever said to me. And it didn't even have anything obnoxious in it. Maybe Lizzy was right about him.

The curtains have all been pulled, and Samantha switches off the lights before sitting cross-legged on the rug. You'd never know it was daylight outside. Lizzy, Rick, and I join her on the floor. The Ouija board is set up in the middle. That little plastic pointer thing is resting in the corner of the board. I haven't used a Ouija board since my sixth-grade lab partner's birthday party. We were trying to contact the spirit of George Washington, because he was the only dead person we could agree on. Everyone accused everyone else of cheating and pushing the pointy thing. Two kids went home crying. I hope this ends better.

"We are ready to begin," Samantha says in a hushed tone. "Everyone join hands." Reluctantly, I take Rick's hand on one side, and Samantha's on the other. "We are going to call upon the spirit of —" Out of the corner of her mouth she whispers, "What's your dad's name?"

"Daniel Fink," I whisper back.

"We are going to call on the spirit of Daniel Fink," Samantha continues. "Mr. Fink, if you can hear the sound of my voice, please send us a sign."

I can hear the sound of my own breathing, along with faint sounds of traffic. A horn honks outside, and Samantha says, "Thank you! We will take that as a sign of your presence and your willingness to speak with us."

I open my mouth to argue, but Lizzy shoots me a look from across the Ouija board. Samantha lets go of my hand, so I let go of Rick's. He and Lizzy keep holding hands until I clear my throat, and she hastily drops his.

"Okay, everyone," Samantha says. "Now gently lay the first two fingers of your right hand on the pointer."

We all lean a little closer to the board and do as she says. She closes her eyes and begins to sway slightly from side to side. "O great spirit of Daniel Fink, we call upon you to answer our plea. Please tell us where we can find the keys to the box you left for Jeremy."

For a few minutes, nothing happens. It's more difficult than one might think to keep your hand resting lightly on a piece of plastic. I begin to get a cramp in my left leg. I stretch very carefully, lest I move the pointer and be accused of cheating. If my father were truly here, I would feel his presence, wouldn't I?

"Do you feel anything?" Lizzy whispers, reading my mind.

"Yeah," I reply. "I feel like an idiot."

Rick snickers. For the first time he's laughing with me, not *at* me or Lizzy.

"Shh!" Samantha whispers loudly. "Now concentrate!"

"What if Jeremy's dad was already reincarnated?" Rick asks. "He might even be a five-year-old by now. He could be little Bobby Sanchez!"

"Shut up!" Samantha says, glaring at him. "Jeremy's father is *not* Bobby Sanchez!"

"How do you know?" Rick asks.

Lizzy pipes in with, "He and Jeremy *do* get along really well. . . ."

"This is ridiculous," I say, pulling my hand away from the pointer. "I knew I should have spent the day figuring out how to be invisible!" As soon as the words are out of my mouth I regret them. What is *wrong* with me? Why do I just hand people reasons to make fun of me?

But instead of laughing at me, Rick says, "You want to learn how to be invisible? I can show you, no problem."

Samantha groans. "Not that again! I thought you wanted to start fresh here. You know, be *normal*."

"Don't listen to her," Rick says, springing to his feet. "She's just jealous she's not able to do it." He takes off down the hall, cape billowing behind him.

Having no other option, I look at Lizzy for guidance. She shrugs. "Couldn't hurt."

"That's what you said about *this*!" I point to the board.

"It's not her fault," Samantha says. "Maybe I did something wrong." She looks so disappointed that I instantly feel bad.

"No, you were great," I say, trying to sound sincere. "I'm not sure I really believe it's possible to contact my dad. But thank you for trying. I know you were only trying to help." I hurry after Rick before she can answer.

As I turn the corner, I hear her say to Lizzy, "He's so sweet! Are you sure you guys aren't dating?"

"I'm *positive*!" Lizzy replies without hesitation.

I'd blush at being called "sweet" if I weren't still under the dark cloud of my existential crisis. By the way, I looked up existentialism, and the definition is: *an analysis of individual existence in an unfathomable universe and the plight of the individual who must assume ultimate responsibility for his acts of free will without any certain knowledge of what is right or wrong or good or bad.* I had to read the definition twice before I could understand it. One word sure can cover a lot of ground!

Rick's bedroom is easy to pick out by the big skull and crossbones sticker. I knock on the door, half-hoping he will have disappeared and won't be in there. What am I doing? Why am I trusting him?

"Come in and take off your sneakers," he calls out.

I tentatively push the door open and find him on the floor, surrounded by books. As I pull off my sneakers, I notice a colorful poster with all these lines and shapes hanging over his bed.

"That's a Sri Yantra diagram," Rick explains. "The interconnecting triangles are supposed to lead you into a hypnotic state. It will be part of our training."

I join him on the floor and peek at the book titles. *The Dummy's Guide to Mysticism*, *The Holographic Universe*, and *New Physics: It's Not Your Father's Physics*. My heart quickens. These are the types of books *I* would read! Well, maybe not the mysticism one. I'm more of a science guy.

"Did you read all these?" I ask.

"Twice! And in order to become invisible, you've gotta understand the nature of reality. Now, you know there's no such thing as objective reality, right? Like an actual, tangible reality?" First Mr. Rudolph tells me the word *meaning* has no meaning, and now this? Doubtful, I ask, "How is reality not real?"

"Everything we think we know is really only perceived by our senses," he explains patiently. "The sounds we hear are just waves in the air; colors are electromagnetic radiation; your sense of taste comes from molecules that match a specific area on your tongue. Hey, if our eyes could access the infrared part of the light spectrum, the sky would be green and trees would be red. Some animals see in completely different ways, so who knows what colors look like to them. Nothing is really how we perceive it. Get it?"

I nod again, astounded by what he is telling me. If the sky isn't reliably blue, what hope do I have of finding the meaning of life? How can I find the meaning of life in a world where the sky could actually be green? Or orange?

He continues. "Matter — the stuff that all of us are made of — is really a wave of energy, only in a different form. The electrons buzzing around inside of us are everywhere and nowhere at the same time. Look down at your hand."

I turn over my right hand and stare at my palm.

"If you had an atomic microscope, you'd be able to see the atoms making up the skin on your hand. At the center of each atom is a nucleus with neutrons and protons and electrons, right?"

"I don't really know," I admit. "We don't have chemistry until next year."

"Trust me, that's the way it is. But the really weird

thing is that the rest of the atom, the other ninety-nine–point–nine-nine of it is empty. Between each atom is a void. There is truly nothing holding us — or anything else for that matter — together."

I stare so hard at my hand that my eyes start to sting.

"When you realize you're just a wave of energy," he says, with the air of someone coming to the punchline, "you can disappear."

My eyes widen. "When do I start?"

"Right now," Rick says. "Stand about a foot in front of the poster. Stare directly at the center of the design, but relax your eyes so they cross a little. Nod when you've got it."

I try to relax my eyes, but each time I do, they start to close. Finally, I just look at the poster like I'm looking at something much farther away, and it seems to work. I nod to Rick.

"Great," he says. "Now visualize a white light, and imagine yourself inside that light. The white light is getting really bright. It's starting to absorb the objects in my room."

"It is?" I ask.

"Yes. No talking! Now, see yourself getting blurry from inside the light until you can't see the light anymore."

My head gets lighter as I imagine the white light around me. It's like the whole world is within that poster, and the edges of the design start to fade.

"Is it working?" I ask excitedly. "Am I invisible?"

Rick shakes his head. "Nope. I can still see you. Keep trying."

I stare for another few minutes until I fear I may go cross-eyed for good. Sighing deeply, I reluctantly turn away from the poster. "How long did it take you to be able to do it?"

"Me?" he asks, surprised. "I've never actually tried it."

I stare at him suspiciously.

"Hey, I never said I could do it, I just said I could teach *you* how."

"I bet you never even read those books!"

He shrugs. "Read, skimmed, browsed, same difference."

I quickly tug on my sneakers, putting them on the wrong feet and not stopping to correct them. Afraid to hear the answer, I nevertheless ask, "Did you make up all that stuff you told me, about the nature of reality?"

"No," he says sincerely. "I swear. That's all true."

I'm relieved to hear that. But I'm still angry that he made me believe, even for a minute, that he could make me invisible. Without saying good-bye, I leave his room and almost trip over my feet as I run down the hall. When I pass Samantha's room, I can hear her and Lizzy listening to music and laughing.

Rick catches up with me as I'm halfway out their front door. "Why would *I* ever need to be invisible? That's only for little kids!"

I'm only one year younger than him, but I don't turn around to remind him of this. I have only myself to blame for trusting him.

And maybe Lizzy. Definitely Lizzy.

Chapter 13: The Telescope

Mary places a tall glass of lemonade in front of each of us, and a plate of chocolate-chip cookies in the middle of the white patio table. She has melted a mini Reese's Peanut Butter Cup in the center of each cookie. When she sees my joyful expression, she winks at me. And I thought nothing could get me out of my funk.

We're sitting in Mr. Oswald's back garden, because his desk drawers are being packed up. I had no idea there were gardens in Manhattan other than in the parks. The sounds of the street are muffled from here, and there's actually a bird or two chirping away in the small trees. It is very peaceful.

"May I see your notebooks?" Mr. Oswald asks, holding out his hand. I unzip my backpack and hand mine to him. Lizzy pulls hers out of her front pocket and apologizes for mangling it.

It had taken me the full H.O.J. last night to write down my observations from the experience at Mr. Rudolph's. I kept confusing what he had told us with what Rick had said about how at the deepest layer, nothing is connected. All night I felt like if I closed my eyes, I would float away into a void of nothingness. I know I should have recorded the visit right after we got home from it, but I was too busy wallowing in my identity crisis. Which, as peaceful as it is to watch butterflies flutter by, I have not entirely come out of.

I watch Mr. Oswald's face as he reads Lizzy's notebook

first. Every once in a while he smiles, or nods, or looks puzzled. I glance over at Lizzy, and she's squirming a bit, sticking and unsticking her bare legs from the plastic chair.

"Very good, Ms. Muldoun," he says, closing her notebook and passing it back to her. "You have quite an eye for observing the tiny details of people's surroundings." Lizzy beams as she takes the notebook from him. "Perhaps next time," he adds, "you can address a bit more of what the people you meet have to say, and how it made you feel. All right?"

Lizzy nods uncertainly, still clearly pleased with the previous compliment.

"And I hope you are enjoying your new lamp," he adds with a smile.

"Oh, yes," Lizzy says happily. "My dad put a light bulb in it and attached a new cord, and it works great! It makes our living room much more colorful." Then she hurriedly adds, "I told Mr. Rudolph not to give it to me, honestly."

Mr. Oswald smiles warmly. "I know. He told me."

"You spoke to Mr. Rudolph?" I ask, surprised.

He nods.

"Did he, er, say anything about us?"

"Only that he enjoyed your visit very much."

"Oh, okay, good," I reply, relieved. Maybe Mr. Oswald wouldn't like it if he knew we had asked him about the meaning of life. It's not like it's part of our job description. It isn't his fault we're doing this instead of looking for the keys to my dad's box and learning the meaning of life from it.

As he opens my notebook and begins to read from the beginning, I can't help but apologize for it up front. "I'm sorry about the randomness of what I wrote, Mr. Oswald. There's been a lot to absorb."

Without looking up, he says, "Never apologize for writing your truth, Mr. Fink. There are no right or wrong answers."

I think he must be wrong about that. If there were no right or wrong answers, everyone in school would get straight *A*'s.

Lizzy slurps her lemonade and says, "I was worried Jeremy wasn't going to write anything at all. You see, he's been having an existential crisis."

I would kick her, but she is across the table from me.

Mr. Oswald raises his eyebrows. "Is that so?"

Lizzy nods. "And then he tried to become invisible."

I am tempted to throw my lemonade at Lizzy, but violence never solved anything.

Mr. Oswald looks at me. "You have been busy indeed. Now lets see what we've got here." As he reads, Mr. Oswald mumbles, "Very interesting point here. And this one, too. Not sure what you mean by that, but I see where you're going. Hmm, yes, hadn't thought of it quite that way. Very good. Very astute."

I redden as he hands the book back to me. I hurry to stick it deep in my backpack. Mr. Oswald turns to Lizzy. "Ms. Muldoun, why are you here?"

Lizzy puts her hands on the arms of her plastic chair like she's about to push herself up. "Er, do you want me to leave?"

Mr. Oswald laughs. "No, no, of course not, I mean, why are you *here*?"

Lizzy tries again. "Because of a little misunderstanding at an office building?"

"No, no, not that," Mr. Oswald says. "I meant, why do you think you are here on earth at this point in our history?"

"Oh," Lizzy says. "I don't know. I haven't thought about it."

"Jeremy here has given it a lot of thought. As his best friend, do you mean to tell me you haven't thought about it some yourself?"

Lizzy shifts around uncomfortably in her seat. She pulls at the straw in her now empty glass.

"I really don't know," she mumbles. Then she abruptly stops fidgeting and says, "If you know so much, why don't *you* tell us why we're here?"

I cringe at Lizzy's forwardness, but Mr. Oswald laughs and says, "In my day, Lizzy, you'd be what's known as a spitfire."

"Thanks," she says, puffing out her chest. "I think."

"But I'm afraid I can't answer that question for you. In fact, I am not so sure it is the correct question in the first place."

That figures. When I asked Mr. Rudolph about the meaning of life, he said the same thing. That I had the question wrong. How am I supposed to learn the answers if I keep messing up the questions? It's moments like this when I would sell my left foot for a bag of Sour Patch Kids.

Mr. Oswald waits patiently as a bumblebee swoops down, buzzes around his glass, and flies off. "If I were you," he says, "I'd be more interested in *how* we are here.

Why is there something, instead of nothing? Perhaps if we understood *that*, we'd know the why of it."

I slump a bit in my seat. "But how am I supposed to figure *that* out?"

He gestures behind him for James to come forward with the small brass telescope. I wonder how long he's been standing there.

"It just so happens," Mr. Oswald says, taking the telescope and holding it out to me, "that today you'll be meeting someone who just might know the answer."

Lizzy groans. "Is it too late to pick up trash in Central Park?"

We've been in the car for less than ten minutes when James pulls up in front of the Museum of Natural History and neatly backs up into a spot. "Everyone out," he says over his shoulder.

"But aren't we going to return the telescope to —" I glance down at the envelope on my lap. We hadn't even gotten a chance to open it yet. "To Amos Grady? The kid from Kentucky?"

James nods. "He's now Dr. Amos Grady, a prominent astronomer. You're going to bring the telescope to him at his office in the museum."

"Hey, I remember this place," Lizzy says, peering at the large banner hanging from the roof of the building. "We came here in sixth grade to see that show at the planetarium. I fell asleep, and you pinched me so hard I bruised! Remember, Jeremy?"

It all came flooding back to me. "You were snoring! I

still don't understand how anyone can fall asleep watching the birth of a star in a distant galaxy!"

"How could anyone *not*?" she counters. "I'm tired just looking at the museum from out here!"

Before I say something I might regret, I pick up the telescope, which we'd wrapped in bubble wrap, and get out of the car. James plunks eight quarters into the meter. Lizzy steps out and makes a big show of yawning.

"She's hopeless," I complain to James as we climb the stairs to the front entrance.

James shakes his head. "If everyone were interested in the same things, imagine how boring life would be. What if everyone wanted to be a chef? There'd be lots of people making meals, but no one growing the food, delivering it to the market, stocking it on the shelves. Right?"

"Still," I grumble. "It was a *new star*."

The museum is full of parents dragging kids by the hands or hurrying to catch up with them. One boy sits cross-legged on the floor, wailing that if he can't see the dinosaurs again he's not moving from that spot. James walks up to the security desk, and we hang back and look around.

A mom drags the screaming dinosaur kid past us. Balancing the heavy telescope in my arms, I say to Lizzy, "See? Now *that* kid is showing the right amount of enthusiasm."

She puts her hands over her ears. "If I were his mother, I'd leave him here."

"Mothers don't leave their kids somewhere just because they cry."

"Oh, really?" she asks, not looking at me. "Why *do* they leave them?"

I should have seen that one coming a mile off. I rarely think about Lizzy's mom, and Lizzy almost never mentions her. I feel like a jerk.

"Sorry," I mumble, reaching out my foot to tap the toe of her sneaker.

"Don't worry about it," she mumbles back.

James marches back over. "I used the security guard's phone to speak with Dr. Grady. He's expecting us in the astrophysics lab downstairs. Follow me." James consults a map in his hand and heads across the main level toward the archway that says ROSE CENTER above it.

My heart leaps, and I almost trip over my own feet in my hurry to follow him. We're going to a real science lab! In the greatest museum in the world!

"Whoa, there, nerd boy," Lizzy says, coming up from behind. She lifts the telescope out of my arms. "You're so giddy you almost dropped this."

I don't know which bothers me more, being called nerd boy, or giddy. "All great scientists were nerds," I tell her. "If Albert Einstein had played football, do you think he would have come up with the theory of relativity?"

"Am I supposed to know what that is?"

"I can't explain it to you now," I reply. "But it's very important!"

We pass under the archway and into a large open space with a tall winding stairway full of charts and graphs about the universe. The ceiling and the walls of the room are all made of glass. It's completely different from the rest of the museum.

"Hey, do you have this guy's envelope?" Lizzy asks as we follow James into the room.

I pat the pockets of my shorts until I find it. "I can't believe we almost forgot to read this." I slit open the top, narrowly avoiding a paper cut, and quickly unfold the piece of paper. I read the details out loud, taking care not to bump into anyone while I read.

```
Oswald's Pawn Emporium
Date: April 3, 1944
Name: Amos Grady
Age: 15
Location: Brooklyn
Item to Pawn: Telescope
Personal Statement of Seller: This telescope
used to belong to my grandfather. Looking in
it was his favorite thing to do in the world.
He left it to me in his will. I need the
money for my track team uniform. The cleats
are very expensive and my parents can't af-
ford it. I need to run track in order to get
the scholarship to MIT next year. My grand-
father would understand. I know he would. I
am almost certain.
```

The photo shows a boy with very curly hair grasping the telescope in his arms. I peer a little closer. I think those are tears in his eyes.

Under the photo it says:

Price: *$45.00 (Forty-Five Dollars)*
Signed by: *Oswald Oswald, Proprietor*

I fold the letter back up and stick it in the envelope. I don't want Lizzy to see that young Amos was crying.

"What does his picture look like?" Lizzy asks. "Is he cute?"

I stop where I am. James is already halfway across the exhibit, but I figure he won't go too far without us. "Why would you ask that?"

She shrugs. "Track runners are usually cute. Track and baseball have the cutest guys. Football and hockey, not so much. Everyone knows that."

"Keep in mind," I tell her, "this particular track runner would be in his seventies now."

Lizzy snorts. "I didn't say I wanted to date him." Then she says, "Don't move, and look down."

I freeze in place and slowly look down, unsure of what I'm expecting to find. All I see at first are numbers flashing up at me in red: 18 LBS. It turns out I'm standing on top of a scale, which is built right into the floor. Ah ha! So they *can* build scales into the ground. I knew it!

"Wow," Lizzy says. "I knew you were skinny, but I didn't think you were *that* skinny!" I look around for an explanation of the scale, but I don't see one.

A man with wild white hair, a white lab coat, and big round glasses approaches. He has a little skip to his step. He reminds me of a poster of Albert Einstein my old science teacher had hung on the wall. To my surprise, James is with him.

The old man points down at the scale and says, "That's what you would weigh if you stood on the moon. Less gravitational pull."

My eyes widen. "Cool!"

"Let me try," Lizzy says, thrusting the telescope into my arms and stepping on the scale herself. "Seventeen pounds!" she announces.

"If you stood on the sun," the old man says, "you'd weigh over a ton."

"Wow," Lizzy says, nodding. "No one would mess with me then!"

James clears his throat. "This is Dr. Grady," he announces. "Dr. Grady, this is Jeremy Fink and Lizzy Muldoun. The good doctor apparently couldn't wait for us to get to his lab."

Dr. Grady smiles sheepishly. "You'll have to forgive my impatience. We scientists are a curious bunch. A man gets a cryptic call saying two young people have something that belongs to him, and, well, he can't just sit in his office and wait."

"You guys know the drill," James tells Lizzy and me. "I'll be waiting in the dinosaur exhibit. Come meet me when you're done."

"See ya, James," Lizzy replies. I don't say anything. I'm too busy staring at Dr. Grady in his white lab coat. A real scientist! The things he must know about the world!

"Is that it?" Dr. Grady asks.

I must look puzzled, because he reaches over and taps the telescope in my arms.

"Oh!" I exclaim, reddening. "Yes, this is it." I pass the telescope to him, and he sits on a nearby bench to unwrap it. He stops after uncovering the top half. To my surprise and horror, he drops his head in his hands and begins to weep. Lizzy's eyes look like they're about to pop out of her head.

"What do we do?" she whispers in a low voice.

I shake my head, at a total loss. The only time I'd seen a grown man cry was my dad during an episode of *Antiques Roadshow*, when the copper pot some guy bought at a yard sale turned out to have belonged to Benjamin Franklin.

This is very different.

With one final heave of his shoulders, Dr. Grady wipes his eyes with the back of his hand. "I'm sorry, children," he says. "I've always been a crier. The kids at school used to tease me mercilessly."

I hold the envelope out to Dr. Grady, and he slowly reaches up for it. The occasional whimper sneaks out of him as he reads the letter.

I blame my inability to comfort him on Mom not letting me have a real pet.

Dr. Grady tucks the letter in his coat pocket and turns his attention back to the telescope. "I never dreamed I'd see this again," he says, eyeing it lovingly. "You must tell me how it came to be in your possession."

I open my mouth to answer when Lizzy says, "We'll tell you on one condition."

I glare at her. What does she think she's doing?

Dr. Grady looks amused. "And what would that be?"

"That you tell us the meaning of life," she says plainly. I shake my head at her.

"No, wait," she says. "I mean the *purpose* of life. That's what I mean, right?"

I shake my head again. Dr. Grady turns his head back and forth between us.

"Oh, right. Duh!" Lizzy says. "I mean, *why* are we here? *That's* what I want to know."

I sigh. "What she means to say is, *how* are we here? Why is there something instead of nothing? Mr. Oswald thought you might know."

His eyes widen. "Old Ozzy is still alive? Impossible! He was ancient when I was a boy!"

"No, no," I assure him. "Our Mr. Oswald is his grandson."

Dr. Grady pushes himself off the bench. "Well, that's a relief," he says. "For a second there I thought Old Ozzy fashioned himself a time machine."

My ears perk up. If anyone would know how to build a time machine, it would be Dr. Grady.

"Go on," Lizzy says, reading my mind as usual. "Ask him. You know you want to."

"Ask me what?" Dr. Grady says, carefully lifting the telescope. "Something more important than how we all got to this backwater edge of the Milky Way?"

I can't seem to make myself ask the question. All of a sudden, it just sounds silly.

"He wants to know how to build a time machine," Lizzy reveals. "He's been trying to do it for five years."

"Not trying, exactly," I hurry to explain. "Mostly reading about it. About going back in time, that is. Not to the future or anything like that. I don't think that's possible."

He smiles. "I'm sorry to say that time travel is still theoretical at this point. But you're right, all the known laws of physics indicate that travel to the future is likely impossible. Travel to the past though, well, I'm not writing that off. But since there would be no way to return to the future, there would be two of you in the past and none of you here in the present. Theoretically of course. Very messy. Quite impractical. Now why would a young man like yourself want to do such a thing?"

My throat tightens. Thankfully Lizzy doesn't try to answer for me.

"Why don't you two wait here," Dr. Grady says kindly. "I'll run this back to my office and then I'll show you around. We can chat some more."

I nod mutely, and we sit down on the bench. I stare up at the huge metal ball hanging from the ceiling, with the words THE SUN printed on it. A tiny ball hangs beside it. THE EARTH. How did I miss those before? One snip of a chain and they would crush us. The sign hanging next to them says, MORE THAN ONE MILLION OF OUR EARTHS WOULD FIT INSIDE THE SUN.

I feel very small.

Chapter 14: Life, the Universe, and Everything

"Are you okay?" Lizzy asks. "You look a little freaked out. More freaked out than usual, I mean. I hope you didn't mind me asking about the time machine. Did you understand all that mumbo-jumbo?"

I pull myself away from the models of the sun and earth and take a deep breath. "Basically, he told me that even if I found a way to go back in time to save my father, I couldn't really save him. I couldn't bring him back with me. And if I could never get back, then I'd be leaving my mom without both my dad *and* me."

"But, hey, there would be two Jeremy Finks in the past. That wouldn't be so bad, right?"

I shake my head. "One of me is plenty."

"But maybe the other Jeremy could do your math homework while you — the real Jeremy — hung out with me. Two Jeremys would mean there'd be one more person on earth who could stand to be around me."

"First off," I reply, "I like math. But thanks for trying to make me feel better. And I'm not the only person who likes you. Your dad, for one."

"He *has* to, I'm his daughter."

"Well, Samantha seems to like you."

Lizzy shrugs. "I heard her tell Rick she thinks I'm 'entertaining.'"

"Well, that doesn't sound so bad."

Lizzy makes a face. "*Dogs* are entertaining."

I shrug. "Not all of them."

Lizzy smiles. At that moment Dr. Grady appears. He has taken off his white lab coat, but still looks like Einstein. "Come on," Lizzy says, pulling me to my feet. "Let's go find out how we got to this — what did he call it? — backwater edge of the Milky Way."

"I have reconsidered your question, Mr. Fink," Dr. Grady says, clasping me on the shoulder. "There is, in fact, a way to see into the past whenever one wishes. I'm afraid it's not exactly what you're looking for, but it is as good a place as any to start finding the answer to your first question — how we came to be here, and may even answer *why*. Follow me and keep in mind, this is just the scientific explanation based on what we can observe and measure with our current equipment."

He leads us to the top of the winding ramp. Most people are going in the opposite direction, so we have to fight our way through. "You have heard of a light year I imagine?" he asks. I nod. Lizzy nods, too, but I think she would nod at anything if it meant not having to listen to an explanation. I don't think Dr. Grady is convinced either, since he explains, "If an object — a star, for instance, like our own sun — is eight hundred light years away from Earth, it would take light leaving that object twenty million years until it reached our eyes. So when you look at that object, you are seeing it as it appeared eight hundred light years ago, not as it looks today. It might not even exist anymore.

"Every time you look up at the stars," Dr. Grady continues, "you are looking into the past."

He points to a map of the night sky, and I recognize some of the constellations we learned about in school. He catches sight of Lizzy checking her teeth in one of the shiny display cases. "I'm not boring you, am I? We could just check out the gift shop if you'd prefer."

I try to give Lizzy a kick, but she moves away too quickly. She nearly topples right into a model of the solar system. "Please, go on, Dr. Grady," I urge.

"Okay, then. Roll up your sleeves, and I'll give you a quick lesson in the history of the universe. Ready?"

"Um, we're wearing short sleeves," Lizzy points out.

"It's an expression, my dear. Like, 'It's the journey, not the destination.' Shall I continue?"

"What journey do you mean?" Lizzy asks.

"Why, life, of course."

"Oh," Lizzy says. "Right."

Dr. Grady takes a few steps down the ramp and points to a quote engraved on the wall. He reads it out loud: "'The universe is queerer than we suppose, and queerer than we *can* suppose.' This brings us back to your original question — how did we come to be here in this strange, mostly unknowable place? For the answer to that, we have to start at the beginning. About thirteen-point-seven billion years ago, there was nothing that we can measure. No space. No time. Then suddenly, there was something. This something is called a singularity — a point so dense and hot that it contained all the matter that will ever fill the universe. No one knows where it came from. Maybe a supreme being placed it there for all we know, or it came from some whole other universe we know nothing about. But we *do* know what came next."

Before I can stop myself, my hand shoots up in the air. Lizzy laughs, and I quickly lower it. "The Big Bang?"

"Exactly!" Dr. Grady says, rubbing his hands together excitedly. "But don't think of it as a bang, or an explosion, it was actually a massive *expansion*, like blowing up an unimaginably tiny balloon to an unimaginably huge balloon that is still expanding."

Dr. Grady pauses, running his hands through his hair. It doesn't do much good because it bounces right back up anyway. Lizzy begins to hum softly to herself. I elbow her in the ribs. She shoots me a dirty look, but stops humming. Dr. Grady doesn't seem to notice.

"All the matter and energy in the universe," he explains excitedly, "including us, are inside this balloon. The planets, the stars, you and I, we all came from the very same stuff, at the very same point in time, thirteen-point-seven billion years ago. The universe unfolded at many times the speed of light, spewing forth subatomic particles, and creating things like gravity and electromagnetism. Stars formed from gasses and dust clouds, and the debris and ice spun off to create the planets. With me so far?"

I nod, my brain spinning. So I wasn't really born twelve (almost thirteen) years ago? I was really born 13.7 billion years ago? Mom owes me a lot of birthday presents!

"Let's bring it closer to home now," Dr. Grady says

happily. It's great watching someone who loves what he does. Dad was like that, at the comics store. Mom loves the library, and Lizzy's dad loves the post office. I wonder if I'll ever find something I love as much. I tune back in to hear Dr. Grady say, "Our own solar system was formed 4.5 billion years ago. It took about another billion years until the surface of the earth cooled. Pretty much as soon as life could begin, it did. Out of the primordial soup — some basic chemicals and gasses mixed with UV radiation and lightning — arose the building blocks of life: amino acids. These were followed by bacteria, then single-celled organisms, multicelled organisms, plants, invertebrates, vertebrates, reptiles, and mammals, all adapting to their ever-changing environment over billions of years."

A group of teenagers dressed in white lab coats approaches, trailing after an older woman who looks like the female version of Dr. Grady. The kids each carry a clipboard. Lizzy nudges me and whispers, "That's you in five years!"

"Very funny," I whisper back. But I stare at their faces as they file by. Their eyes look eager and bright. It wouldn't be so bad to look like that.

Dr. Grady waits for the group to pass and continues. "It may be not very appealing to think that we came from the same sludge that produced the amoeba, but we all have a common ancestor; our DNA shares the same chemical structure. You, I, and the fruit fly all have the same blueprint for life. All life on this planet is connected — some people can feel it more than others, on a spiritual level. If there is life on other planets, it will likely have evolved very differently from us. The chance of duplicating what happened here is close to zero."

"How come?" I can't help asking.

"Trust me," Dr. Grady says. "We are here because over billions of years, countless variables fell into place, any of which could have taken another path. We are essentially a beautiful fluke, as are the millions of other species with which we share this planet. Our cells are composed of atoms and dust particles from distant galaxies, and from the billions of living organisms that inhabited this planet before us."

He pauses here and wipes a little tear from his eye. To be polite, Lizzy and I look away.

"So now you know the scientific explanation of *how* we got here," Dr. Grady says, clearing his throat. "As you can see, it also answers the question of *why* we are here. Physics tells us we're here because gravity keeps us from floating away into space. In the most basic biological terms, we're here because some of the earliest inhabitants of this planet — bacteria — allow us to be. Our bodies would not be able to function without the jobs they perform for us — in the air around us, on our skin, and inside our organs. We think we're the most powerful species on the planet, but we're far from it. We would not live for one day without them, but bacteria are so adaptable, they will be here when the sun burns out. Bacteria and cockroaches!"

I look at Lizzy, who has started squirming. I have no doubt she's thinking about the bacteria living on her body. Somehow I thought the answer to why we're here would be a little more, I don't know, glamorous?

Lizzy begins scratching. Long red welts appear on her arms.

"I fear I have rambled too long," Dr. Grady says, consulting his watch. "I hope I didn't overwhelm you."

"No, it was great," I tell him honestly. I have a million questions to ask, but I'm pretty sure Lizzy will kill me if I do. "Oh," I say, suddenly remembering the bargain Lizzy made, "your telescope came from —"

He puts up his hand to cut me off. "I changed my mind. Let it be a mystery as to why it has returned to me after fifty years. I've spent my life trying to find rational explanations for life's mysteries."

"Okay," I say with a smile. Lowering my voice, I ask, "Maybe someday I could . . . come back?"

"Of course," he says, slapping me on the back and grinning. "And you won't even have to bring me anything."

We shake hands, and I turn to Lizzy. "Are you ready to go?"

She nods frantically.

"Are you all right, Lizzy?" Dr. Grady asks, his brow crinkling in concern.

Lizzy nods again. "I'll be okay as soon as I can get into a *really* hot shower."

He laughs. "Remember, bacteria are friendly, for the most part. You don't want to wash, or scratch, them all away."

Lizzy hastily sticks her hands in her shorts pockets to keep from scratching anymore. I know she's not convinced. We head for the archway that will lead us back to the dinosaur exhibit and James.

"Never forget," Dr. Amos says as we enter the exhibit, "as immense as the universe is, and as much as we will never know about it, there is only one Jeremy Fink, one Lizzy Muldoun. One Amos Grady. That makes each of us special and unique beyond comprehension. Why are we here? In my opinion, we're here because we won the evolutionary lottery. We're here because as far as we know, this is the only place we *can* be."

"So basically what you're saying is," Lizzy says, scratching her thighs from inside her pockets. "We're here because we're here?"

"Precisely!" Dr. Grady says.

Lizzy pinches me on the arm. "Does that work for you, Jeremy? Or is your existential crisis gonna continue?"

My brain is still spinning from all Dr. Grady has said. But spinning in a good way. "You know it takes me a long time to sort through things," I reply. "I can't make decisions at the drop of a hat like you can."

"How true. Once," Lizzy begins, scratching her belly now as we walk, "when we were six, Jeremy's parents took us for ice cream. It took him so long to decide between chocolate and vanilla, that eventually the guy had to close the shop and he didn't get anything."

I sigh. I liked it much better when Lizzy was consumed with tearing away layers of her skin. Dr. Grady chuckles and says, "Coming to terms with why we are here and the meaning of it all can be a lifelong quest. Someday when you two are old and married, you'll look back at —"

"AAAAH!!" we scream in unison.

"We're not getting *married*!" I exclaim.

"At least not to each other!" Lizzy adds.

At that moment, the life-size dinosaur skeleton looms into view. No doubt anxious to change the subject, Dr. Grady says, "If a meteor hadn't struck the earth and made that guy extinct, mammals wouldn't have grown any bigger than a large rat or a small pig. You and I wouldn't be here. So it worked out well for us." He looks up at the dinosaur fondly. "Not so well for him, though. There's your friend," Dr. Grady says, pointing to James. James is standing behind one of the dinosaur's huge front legs. He's leaning over the railing and peering so close that his nose is almost touching it.

"It's not real," Dr. Grady says when we approach.

"No?" James says, clearly disappointed.

Dr. Grady shakes his head. "But the other leg is."

James immediately rushes over to that leg and peers closely again. I follow him. "I didn't take you for a dinosaur guy."

James nods. "My father used to collect fossils and bones. He once found a mollusk that was over a million years old."

"Wow!" I say, truly impressed. "My dad's greatest find was a scratch-off lottery ticket worth twenty-five bucks stuck inside a book he found on the street!"

"Hey," James says, cocking his head. "What's wrong with Lizzy?"

I turn to see Lizzy in the corner of the exhibit, scratching her head crazily. She has pulled her ponytail out, and her hair is now sticking up in every direction. "Oh. That's because Dr. Grady told us that bacteria basically cover us from head to toe, inside and out."

"We'd better take her home," James says.

I look for Dr. Grady to say good-bye, and find him engrossed in a conversation with a father and his two young boys. He waves and salutes as we leave.

In the car on the way home, Lizzy curls up on the seat, occasionally twitching, and I realize that I feel much better. The dark cloud that was pressing down on me isn't there anymore. Mr. Oswald was right. Knowing how we got here helps. Even though it is totally overwhelming how huge the universe is, and what a small part of it we are, it's comforting somehow to understand where we fit in. And it's exciting to think of how many more H.O.J.s I can fill learning more about it. I'm tempted to torture Lizzy by making her do a recap with me of everything we learned today, but I decide to spare her.

No matter how much I've learned this week about life, the universe, and everything, I'm not sure I'm any closer to knowing what's in Dad's box. I reach into the minifridge and pull out a soda. I'm about to pop the top when an idea hits me — something I should have thought of the day Mom handed me the box. It's so obvious!

I lean forward and shake Lizzy on the leg. She moans. I take that as a sign that she's listening.

"How'd you like to go to Atlantic City?"

She opens one eye. "Are there bacteria in Atlantic City?"

"Nope," I lie.

"Okay," she says, and closes her eye again. A second later she opens it. "How are we gonna get to Atlantic City?"

"I'll think of something," I reply. I wait for her to ask me *why* we're going to Atlantic City, but she doesn't.

By the time Mom gets home from work, I still haven't thought of a plan. I had spent most of the afternoon watching Ferret chase Cat around the fish tank. Dog and Hamster just swam by leisurely, looking amused. Needless to say, they didn't give me any ideas. Many times I considered knocking on Lizzy's door and asking for help, but she was taking the longest shower on record. And, she's always the one who comes up with the plans. I should be able to do *one* on my own.

Mom knocks on my door and then pushes it open. She's wearing a button that says READING IS FOR WINNERS. "How was your day?" she asks, taking a sip of iced tea.

"It was really good," I tell her. "We went to the Museum of Natural History!"

"That's some rough community service you guys are forced to endure."

I grin. "It's not all fun and games. Today in the limo they were out of Coke. I had to have Pepsi."

"But you like Pepsi better anyway."

"True, but I didn't have a *choice*."

She shakes her head at me. "Before I forget, Aunt Judi has an art exhibit in Atlantic City on Sunday. Do you and Lizzy want to come?"

I hear her say the words, but I can't absorb them. I am *never* this lucky.

"Did you say Atlantic City?" I ask, holding my breath.

"I did. The show is at one of the casinos on the board-walk. They're trying to improve their image by supporting local artists."

Still not willing to believe it, I say, "Did you say the boardwalk?"

She walks over to me, lifts up a lock of my hair, and peers into my ear. "Are you developing a hearing problem?"

I shake my head, and my hair falls back into place.

"Are you interested or not?"

I nod enthusiastically.

"So this is what it's going to be like living with a teenager," she says with a sigh. Then she tousles my hair like I'm five, and closes my door.

Chapter 15: The Boardwalk

Lizzy has pushed aside her coffee table and is practicing her hula-hooping routine.

I toss her a banana from the bowl on the table. She catches it easily. "I still can't believe you pulled it off," Lizzy says, beginning to peel the banana. Her accompanying music is playing on the CD player. It had taken her hours to pick out the perfect hula-hoop song: *"You spin me right round baby right round. Like a record baby right round, round, round."*

"Honestly, I can't take the credit," I reply. "We owe it to Aunt Judi and her art show."

Lizzy shakes her head. "Somehow you made it happen. I don't know how, but you did."

As much as I'd like to believe I could perform feats of real magic, I gave that up a few years ago when I stared at a spoon for two hours, trying to make it bend. All that happened was that I got a monster headache and felt really stupid.

Lizzy tosses her banana peel over her shoulder, and accidentally brushes her arm against the hoop. It instantly falls. "Ugh," she says, picking the hoop back up and placing it around her waist again. "I'm never going to be ready. And we're not any closer to opening that box. But maybe we will be after tomorrow."

"How?"

Lizzy picks up the hoop and places it around her waist. "We'll just ask the fortune-teller when we find her."

"*If* we find her," I reply, realizing Lizzy has known all along why I want to go. The whole thing really is a long shot. After all, the fortune-teller was already ancient when Dad met her. She'd be thirty years older now. I toss Lizzy the football, and it slides right out of her hands. We're going to have to step up the practices if we want those Snickers bars.

The next morning Mom wakes me up at the crack of dawn. "Aunt Judi will be here any minute," she says, raising the blinds. I groan and put the alligator over my eyes. Who knew the sun was even *up* this early?

She lifts the alligator off and places him on my desk, next to Dad's box. Then she pulls a pair of shorts and a T-shirt out of my dresser drawer and tosses them on the bed.

"I've been dressing myself for some time now, Mom," I tell her, forcing myself to sit up.

"Sorry," she says, not sounding very sorry if you ask me. "We're in a hurry." She leans over and pounds on the wall with her fist. Then she lifts up the solar system poster. "Get up, Lizzy!" she yells through the hole.

I stare at her in shock, fully awake now. "You *know* about that?"

She laughs. "I'm a mother. Mothers know everything."

"They do?" This is news to me.

"Of course," she says, holding up my T-shirt and shorts in an attempt to hurry me along. "Like I know that when we get to Atlantic City, you and Lizzy are going to come up with some excuse to leave the exhibit so you can look for the fortune-teller your dad met on his thirteenth birthday."

My jaw falls open. She leans over and pushes up on my chin.

"Do you have ESP or something?" I ask when I am finally capable of speech.

She smiles cryptically and doesn't answer. Then she pounds on the wall again and pulls aside the poster.

Lizzy's muffled voice comes through. "I'm up! I'm up! Geez!"

Twenty minutes later, Lizzy and I are crammed in the backseat of Aunt Judi's station wagon. We are sharing the seat with ten sculptures wrapped in foam. The car smells like a combination of stale coffee and feet.

"I miss James," Lizzy whispers. I nod in agreement. The car isn't even my aunt's. It's shared among all the artists working in her building. It is so old it honestly has an eight-track cassette player. We're talking *1960s* old. It will be a miracle if we make it to New Jersey without the engine overheating or all four tires spinning off in opposite directions. I am somewhat surprised that Mom would risk our lives in this thing. She doesn't seem too worried though. She has her arm out the window and her hair is flying all around. Unlike me, she likes venturing out of the city. I'm always afraid water from the Hudson River is going to flood the tunnel. I really should spend an H.O.J. finding out how the tunnels were built.

"Do you want me to put on some music?" Aunt Judi calls back to us.

I shudder at the thought. Anything that is on eight-track is probably not something I want to hear. Still, if there's no music, we'll have to listen to Mom and Aunt Judi discuss "the role of the artist in today's society." I lean forward and ask, "What are our choices?"

Aunt Judi shuffles through the cassettes on her lap. "Bread, KC and the Sunshine Band, or the Jackson 5."

Lizzy and I exchange quizzical looks. "Just to clarify," I say, "those are musical groups?"

She and my mother laugh. "Of course they are," Aunt Judi says.

"Surprise us," Lizzy says, rolling her eyes.

A few seconds later the sounds of disco cackle through the old speakers. *I want to put on my my my my my boogie shoes.* I settle far back in the seat for what will no doubt be a very long drive.

"What do you mean they can't come in?"

Lizzy and I shrink back to the wall. When my mom raises her voice, which is rare, people cower. The casino security guard isn't cowering though. He is folding his meaty arms across his wide chest.

"No one under eighteen gets on the casino floor," he booms.

"They aren't going to *gamble*," she insists. "My sister is in an art exhibit. We only need to walk through the casino to get there!"

He shakes his head and glances around. "I don't see no art."

"She went in through the loading zone," my mother

says, clearly getting exasperated. "We are supposed to meet her now."

He shakes his head again. It occurs to me that if Mom already knows we're going to make some excuse to leave, it might as well be now. I reach over and pull on the sleeve of her blouse. "Um, Lizzy and I can walk around the boardwalk and sit on the beach. We'll meet you back here in a few hours?"

She sighs and gives us both long looks. "All right," she finally says. "But be careful. Stay together. You have your sandwiches?"

I pat my backpack and nod.

"Meet back here for lunch at noon, okay?"

"Don't worry, Mrs. Fink," Lizzy says, throwing her arm across my shoulders. She has to stand on her tiptoes. "I'll keep him out of trouble."

"And who will keep *you* out of trouble?" she asks wearily.

"Who, me?" Lizzy asks. "My troublemaking days are all in the past."

While my mom searches for a response, Lizzy and I hurry to the exit doors and burst out onto the boardwalk. Since it's barely 9:00, hardly anyone is around. We pass casino after casino, and a lot of hot dog and T-shirt stands. Most of them are still closed. "Where is everyone?" Lizzy asks.

"Sleeping," I reply.

"Or at church."

I shrug. "I guess."

"Maybe we should go."

I stop walking. "To church?"

Lizzy points to an old wooden building right on the edge of the beach. THE ATLANTIC CITY SPIRITUALIST CHURCH. ALL ARE WELCOME. SERVICES BEGIN AT 9:30.

"We're right on time," she says, pulling me toward the building. From the looks of it, the church was probably once a T-shirt shop!

I pull back. "Are you serious? I can't go in there!"

"Why not?"

"For one thing, I'm part Jewish. We don't do churches."

"*All are welcome*," Lizzy says, tapping the sign with her finger. "That means you, too."

"Why do you want to go so badly?" I ask, suspicious. "Something to atone for?"

"Very funny. I just want to try it. Learning all that stuff about the universe has made me curious, that's all. What's the worst that could possibly happen?"

"I don't know. They could chase us out with pitch-forks and torches."

Behind us a woman says, "We got rid of the pitchforks years ago, didn't we, Henry?"

"We sure did," a man's voice replies. "Except for that one time. But that guy really deserved it."

Cringing, I slowly turn around. An elderly couple is standing a few feet away, holding hands and grinning.

"Sorry about my friend," Lizzy says, approaching them. "He doesn't get out much."

"No worries," the woman says. "We didn't mean to

make fun. We're a wacky bunch. If you'd like to give the service a try, please don't feel shy. You can sit in the back so you won't feel awkward about leaving in the middle."

"What do you say?" Lizzy asks.

Her expression is so hopeful, how can I say no? "All right." I thrust my hands into my short's pockets. "But you have to promise to leave if I ask you to."

"I promise," Lizzy says, pulling me toward the open door. As soon as I step through the threshold I relax a little. It really doesn't seem too threatening. Long windows in the back face the wide beach with the ocean behind it. About twenty rows of folding chairs are set up in front of a small stage. Maybe fifteen people are already sitting down. I don't see any crosses, or anything really religious at all. Then out of nowhere, a woman in a flowing white dress places a bible in my hand. I look up in surprise, but she's already moved on to the next person.

"How come she didn't give you one?" I ask Lizzy when I see she's empty-handed.

"She said we're supposed to share," she says, pointing to two seats in the back row. "Come on, let's go sit down."

I follow, in a bit of a daze. "When did she say that?"

Lizzy rolls her eyes. "Right before she handed it to you."

I shake my head and sit in one of the hard plastic chairs. The seats are starting to fill up with people from all walks of life. Some in dresses and suits, one guy in tattered pants without any shoes, a surfer complete with surfboard, and a few Goth teenagers. Everyone says hello to each other like they're old friends. A few smile at us, and we smile back like we do this all the time. I open the Bible, and am surprised to find it isn't a bible at all. It's a song-book!

I turn to Lizzy. "What kind of church *is* this?"

She shrugs. "Beats me."

I slide down in my chair. A few minutes later, the minister, or whoever he is, instructs us all to stand and to open to page three in the book. I expect to find a religious hymnal, but instead page three is the lyrics for "The Wind Beneath My Wings." I do a double-take, and then tilt the page so Lizzy can see it. Mom is a big Bette Midler fan, and I've had to sit through the movie *Beaches* more times than any boy should ever be subjected to.

Lizzy giggles and whispers, "Did I ever tell you you're my hero?"

I reply with the next line, "You're everything, everything, I wish I could be."

"Really?" she says, looking up from the page.

I mouth *No* and shake my head.

As the whole congregation sings about flying higher than an eagle, I actually feel moved. Hearing the song sung by this big group in this church on a beach is really uplifting. No one would guess that thirty feet away, people are playing blackjack and slots while extra oxygen is being pumped through the vents to keep the gamblers from getting tired.

Maybe this is why people go to church. For a sense of belonging, of escaping the everyday routine where people don't generally burst into group song. I've only been here ten minutes, and I feel it already. I also feel Lizzy tugging at my shirt. It takes only a second to realize I'm the only one still standing. I hurriedly sit down.

The minister begins talking. He welcomes all the old faces and the new ones. Then he says, "Mankind is the eye through which the spirit of God views his or her creation. Let us today, on this beautiful Sunday morning, be vessels through which we can see the infinite. For there rests our true natures. We are spiritual beings having an earthly life. When our life here is done, we return to the source. What is life? Life is love. Do not make the mistake of thinking loving is easy; it is not. We must love ourselves, not just other people. We must be awake. Do not sleepwalk through your life. Enjoy it fully, because none of us gets out of here alive."

People laugh a bit at the last part. Lizzy leans over and whispers, "Wow, that was deep."

I nod. I'm thinking about what he said about returning to the source. Is that where my father is now? In the source? Just as I'd never really thought about the meaning of life before all this, I'd never really thought about what happens to you after you die. Even when Lizzy made me do that séance last week, I didn't really think about it. Do we really get reincarnated like Rick said? Are Heaven and Hell real, and not just something they scare you with in Sunday school? Or is the end just the end, like a blank screen, over and out, thanks for the ride? I bet the meaning of death is tied to the meaning of life. This is something I really should have considered sooner.

The minister guy is still talking. "Now is the time for healing. Anyone who would like to participate, please take a seat in the row of chairs on your left. Our healers tap into the life force of the universe. They can help anyone who is in physical, mental, or emotional distress. They are waiting to help you." He points to a group of about ten chairs set apart from the others. Each chair has a man or a woman standing behind it. People are starting to get up from the audience to make their way over to them.

I watch as the chairs fill up one by one. I turn to Lizzy to see what she thinks of all this, but to my utter disbelief, she's not in her seat! Did the healing stuff push her over the edge, and she left without telling me? I look around wildly, and finally spot her in the last place I had thought to look — in one of the chairs in front of a healer-woman. My mouth falls open. The healer looks around sixty, with gray and brown hair hanging all the way to her waist. She has her hands on Lizzy's shoulders and is whispering something in her ear. Lizzy's eyes are closed, her hands folded in her lap. I blink twice to make sure I'm not seeing things.

In a minute, the woman moves her hands from Lizzy's shoulders to the top of her head, and then back to her shoulders. Up and down the row, the healers are doing the same things. Some have their eyes closed, too. A line of people are waiting for their turn. One by one, someone gets up from a chair, thanks the healer, and another person takes the seat. I am dying to know what Lizzy is feeling up there. Not to mention why she went in the first place! Trying not to make any noise, I carefully unwrap the corner of one of my peanut butter sandwiches and nibble on it while I watch, fascinated.

Finally it's Lizzy's turn to open her eyes and thank her

healer. She quickly makes her way back through the rows of seats until she reaches me. "Come on," she says, grabbing my arm and causing me to drop my sandwich. Luckily it is still mostly wrapped. I bend down to pick it up from the floor.

"Come on! Let's go!" Lizzy says, a sense of urgency evident in her voice.

"Huh? Why? What was that all about up there?"

"Just let's go," she says. Then without waiting for me anymore, she heads out the front door. I quickly shove the sandwich back into my bag and slip out after her, leaving the songbook on my seat. I feel a little rude leaving in the middle of the service, but maybe not too many people noticed.

Lizzy is pacing back and forth outside. I can't read her expression. She doesn't look upset or angry or calm or contemplative, or anything, really.

"Lizzy?"

She stops pacing.

"Why did you want to leave? Why did you go up there?"

She doesn't answer.

"Is everything okay?" I ask, starting to feel concerned. "Why did you need healing? What did it feel like?"

"I'm fine," she says. "Don't worry. I just really don't want to talk about it, okay?"

"But —"

She shakes her head.

We walk in silence in the same direction we had been heading earlier. Every few feet I sneak a glance at Lizzy, but she's looking straight ahead. The stores are mostly open now, and the boardwalk has a lot more people on it. A group of businesspeople with badges around their necks hurries past us. There are a few families and some couples holding hands. We approach a woman sitting behind a table, but it turns out she's offering temporary tattoos for five dollars, not fortunes.

"Wanna get one?" Lizzy asks, breaking her silence.

"It's just one surprise after another with you today."

"I'm gonna do it."

"Why?"

"Why not? It washes off in a week."

I guess I can't argue with that. We walk over to the board that shows all the different designs. "How about this one?" she says, pointing to a set of Chinese symbols. Underneath it is the English translation. I lean closer to read it. LIFE.

"Don't you think that's appropriate?" she asks. "You know, since we're on this whole meaning-of-life quest."

"Where would you put it?"

"On my upper arm, I guess."

"Like a sailor?"

"Trust me," she says, rolling her short sleeve up onto her shoulder. "It's not gonna say 'MOM' in a big heart."

"Y'all ready?" the tattoo woman asks, cracking her gum. I don't think the tattoos that cover her own arms are temporary.

"It's just her," I say quickly, backing away and pointing at Lizzy.

"Which one'd ya choose?" she asks.

Lizzy points to the one she wants.

"Ah, life," the lady says in her Texas drawl. "That's a fine choice." She directs Lizzy to sit down on the stool. She then wipes Lizzy's arm with a tissue. "To get off any sweat," she explains. "We want a nice clean surface." She takes out a very thin brush, and a bottle of henna. Glancing over at the design every few seconds, she begins painting it on in tiny strokes.

I clear my throat. "You wouldn't happen to, uh, know of any fortune-tellers around here?"

"What kinda fortune-teller?" she asks. "We got the kind who can tell your fortune with cards, and one who can hold an object of yours and tell ya who you're gonna marry. And we got some regular palm readers, too."

"Palm readers," I say.

"Jeremy!" shouts Lizzy, "Don't bother the woman while she's putting on my tattoo!"

The woman laughs. "Don't worry, honey. I been doing this so many years I could tap dance and fry an egg and still not mess up. So what kinda palm reader y'all lookin' for?"

I realize I don't know much about her at all. "Well, she'd be old. Very, very old." The woman laughs again, and this time her brush actually slips a little. She quickly wets the corner of a paper towel and fixes it. Lizzy glares at me.

"Old compared to me?" she asks. "Or old compared to you? Kids your age think everyone over forty is old!"

"Old compared to anybody," I say. "And she has an accent. Like, Russian or something."

The woman finishes Lizzy's tattoo and stands back to give it a final look. "Russian, you say? Big hair? Big —" She pauses and then says, "Teeth. Big teeth. Sound like her?"

"I don't know," I reply honestly. "My dad never mentioned her teeth."

She chuckles. "Check out the little shop right past the Tropicana, a few casinos down the way. I think they speak something funny like Russian in there."

I start to say thank you for the information, but at the same time Lizzy says, "Hey, you must know a lot about life, you know, from working here?"

I feel my face reddening, but I don't stop Lizzy from asking what I know she's about to ask.

"I've seen it all, honey. Why you askin'?"

"We're on a quest to find out the meaning of life," Lizzy explains. "We kind of have a deadline."

The woman makes one final flourish with the tiny paintbrush on Lizzy's arm, then stands back to admire her work. With a satisfied nod, she says, "Five bucks, please."

Lizzy stands up from the stool and twists her shoulder so she can see the tattoo. "Cool." She digs into her pocket and hands over a rumpled five-dollar bill.

"The meaning of life," the woman says, tucking the bill down the front of her shirt. "That's an easy one. God's love gives life meaning. I just follow the path He sets out in the Good Book. That's all I need to know. You follow His guidelines, it's almost like a map through life to Heaven. You don't ever gotta worry if you're making the right choices or not, 'cause it's all right there for you."

She looks like she's about to say more, but a family of six with big cameras around their necks have swarmed the table.

"But how do you know you're following the right religion?" Lizzy asks. "The right path?"

The woman raises her eyebrows like no one's ever asked her that before. Then she smiles. "I don't know it in my head, honey. I feel it in my heart."

"But —" Lizzy is cut off by a crowd of noisy college kids who have swarmed the tattoo display and are daring each other to get the ugliest ones.

"Uh, thanks for everything," I tell the woman loudly, grabbing onto Lizzy's arm before she can pry any more.

The woman looks up from her new customers and nods at us. "My pleasure, honey. Hope y'all get good fortunes."

As we walk away, Lizzy says, "I just don't understand how there can be so many different religions with everyone thinking theirs is the right one."

"I don't know. I guess that's why there are so many wars."

Lizzy doesn't answer. Her head is twisted around and she's busy admiring her tattoo. I have to steer her away from bumping into people.

"Does it bother you that no one will be able to read that?" I ask. "Unless they're Chinese, that is."

She shakes her head. "I know what it means; that's enough. I can't wait to watch my dad freak out until I tell him it's only temporary."

We walk past the Tropicana, and just like the lady had said, we're right in front of a shop that says PALM READINGS, FIVE DOLLARS.

Neither of us makes a move to go in. "I guess everything on the boardwalk is five dollars," Lizzy jokes.

I still don't move. "What if she's not there? Or worse

yet, what if she is? What am I going to say? That if she hadn't given my dad that fortune, he might have been more careful?"

"Do you really believe that?"

I shrug. "Maybe a little."

"I thought you were going to ask her where the keys are."

"Yeah, that, too."

"We don't have to go in if you don't want to."

I take a deep breath and push open the door before I can change my mind. "I'll never know if I don't try." We step into a room covered in pink-and-orange silk tapestries. Incense burns on a table in the middle of the room. Crystal balls of all sizes line the shelves. A beaded curtain separates the main room from another behind it.

"Okay, this place is freaky," Lizzy says. "Let's make this short and sweet."

I step up to the beaded curtain. "Um, hello? Anyone?"

I hear a rustling sound in the back. A hand with long bright-pink fingernails pushes through the curtain. I jump back and almost knock a crystal ball right out of Lizzy's hand. The woman attached to the hand isn't more than thirty years old. She doesn't look like she has very big teeth, either.

"Zat is not a toy," the woman says, taking it from Lizzy and returning it to the shelf. "Now, vould you like a reading?" She looks expectantly at us.

We shake our heads. "We must have come to the wrong place," I tell her, turning toward the door.

"Nonsense!" she exclaims. "No von comes into Madame Zaleski's House of Palm by mistake. Greater forces, zhey have brought you here."

Her name, Madame Zaleski, rings a bell. Dad must have said her name once.

"Are *you* Madame Zaleski?" I ask.

She gives a little curtsy. "At your service. Now, who is zhe first to go?"

"But you can't be her," Lizzy says, peering closely at the woman. "You'd have to be at least ninety years old!"

The woman narrows her eyes. "You zink I look ninety yeers old?"

"No, no, of course not," I say, glaring at Lizzy. "Is there another Madame Zaleski who used to work on the boardwalk? Like, thirty years ago?"

The woman's face softens. "Ah, Grandmama. She taught me everyzing I know. Shame vat zhey did to her."

Lizzy and I exchange a look. "Um, what did they do to her?" I ask.

"Zhey kicked her off zhe boardwalk, zat's vat zhey did! After twenty years!"

"Why?" Lizzy asks.

The woman brushes off the question with a flip of her hand. "Over a piffle! A nothing! Zhey said she vas scaring people. Zat she told zhem all zhe same thing."

A chill begins to crawl up my spine. I force myself to ask, "What did she tell them?"

She waves her hand again. "Zhey claim she told all zhe men zhey vould die ven zhey vere forty years old."

The chill now extends down my legs and out my arms.

Lizzy grabs onto my arm. Tight. So tight that she's cutting off my circulation. I choose my words carefully. "So what you're saying is that your grandmother was a fraud? Not everyone she told that to actually died when they were forty, or, say, thirty-nine?"

"Of course they didn't!" she says. "Grandmama wasn't a fraud, exactly. She just liked to mix things up a little. It gets boring saying the same old things. 'You'll meet the man of your dreams on a train!' 'You will have two children, a boy and a girl.' 'You'll travel a lot.' Read the small print." She pulls two business cards out of the pocket of her long skirt and hands one to each of us. The card says FOR ENTERTAINMENT PURPOSES ONLY.

"Hey!" Lizzy yells, looking up from the card. "What happened to your accent?"

The woman shrugs. "You want a reading or not? I gotta nail appointment in a few minutes."

"You know, I think we'll skip it this time," Lizzy says. "Come on, Jeremy. Let's get out of here."

I honestly don't think my feet will move. I'm tempted to scream. My eyes begin to sting from holding back the tears I refuse to shed in front of the woman. I look her right in the eye and say, "Since he was thirteen, my father thought he was going to die when he was forty. He lived his whole life that way. He died a few months before his fortieth birthday." Lizzy puts her hand back on my arm, but I shake it off. "Your grandmother cursed him!"

The woman flinches. Then she says, "I am very sorry for your terrible loss. But Grandmama did not curse him. If anything, she blessed him."

"How do you figure that?" Lizzy growls.

"We all live as if we are going to live forever. When you know you won't, life looks different."

"Yeah, shorter!" Lizzy says. "Jeremy, can we go now?"

"Just one more thing," I say. "Where are the keys to the box my father left me?"

"Jeremy!" Lizzy says. "How can you believe anything she says now?"

I don't reply. The woman closes her eyes. In that second, Lizzy grabs a stick of incense from the pile and shoves it in her pocket. It doesn't even bother me.

Madame Zaleski's eyes pop open. In a trancelike voice she says, "You have already been very near to zhe keys vich you seek. You vil find zhem, but it vil take much vork." She shakes her head like she's clearing it. Holding out her hand, she says, "Five dollars, please."

"You have *got* to be kidding!" Lizzy says. "You're lucky we don't sue you! Come on, Jeremy."

I let Lizzy lead me out the door. The woman doesn't try to stop us. We walk across the boardwalk, down a few wooden stairs, and onto the beach. All the while Lizzy is muttering "Some nerve!" and "That stupid accent was back at the end!" and "We should *still* sue her!"

About halfway to the water, I plop down on the sand. It feels warm under my hands. Lizzy sits down next to me. "Are you all right? You haven't said anything."

The sand starts to swim in front of my eyes and I quickly wipe away the tears. "It was just an accident," I say softly.

"What was?"

214

"My dad's death. It wasn't his destiny to die young. It was just an accident."

Lizzy doesn't reply. I watch as she scoops up a handful of sand and lets it run through her fingers. "Does that make it easier, or harder?"

"I don't know. Different, I guess. It makes me want to know what's in the box even more. I hope whatever it is, at least part of it is a letter. I want to know what he was thinking when he made it for me."

"You already know. Even if we never find the keys. You already know what he was thinking."

"I do?"

She nods.

"You know what I don't know?" I ask.

She shakes her head.

"I don't know why you went up to be healed."

"Neither do I," she replies.

"Really?"

She nods. "Do you always know why you do something?"

"Yes."

"Well, I don't."

"So what was it like?"

"It was . . . different. I felt . . . quiet. Like for a minute, my brain was quiet."

We don't say anything for a minute. I watch two kids building a sand castle down by the water. A few seconds later the tide washes half of it away. But they don't seem to mind. They just start right back up again.

"What do you think about what the fortune-teller

said?" I ask. "That we've already been very near the keys? What does that mean? Our apartments? The flea market? The store? If they really were in Harold's office, we for sure can't go back there."

"We can't believe anything that comes out of her mouth. She just wanted her five dollars. Now come on," Lizzy says, standing up and brushing the sand off her legs. "Let's see if we can sneak into a casino and win a few bucks!"

"Didn't you tell my mother that you left your trouble-making days behind you?"

"Hey, in Europe you can gamble when you're younger. I saw it on TV."

"We're in New Jersey, remember?"

She shrugs. "So we'll talk with a foreign accent."

"Anything other than Russian!"

"I don't think that even *was* Russian," Lizzy says. "Come on. I'll race you."

Before I can respond, she takes off toward the board-walk. I can't believe she managed to make me feel better. I watch her run, her ponytail bobbing behind her. I know with my freakishly long legs I could easily overtake her, even with her head start. But I don't. Because that's what best friends do for each other.

Chapter 16: Flotsam and Jetsam

Needless to say, we didn't get into any of the casinos. Lizzy tried basically the only thing she remembered from French class last year. "*Bonjour. Je ne comprend pas anglais*," she told the security guard at Bally's, but he just laughed at her. After slices of pizza for lunch, Mom took us into Aunt Judi's exhibit by sneaking us through the loading dock. If I thought my aunt's artwork was weird, her sculptures were practically normal compared to some of the others on display.

The ride home was much more comfortable, since Aunt Judi had sold four sculptures to some high roller who won five thousand dollars at roulette. "Always bet on your birthday," the man had advised me, puffing on a cigar. "It's your luckiest number." I told him I'd remember that.

Now I'm back in my bedroom trying to record my observations from the museum. This is the third H.O.J. that I've worked on it. Dr. Grady told us so much, I want to make sure I do it justice in my notebook. After filling my trash can with crumpled pages, I finally wind up with this:

At the museum I learned that the universe is a lot more enormous than I thought. Every day, suns are born and die. Ours will die, too, one day. In the scheme of time, we are a new arrival to this place and are lucky to be here. In all of history, there will only be one Jeremy Fink (unless I do that time machine thing, and then there will be two of me, but I don't really see that happening anymore), and only one of everyone else, too. I feel closer to Dog and Cat and Hamster and Ferret now, even though they are fish and I'm human. We are all connected at a deep, chemical level. We are inside the universe, and the universe is inside us. Even if we're here for no other reason than because we're here, I don't think it relieves us of deciding what our own purpose here is. I still have to figure that out, but I don't feel like I need to know right this instant anymore. I think I can wait to find out how many apples are inside me. (That last part came from Mr. Rudolph the other day.)

The next morning, I'm in the middle of getting dressed when the phone rings. Mom answers it. A minute later she finds me in the bathroom brushing my teeth. "That was James," she says. "Mr. Oswald isn't feeling well. James said he'll call us in a few days to see if Mr. Oswald is ready to have you come back to work."

I put down the toothbrush, my mouth still filled with foam. "Is he okay?"

"He said it wasn't anything serious. I'm sure you don't need to worry. This will give you time to practice for the fair. We leave in a week."

My eyes open wide. "It's only a week away?"

She nods. "The fair is earlier this year, so your grandmother and I planned the trip accordingly. I'm sorry, I thought you knew the dates."

I shake my head. "But that means I'll be there during my birthday."

"Is that a problem?" she asks, handing me a towel to wipe my mouth.

"It means I have even less time to find the keys to Dad's box."

"Are you still caught up with that?" she asks worriedly. "I hope it's not ruining your summer. Your dad wouldn't have wanted that."

I quickly shake my head. "No, it's not ruining my summer. It's just making it . . . different. That's all."

"I have to leave for work now," she says. "Remember, things have a way of working themselves out. Not everything is in our control."

"I know, Mom. Believe me, I know."

"Good, because this morning you're having oatmeal for breakfast. I didn't forget our agreement that you'll eat one new thing each week. It's warming on the stove. Whole grain with peaches. You'll love it!"

My stomach grumbles in protest.

"And I'll know if you put it in the garbage disposal."

I roll my eyes. "Because mothers know everything."

"That's right," she says, looking in the mirror to attach today's pin, READING ISN'T ONLY FUNDAMENTAL, IT'S FUN. "And don't even think about feeding it to the fish."

After she leaves, I force myself to sit down and have a few spoonfuls of the glop in the pot. I bite into a piece of peach and almost gag. I have to pull it out of my mouth. Peach is one of my favorite flavors of Mentos. Why can't

I eat a real peach? Determined not to let it get the best of me, I pick out another piece of peach, use my napkin to wipe off the pieces of oatmeal stuck to it, and pop it in my mouth.

Ten seconds later my stomach rebels, and I am kneeling over the toilet bowl saying goodbye to my first bowl of oatmeal. It looks exactly the same in the toilet as it did before I ate it. That's just not right.

I return to my room to find a note from Lizzy.

> Meet you outside to practice at noon? Dad won't let me hula in the living room ever since I broke his great aunt's vase.

I scribble *Okay* and stick it back through the hole. I plop down on my bed with a comic, but before I open it, the words from the palm reader start running through my head. What if the keys are right here, under my nose? After all, I didn't really search the apartment. Mom said they weren't here, and I believed her, but what if she was wrong? Only one way to find out. I toss the comic book aside.

Starting in the kitchen, I open every drawer as far as they'll go. Underneath all the take-out menus I find a lot of buttons and paper clips and Post-it pads. Beads galore. Marbles, stamps (not old ones), an old postcard Grandma sent from a trip to the world's largest ball of yarn, and assorted Tic Tacs. I find three keys, but I recognize them as being the front door keys of Dad's store.

There aren't any drawers in the living room, but I look

behind the drapes and under the coffee table and behind the bookshelves. I reach under Mongo, and my hand lands on something squishy. I grab hold of it, and pull out an orange bunny Peep from a long ago Easter. Even *I* wouldn't eat it now. The scary thing is, it still looks perfectly fine. Dusty, but fine. I think Dr. Grady was wrong. At the end of the world will be bacteria, cockroaches, and Peeps.

I feel weird looking through Mom's room. I step inside, but then I hurry back out. I can't do it. I'll take her word that they just aren't here.

I slip a note through the wall and ask Lizzy to check in her apartment. After all, Mom had said that's where the box was kept for a while. She writes back that she'll check. Twenty minutes later I pull out a note and find two keys wrapped up in it.

These were both in a little tray on my dad's dresser. What do you think?

I turn the keys over in my hand. They're a bit smaller than the ones I think we need, but it's worth a try. I bring them over to my desk and sit down in the chair. I slide the box toward me, but I can see without even trying that they're definitely too small. I try them anyway, then wrap them back up and send them through. No note is necessary.

At noon I meet Lizzy on the sidewalk. The hula hoop is zooming around her waist, and she's wearing her old fake-grass skirt. It's much shorter now than when she was eight. She's gotten very good in the last week. Her props are on a towel next to her. I pick up the football and toss it to her. She catches it neatly this time.

"The crowd roars," she says, holding it above her head as she twists her hips.

Walking toward us with a grocery bag swinging from each hand is Rick. I haven't seen him since the whole invisible thing. Lizzy doesn't notice him, since she's facing the wrong way, and I don't want her to get distracted. Lizzy tosses the ball back to me, and I catch it. Maybe he'll walk by quietly, and she won't even notice. No such luck.

"What on earth are you doing?" Rick asks, stifling a laugh.

"What does it look like?" Lizzy says.

"It looks like you're playing with a hula hoop. And you're wearing some kind of grass skirt."

"So what if I am?" Lizzy says, sticking out her chin. "Hula is a national sport in Hawaii."

"Last I checked, this is America," Rick says.

"Hawaii *is* in America!" I point out.

"You know what I mean," he says, but turns away from Lizzy and heads up the stairs. Before he disappears inside, he calls out, "Good luck at the tractor pull!"

"For the last time," Lizzy yells, "we are NOT doing the tractor pull!" Her hula hoop falls to the ground and wobbles for a few seconds before coming to a rest.

"When we win first place," she says, hands on her hips, "he won't be laughing anymore."

"And we won't let him have any of our Snickers," I reply, lifting up her hoop and handing it to her. "Now let's see you peel that banana again."

We practice the routine pretty much nonstop for the next two days, until Lizzy claims she now has a permanent red mark around her waist. By the time James calls on Thursday morning to say he's coming for us, we have the routine down cold.

"James!" Lizzy says as we slide into the cool backseat. "We missed you!"

"The limo hasn't been the same without you two," he replies, pulling away from the curb.

"Is Mr. Oswald okay?" I ask.

"He likes to say he has 'old bones.' Sometimes it's hard for him to get around much. But he's better. He's looking forward to seeing you both."

Hearing that makes me feel good. Lizzy smiles, too. Neither of us has said it, but I, at least, have started thinking of Mr. Oswald sort of like a grandfather.

"So what are we returning today?" Lizzy asks.

James shrugs. "I get my assignment when you do." And with that, he puts up the window divider.

I lean back and enjoy the scenery. Usually all the people on busy streets like Fifth Avenue freak me out a little, but today it doesn't bother me. After all that stuff about everyone being connected, I feel warmer toward my fellow man. I munch contentedly on a sandwich.

"Jeremy?" Lizzy says, startling me. "I did something I never told you about."

I let the sandwich fall to my lap. My mind races with all the things Lizzy might have done. Opened the box somehow? Stole something really big? Kissed a boy? Rick! I bet she kissed Rick! When, after the séance? Or the tractor pull comment?

"It had to do with Mabel Billingsly," she says. "The woman with the *Winnie-the-Pooh* book?"

I breathe a sigh of relief. "What about her?"

"You know how Mr. Oswald said I should pay more attention to what people say and how it makes me feel?"

I nod, unable to imagine where this story is going, but grateful that it won't end with her kissing Rick. Not that I'd care if she kissed someone, just not him.

"So that night I looked up Mrs. Billingsly's phone number, and I called her."

"You did?"

She nods. "And I asked her what she thought the meaning of life was."

"No way."

"Way."

"What did she say?"

"That's the weird part," Lizzy says, taking a sip of soda and placing the can back in the cup holder. "She said the meaning of life is friendship. But the thing is, she lost her best friend sixty years ago by selling that book, but all this time, that's what was most important to her."

"Wow."

"Yeah. So I got to thinking, what if we tried to track down her old friend — the one with the funny name — and maybe we can get them back together?"

"Bitsy," I say. "Her name was Bitsy Solomon."

"Right! Bitsy! So what do you think?"

"She died a few years ago," I say quietly.

"Oh," Lizzy says, frowning. Then, "How do you know that?"

I told her what I learned on the Internet, and about Bitsy naming her foundation after the necklaces they both wore.

"Wow," Lizzy says. "Do you think Mrs. Billingsly knows?"

"Probably."

Neither of us says anything for a minute, and then Lizzy says, "You know what all this means, right?"

I shake my head.

"It means if you piss me off, and we don't stay friends, that sixty years from now you'll regret pissing me off."

I pop open a can of 7-Up. "I'll keep that in mind."

"You'd better," she says, and turns to the window. She stares out for the rest of the ride.

Mr. Oswald opens the door for us. For the first time he's in regular pants, a button-down shirt, and a white brimmed hat. Even though he looks a little frailer than the last time we saw him, he looks much better in these clothes than in his usual suit. More natural or something. Lizzy surprises all of us by running up and giving him a hug.

He laughs. "What's that for?"

Lizzy doesn't answer and doesn't let go.

"Honestly," he says, "I'm not dying! Just needed to rest the old bones for a few days."

I pry Lizzy away, and Mr. Oswald straightens his shirt. As we file inside, I can see nearly the whole house is boxed up now. His office shelves are still full though. I wonder what we'll be delivering today. The old globe? A baseball glove?

"Notebooks?" he asks.

We fish out our notebooks and hand them over. He takes them and sits in his big leather chair. To my surprise, he flips open the front cover of each one, scribbles something, and slides them back to us. I open mine to see that he has written his name and the date.

"You're not going to read them?" I ask.

He shakes his head and folds his hands together. "Your observations of life are your own. You don't need me or anyone telling you how to do it anymore."

"We don't?" Lizzy says. "What if the community service people want to collect them?"

"They probably won't," Mr. Oswald says. "But that's why I signed them, just in case."

"Mr. Oswald?" I ask as I slip my notebook in my backpack.

"Yes, Jeremy?"

"Did my mom tell you we're going away to New Jersey on Saturday? I hope that's okay. I'm sorry we'll be missing work."

He smiles, but it's a sad smile. "This is our last day together."

"Huh?" Lizzy and I say together.

"My move is happening sooner than I expected. I'll need to wrap up a lot of loose ends before I go."

My stomach clenches. I know I should be glad that we have our freedom again, but all I feel is a sense of loss.

"No more limo rides?" Lizzy says.

"I'm afraid not," Mr. Oswald replies. "But to show my appreciation at how well you both did, I'd like you both to choose something from my shelves. Anything you like."

Lizzy is already halfway out of her seat.

I start to get up, too, but then hesitate. "But don't these still need to be returned to the people who pawned them when they were kids?"

Mr. Oswald shakes his head. "The telescope was the last one. The rest of these objects have found their way to me over the years in the traditional manner. Go on, take a look."

Lizzy makes a beeline for the creepy blue-eyed doll. I guess that's what happens when your dad gives you trucks instead of dolls to play with as a baby. Mr. Muldoun swears he tried to get her to play with a Barbie, but she threw it out the window.

I scan the shelves, but I can't pick out anything that I really need. The old record player is kinda cool, and there's a huge dictionary on a stand, which is very tempting.

"Having trouble?" Mr. Oswald asks, stepping up behind me.

"I just can't choose."

"How about that suitcase?" he suggests, pointing to a

hardback suitcase on the bottom shelf. "You could use it for your trip."

I hadn't really noticed it before. I bend down to take a look. It's one of those old-fashioned suitcases, covered with stickers from exotic ports around the world. At first I think it's just manufactured to look that way, but upon closer inspection, I see they are all real. The stickers have dates on them from the twenties up to the fifties. It's actually very, very cool. I could put books or comics in there. Or anything, really. "Thanks!" I tell him. "It's great." I close my hand around the handle and figure I would easily lift it off the shelf. Instead, I almost fall forward when I try to lift it.

"Oh, right!" Mr. Oswald says. "I'm sorry about that. I forgot that's where I stored the flotsam and jetsam people left in all the old furniture I've bought over the years."

Lizzy asks, "What the heck is flotsam and jetsam?"

"Little things like safety pins, pencils, buttons, keys. Things that have a way of getting stuck in the backs of drawers. I have a hard time throwing anything out." Lizzy and I exchange an excited look while Mr. Oswald chuckles and says, "But of course one look at my home would tell you that much. I'll have James empty the suitcase for you, and then you'll be —"

"No!" Lizzy and I yell at the same time.

Mr. Oswald steps back a foot.

I hurry to explain. "If it's okay, can I take it with the flotsam and jetsam inside?"

"Of course, but why?"

I open my mouth to explain, but glance at Lizzy first. She nods, so I say, "You remember that box I showed you? The one with all the keyholes?"

"Of course. An interesting box. Unusual."

"Well, we kinda have only one more week to find the keys to open it."

"And you think they might be in there?" He casts the suitcase a doubtful look.

"We've already tried half the keys in this city," Lizzy says. "So it's worth a shot."

"By all means, take them then. As a collector, I always admire a good quest. I bet your father did, too, Jeremy, from what you've told me about him." He pats me on the shoulder. "I admire such dedication. Looking for one stamp his whole life. Regular people might think doing such a thing would be frustrating, but it's not. There's joy in the search itself. It's exciting."

I nod. "That's how he felt about it. Remember, Lizzy?"

She smiles. "That's why he wanted us to start our own collections."

Mr. Oswald presses the intercom and calls for James to come in and to bring a cart with wheels. While we wait, he says, "Don't get me wrong, finding what you're looking for is wonderful, too. The harder something is to acquire, the more satisfying it is when you finally find it."

James arrives, and Mr. Oswald asks him to bring the suitcase out to the car. James loads it on the cart. "Want me to take the doll, too?" he asks Lizzy, trying to hide a smile.

"That's okay," she says. Then when she sees us all looking at her with expressions of 'oh, isn't she cute hugging the doll,' she hastily throws it on top of the suitcase. "It was getting heavy anyway."

"Thanks for everything, Mr. Oswald," I say, sticking out my hand.

He shakes it firmly. "It was my pleasure working with you both. I hope you find what you're looking for. In more ways than one."

Lizzy shakes his hand, too. "I hope you like it down there in Florida. Maybe you'll meet some nice lady to keep you company."

"Lizzy!" I exclaim.

Mr. Oswald just laughs. "We'll see, we'll see."

The ride home is quiet. We make sure to push all the buttons that we hadn't tried before, and turn on the TV for the first time. All we get is static. I turn to Lizzy. "Did you know that some of the radiation from the Big Bang is inside the static on your TV set?"

"Where'd you learn that one?"

"I've been doing some reading about the universe lately. During the H.O.J."

"That's pretty interesting," she says.

My eyes widen. "It is?" Lizzy has never, in my memory, said any of my factoids were interesting. James pulls up in front of the building, but neither of us gets out. I keep opening and closing the door of the fridge. Lizzy fiddles with the armrest. Finally James opens both of the back doors, and we have no choice.

We stand on the curb as he lifts the suitcase out and

places it on the sidewalk. He hands Lizzy her doll. She glances around to make sure no one we know is watching before she takes it.

"We'll miss you, James," she says. "You're a man of few words."

He chuckles. "Never learned anything by listening to myself talk."

"Are you going to Florida with Mr. Oswald?" I ask.

"For a little while. Help him get settled. He won't need me down there. I guarantee in a month or two he'll have set up shop at some antique show or flea market. He can't stay away from those things. Loves meeting other collectors. It's in his blood."

"I know what you mean," I tell him. "It's in mine, too."

"Be good," James tells Lizzy. He sticks out his hand, but she gives him a hug instead. The doll gets wedged between them. They both laugh.

I shake his hand. "Thanks for everything, James. Keep your eyes out for those mollusk fossils."

"Always do," he says, tipping his hat.

We watch the limo until it reaches the end of the block and disappears around the corner. I look down at the suitcase. There's no way we'll be able to get it up the stairs. "Why don't we sort through this stuff out here? Then we can just keep the keys. I'm sure we'd be able to lift it then."

"You mean separate the flotsam from the jetsam?" she says, already kneeling down next to the suitcase.

"You take the flotsam," I tell her. "I'll take the jetsam."

"You *always* get the jetsam," she says, pretending to pout.

"Do you ever worry if people heard our conversations, they would lock us up?"

"All the time," she says, setting the big doll carefully on the lower step so it looks like she's watching over us. "All the time."

Chapter 17: Milestones

In the time it takes us to sort through the suitcase, half the building passes by. Mrs. Sanchez says we look hungry and brings us tacos. I pretend to eat mine, but stick it in my bag and eat one of my peanut butter sandwiches instead. Bobby asks if he can play with Lizzy's doll, and she reluctantly lets him take it upstairs with him. I think it shows strength of character on my part that I haven't teased her about that doll. It hasn't been easy.

Besides all the things Mr. Oswald had said were in there, we find six dollars and thirty-two cents worth of pennies and nickels, two thimbles, eighteen rusty nails, an old watch with a cracked face, dozens of pull-tops from old soda cans, assorted tin foil balls, three leaky batteries, and more than a few dead beetles.

With only the keys remaining in the suitcase, it is light enough for me to carry alone. "How many you think we've got?" I ask, stopping a few feet away from my apartment door to rest.

"Two hundred?" she guesses.

I nod. "At least. It's gonna take us hours. Days."

"We're gonna have to bring it with us to your grandmother's."

"If we get started tonight, maybe we can finish it tomorrow."

Lizzy shakes her head. "I don't feel very good. That taco isn't sitting well, if you know what I mean. You can start without me though."

I shake my head. "We can wait till tomorrow. Either the keys are here, or they're not." I pick up the suitcase again and drag it the rest of the way, bumping up each stair as we go. "If you need anything, my mom has a pharmacy worth of stomach stuff in the medicine cabinet."

"Thanks," she says with a small moan. "I'm just gonna lie down."

A few hours later, Mom and I are playing cards in the kitchen when Lizzy knocks on the door. She's clutching her stomach and looks pale. "Mrs. Fink? I think I need your help."

Mom jumps up from the table and herds Lizzy into the bathroom. I hear them talking, but can't hear what they're saying. I don't want to intrude, but I'm worried. Lizzy's never sick. She's like me with the iron stomach. I turn the corner to the bathroom in time to see my mom slap Lizzy on the cheek. When she takes her hand away, I can see a red handprint. Then my mom pulls her into a hug, and they both start laughing. Laughing!

My jaw literally falls open in shock. Mom has never hit me, and I know Mr. Muldoun has never hit Lizzy. "Mom! What are you doing? Whatever Lizzy did, it can't be *that* bad! And she's sick, too!"

"Jeremy, it's okay," Lizzy says, wiping away a tear.

I can feel the blood rising to my cheeks. "How is it okay? Mom, why did you hit her?"

"Oh, honey," Mom says gently. "It's an old custom

when a girl becomes, er, when she, um . . ." Mom trails off, glancing at Lizzy like she's unsure she should continue.

"I got my period!" Lizzy shouts. "Congratulate me. I'm a woman now!"

Honestly, if the floor would open up and swallow me, I would go happily. I don't know where to look. I knew all the girls at school saw a special film in fifth grade on "becoming a woman" while us boys were sent outside to play dodgeball. And I had heard whisperings last year of girls who had "accidents" during school and had to tie their sweatshirts around their waists. But I can't say I really understand any of it. Lizzy's having this milestone moment, and I'm not any part of it. Starting to feel like a third wheel, I back up, muttering "Er, congratulations, that's great, er, okay, bye!"

Mom closes the door to the bathroom, and I hear the sound of boxes being opened. I knew Mom kept her "woman" stuff under the sink, but I'd never so much as glanced at the boxes to see what was inside them. I'm in my room when I hear the front door close. A minute later Mom knocks on my door.

"I want to make sure you're all right," she says, joining me on the bed.

I put down the comic I'm reading and nod uncertainly. "It's just weird, I guess."

She nods. "I know. You two are growing up so fast. You're already taller than me, and now this with Lizzy." Her eyes fill with tears. "Where does the time go? Soon you'll be off to college."

There's no talking to her when she gets all sentimental

like this. I keep glancing at the comic in my lap while she goes on about time flying. Finally she gets the hint. I scribble a note to Lizzy, apologizing for acting weird, but when I go to stick the note in the hole, it won't go through. I jam it in again, but it still won't go. I pull the paper out and put my eye to the hole. No wonder it won't go anywhere. Instead of seeing the back of the poster that usually hangs there, all I see is a wad of tinfoil. I knock twice on the wall, but she doesn't answer. I consider sending an e-mail, but we never e-mail each other.

The suitcase by my door beckons. If Lizzy is tuning me out, I might as well get a jump on the keys. I kneel down and unlatch the case. But as soon as I flip it open I know I won't do it. We've been in this together from the beginning. It just wouldn't be right. I start packing for the trip instead.

It's almost noon the next day before Lizzy comes over. "Hey," she says, leaning against my desk. She doesn't look any different.

"Hey."

She notices my packed duffel bag on the foot of my bed. "All packed?"

"Yup. You?"

"Nope."

I'm not used to it being awkward between us, and I'm hoping it goes away very soon.

"Um, I'm sorry about the tin foil," she says.

"It's okay."

"I just need some, I don't know, privacy, I guess. Just for a little while."

"I understand."

"Good."

I suddenly feel embarrassed again, like last night. I have to redeem myself somehow for just ducking away. "Are you, um, feeling better?"

She nods. "A little crampy, but better. Your mom really helped me out. My dad was freaking. He was running around in circles in the living room. It was pretty funny."

"Yeah, my mom's a little freaked out, too. Us getting older and stuff."

"Enough serious talk," she says, sitting down on the floor next to the suitcase. "Let's get to work."

Relieved not to have to talk about it anymore, I quickly grab my box from the desk and join her. Every type of key imaginable stares up at us from the bottom of the suitcase. Brass and copper and silver and yellow and even a few translucent ones. Big and small and fat and thin. Some are so rusty they almost fall apart in our hands, while some look like they were minted a year ago. We keep banging into each other as we try to stick the keys in the holes, but it would take way too long if only one of us did it at a time. Soon we get into a rhythm, and now we're knocking elbows just once every four or five keys. Mom, who's off from work today, brings us grilled cheese sandwiches for lunch. We take breaks only to run to the bathroom.

At four o'clock, the miraculous happens. One of my keys goes all the way into the hole. I grab Lizzy's arm, and she freezes.

"Do it," she says. "Turn it."

I take a deep breath and turn it to the right. Nothing happens. "The other way," she says. "Turn it the other way."

"That sounds familiar," I mutter, remembering the door to Harold Folgard's office, but I do it anyway.

And it turns! It turns easily. I hear a *click* as some mechanism snaps into place. We look at each other in shock and glee. Then we both jump up yelling. We run and yell in circles around the pile of discarded keys. Mom comes in and joins us in the circle. I can't believe that we actually found one after looking in so many places. Our theory was right — if we searched enough keys, maybe we'd find one that worked. And we did!

After the jumping and yelling ends, we eagerly dive back into the suitcase. "Careful not to go too fast and miss one," I warn.

"Don't worry, I'm being very careful. Look for ones that look like the one that worked."

The one that worked was long and silver. We try all the ones that even remotely resemble it, but they don't do anything.

At six o'clock, Mom makes us come into the kitchen to eat. A hamburger for me, veggie burger for Lizzy. Mr. Muldoun joins us. He and Mom have grown-up food. A green pepper stuffed with some sort of rice and tomato and chopped meat glop.

"So what are you going to do while Lizzy's away?" I ask Lizzy's dad.

"Oh, the usual," he says between bites of the dinner

I'm sure he's only pretending to enjoy. "Wild parties, dancing till dawn, that sort of thing."

"And here I thought you'd miss me," Lizzy says.

"Of course I'll miss you," he says. "But I'm glad you're going out to the country. We all need to breathe that fresh air every now and again."

"All those cows don't make the air smell very fresh," Lizzy complains.

"There aren't any cows at Grandma's B&B!"

"There's some kind of funky smell there."

"It's the cats! You love cats!"

"I love *my* cat," she corrects me. "Not all cats. Your grandmother has, what, like, twelve of them?"

I nod. "Twelve cats, twelve rooms. Only cat lovers stay there."

"Hey, Dad, guess what?" Lizzy asks, apparently already having lost interest in the cats.

"I give up."

"We found one of the keys for Jeremy's box!"

He looks at me and grins. "That's wonderful."

"I know! And we still have a lot to go through!"

"You two can get back to it if you like," my mom says. "Just finish your burgers."

Five minutes later, we're back on our knees in front of the open suitcase. Fifty minutes after that, we find our second key. Lizzy's hand shakes as she turns it and it clicks into place. This time we sit very calmly, although my heart is racing. The second key is short and squat. Nothing at all like the first.

"They could all be here," she says, her voice cracking. "You might be able to open the box on your birthday after all."

"I know," I whisper, realizing I never let myself believe it might really happen.

"So what are we waiting for?"

Two hours later I am bleary-eyed and ready to pass out. But still, I forge ahead. Soon Mom knocks on the door and suggests to Lizzy that it might be time to go home.

"We just have about twenty more to go, Mom."

"Okay, but the train leaves Penn Station at nine a.m., so we'll be getting up early."

With eight keys to go, I find the third one. It slides right in. After that, it's a mad scramble to try the other eight. But none of them even go halfway into the last keyhole.

It's over. I can't believe it's over. I stare helplessly at the jumble of rejected keys.

"Well, that bites," Lizzy says.

I don't say anything. Picking up the box with the three keys sticking out of it, I shake it as if it would help. I try pulling on the top. I tug and yank, but nothing budges.

"What are we gonna do?" Lizzy asks.

I look over at the pile of discards and grit my teeth till they hurt. "We could try each one again. It would go faster this time since we'd only have to try it in one hole."

"I can't stand to look at one more key tonight," Lizzy says. "But maybe you can do it during your H.O.J.?"

I'm so tired I don't want to do anything during the H.O.J. except sleep. But I nod. "Okay, that's fine."

"I still have to pack," Lizzy says, getting slowly to her feet. "See you bright and early." I grunt and force myself to retry all the keys in the one remaining lock. None of them work. I am practically delirious with exhaustion at this point.

As a final resort, I retry the three keys that did work in the one empty keyhole. Nothing.

I'm so disappointed I feel hollow. I scribble a note and stick it in the hole. The tinfoil is gone. To be one key short, the day before we leave, is almost worse than being four keys short. Maybe it *is* worse. This has been twenty-four hours full of highs and lows. I'd like to get off the roller coaster.

In the morning I transfer all the stuff from my duffle into the new suitcase. It looks much more grown up than the old canvas bag. A cab honks downstairs to take us to the station. I say a quick good-bye to the fish as Mom hurries me out the door. Lizzy is already on the stoop. She's holding the note I sent last night about not finding the last key. She looks up, and I can see the concern in her eyes. "Are you doing okay?"

I nod and force myself to smile bravely. What else can I do? If I don't smile, I'll cry. I watch the cabbie put our bags in the trunk. "We tried the best we could, right?"

Lizzy crumples the note and sticks it in her pocket. "We sure did. That has to count for something. C'mon, let's just try to have fun at your grandmother's. You know, go with the flow like Mr. Rudolph said."

"I'm not sure I can," I reply honestly.

"There'll be funnel cake," she says.

I smile, for real this time. "And food on sticks. Food always tastes better on sticks."

"That's the spirit," she says as my mom ushers us in the back of the cab.

When we get to the station, Mom leads us to the huge electronic sign that lists where all the different trains are boarding. Our train goes to Dover, New Jersey, and will take about an hour and a half. There's one to Chicago, one to Miami, and even one to Los Angeles. Our train leaves in six minutes, and we have to run across practically the whole station. Lizzy has her hula hoop over one shoulder, and it keeps flying around her head and hitting people. Every few feet she calls out "Sorry 'bout that!" or "Oops, excuse me, sorry!"

We make our train with two minutes to spare. We stash our suitcases on the rack above our heads, but the hula hoop is too wide. Lizzy puts it on the floor under our seat, and we all have to keep our feet inside it so it doesn't slide into the row behind us. Lizzy grumbles that when this is all over, she's going to burn the wretched thing. I remind her that it's plastic, and, therefore, won't burn well and would probably give off toxic fumes.

She mutters something I can't hear and gives the hula hoop a kick.

Grandma is waiting for us at the station. It's been months since I've seen her, but she doesn't look any older. After Dad's accident, she aged about ten years overnight. Since then, she's stayed the same. Grandma is like that Easter Peep that I found. She'll be here forever.

Before we can stop her, she's tossing our bags into her van. Grandma's so used to carrying people's stuff at the bed-and-breakfast that she's gotten really strong. She smiles when she sees the hula hoop. "Are you excited for the talent show?" she asks Lizzy.

I expect Lizzy to grumble, but instead she forces her mouth into a smile and nods. "Jeremy's really excited, too, aren't you Jeremy?"

I'm already in the van at this point. "Oh, very," I mutter.

"Why don't I believe them?" Grandma asks Mom as she shuts the back door of the van.

When we arrive at The Cat's Paw B&B forty-five minutes later, I'm feeling a little carsick. The country roads always get me. In the city, the roads are straight and mostly flat. Lizzy and I stumble out of the van. She looks a little pale, too. Mom asks her if she feels okay, and I hear her whisper that her stomach hurts a little. Mom says she'll give her some Advil, but that it's normal and will go away in a few days. I realize they're talking about women stuff again, not carsickness. I grab my suitcase and hurry into the inn. I'm greeted by six cats in various positions. Some cleaning different body parts with their tongues, some sleeping, one batting around a mouse made of yarn, and another one scratching the leg of a chair. I don't see my favorite though.

Grandma comes in behind me. "I put Tootsie Roll in your room already."

Grandmas are the best!

I lug my stuff up the flight of stairs to the room I always stay in when I'm here. Mom's room is across the hall, and Lizzy's attaches to mine by a door. Tootsie Roll, long and brown, is waiting for me on my pillow. He purrs when I pet him, but not a growling purr, like Zilla makes. Grandma's cats are normal cats, not prehistoric beasts dressed in cat costumes. Grandma put a photo of a family visit to the inn on my night table. It was a few years after she opened it, when I was three. Tootsie Roll was just a kitten then, and Grandma let me name her. I make myself look away from Dad's smiling face in the picture.

I have to unpack all my clothes right away or else I feel really unsettled. While I'm stuffing things into drawers, I hear Lizzy and Mom trudging up the stairs. Mom suggests to Lizzy that she lie down for a few hours. Not to be unfeeling or anything, but if Lizzy's going to be sick this whole week, it's going to be pretty boring.

The suitcase is now empty except for three items that I had carefully wrapped in newspaper. First I pull out my dad's box, and place it on the night table next to the photo. Even though I won't be opening it, I couldn't bear to leave it home alone. Then I unwrap the apple Mr. Rudolph gave me, which is only slightly mushy, and place it on the desk next to the printout of *Care and Feeding Instructions for Your Temporary Cat* that Grandma leaves in every room.

I sit on the edge of the bed and pet Tootsie Roll. The absence of noise is deafening. It always takes me a while to get used to it. Outside the window, a real live deer is nibbling one of the bushes. This place really couldn't be any more opposite from our street.

I put my ear next to the door that divides my room from Lizzy's, but I don't hear anything. She's actually sleeping in the middle of the day. Even when we were little kids, Lizzy always refused to nap. She must really be feeling sick. Not for the first time, I'm glad I'm a boy.

Bored already, I head downstairs to see if I can drum up some interest in a card game. Grandma has most of the rooms filled when the state fair is going on, and usually a guest is in the common room looking for company. Not now, though. The place is quiet as a tomb, except for the cats, of course. Lizzy's hula hoop is leaning against the wall. What the heck, no one's around anyway. I drop the hoop around my waist, move into the center of the room, and start moving my hips in circles.

I'm pretty good at this! I'm a natural! The hoop spins around and around, the little beads inside zooming rhythmically. I bend my knees, still moving my hips, and the hoop is now only about a foot off the ground. Still it zooms around and around. I slowly stand back up. It goes up with me. After a few minutes of this, my carsickness returns. I circle the hoop around my thighs, then knees, then calves, before I let it rest on the ground. From behind me applause and a low whistle break out. I whirl around and trip on the side of the hoop in the process.

Lizzy, Mom, and Grandma are standing there clapping. My cheeks burn, but I manage an awkward bow.

Lizzy walks over and picks up her hula hoop. "How long have you been hiding this secret talent from me?"

"I'd like to know that, too," Mom says.

"I thought you were sleeping," I say to Lizzy accusingly.

"Maybe I should have signed *you* up with the hula hoop for the Young Talent Competition!" Grandma says.

"Calm down, everyone," I say, backing into the main entryway. "I was just goofing around. Let's all forget we saw that."

"Do it again, Jeremy!" Lizzy demands, thrusting the hula hoop at me.

"Wait till I grab my video camera," Mom says, poised to run upstairs.

I see my opening and take it, running at top speed out the front door. I hear laughter behind me. When outnumbered by women laughing at you, I've found the best thing to do is run as fast as you can.

Chapter 18: The State Fair

The next morning Grandma gets us up early. It's the first day of the fair, and she has to drop off her homemade jam and find out what table she's assigned in the table-setting competition. "How come Mom doesn't have to enter anything?" I grumble over scrambled eggs. Normally I would never eat eggs, but I eat Grandma's scrambled eggs because she mixes them with mini M&M's. Mom refuses to try that at home.

"Your mother didn't lose a bet," Grandma replies, pouring orange juice for a yawning Lizzy. "You two did."

"We've learned our lesson," Lizzy says. "We'll never bet on anything again. Now can we go back to sleep? This is supposed to be a vacation."

Grandma shakes her head. "You can sleep in tomorrow. You'll want to be bright-eyed and bushy-tailed for the competition on Tuesday."

"Is that a cat thing?" I ask.

"Is what a cat thing?" Grandma asks, sitting down across from me.

"The bright-eyed and bushy-tailed thing you just said."

"Oh. I don't think so. Could be, I guess."

Lizzy rolls her eyes between bites of egg. "Even on vacation he has to know everything. It's a *saying*, that's all."

"Every saying comes from somewhere," I mutter.

"It's about a squirrel," a man's voice says from behind a newspaper at the next table.

"Thank you," I tell him, vindicated.

He rustles the paper in response.

I turn back to Lizzy. "Now don't you feel better knowing?"

"I'd feel better if I were back in bed!"

"Hey, where's Mom?" I ask.

Grandma pushes back her chair and pours more coffee for the other guests before answering. "She's running some errands for me so I can bring you two to the fair. Now hurry up and finish before all the cotton candy is sold out."

Grandma sure knows how to motivate people!

As soon as Grandma pays the entrance fee and we walk through the gate, I inhale deeply. Funnel cake. Cotton candy. Fudge. Corn dogs. This is what Heaven must smell like. I stop short as we pass a booth that is new this year. A man in a red apron is dipping a Twinkie on a stick into the fried dough they use to make the funnel cakes. It's a fried-dough Twinkie! My mouth waters. I have to wipe the drool off with my shirt.

"Later," Grandma promises.

After he hands the Twinkie to the luckiest little girl in the universe, the man shoves a stick into the end of a Snickers and dips it. *A fried-dough Snickers!* This man is brilliant!

I let myself be pulled away only after Grandma crosses

her heart and swears upon all that is holy that she will let me buy one of each before we leave.

On the way to drop off the jars of jam, we pass the pig races and the tractor pull. Both have huge crowds cheering on the contestants. Lizzy takes a flier announcing the times for each race. "I'm gonna give it to Rick when we get home," she says, tucking it in her pocket. "I'll tell him we won both the pig race *and* the tractor pull!"

Grandma hurries us past the booths where men in costumes are yelling into megaphones: "Come see the World's Smallest Woman! She's here! She's real! She'll even talk to you! Only fifty cents for the experience of a lifetime!" "Come see the World's Largest Horse! All the way from Amish Country! You won't believe how huge he is!"

"Grandma, isn't Amish Country, like, only an hour away in Pennsylvania?" I ask, slowing down. "Should I tell him?"

"I think he knows," Grandma says. "These people will say anything to make a buck."

"Oh, you mean like that lady who guessed our weights last year?" Lizzy asks.

"Exactly," Grandma says.

"Aha!" Lizzy and I pounce.

"So you *admit* she was cheating!" I exclaim. "And you still made that bet!"

Grandma's lips tighten. "Okay, okay, I knew it was a scam. But trust me, you'll thank me after the show."

Lizzy puts her hands on her hips. "And I thought grandmothers were supposed to be sweet and loving and not someone who would trick their grandson and practically adopted granddaughter into losing a bet!"

"Ah, yes," Grandma says, "but sometimes grandmothers need to do what they think is best for their grandson and practically adopted granddaughter by opening their eyes to different experiences. That's the only way you'll learn what you're capable of. Now hurry up, my jams are melting."

Reluctantly, Lizzy and I trail behind as Grandma goes into the Crafts and Cooking tent. Tables full of tomato sauces, jams, cookies, quilts, bird feeders, and pies greet us. Some have ribbons attached to them already. They either say, *Excellent*, *Very Good*, *Good*, or *Fair*. I don't see any that say *Eh* or *Poor* or *The Worst Thing I Ever Tasted*. I wait while Grandma registers at the main table and then sticks a label with the number 22 onto her jars. As she's putting her jam among the others, I ask her if anyone ever loses.

She shakes her head.

I'm about to question her further on why anyone would enter a contest where everybody wins, but I'm distracted by three Asian girls giggling and pointing at Lizzy. I hurry over and pull Lizzy away from the giant pumpkins she's admiring. "Um, for some reason, those girls are pointing at you."

She turns around. "Who?"

I don't need to answer, because the group is now approaching her. The girls keep pushing each other ahead and then falling back, giggling. Finally one of them steps up to Lizzy. "You must really love turnips!" she says, and breaks into another fit of giggles.

Lizzy stares at her, and glances at the table of pumpkins. There aren't any turnips there. "Huh? What do you mean?"

The girl points to Lizzy's arm. "Your tattoo! It says 'turnip.' "

"No, it doesn't," Lizzy says crossly. "It says 'life.' "

The girls now fall on top of each other they are laughing so hard. We exchange worried glances.

"Doesn't it?" Lizzy asks in a small voice.

The girls shake their heads. Lizzy quickly unrolls her sleeve and pushes it down to cover the tattoo. She grabs me by the arm. "Come on, Jeremy, let's get out of here."

We leave the girls behind, although their laughter follows us outside of the tent. It is taking all my self-control not to laugh, too.

"Well, it's official," Lizzy says. "We can't trust *anyone* selling *anything* on the Atlantic City boardwalk."

"Would a fried Snickers on a stick make you feel better?"

"It might."

While we wait for my grandmother to come out, Lizzy licks her finger and rubs at the tattoo. It smears a little, but it's still there. As promised, we stop at the new booth, and Grandma buys us one of each kind. With a fried Twinkie in one hand and a fried Snickers in the other, even Lizzy can't stay angry for long.

"I don't even know what a turnip looks like," she mutters as we find a bench to sit on while Grandma goes to the table-setting event to get her assignment. "How could I love turnips when I don't even know what they look like?"

"You couldn't," I say, taking a bite of first the Twinkie, then the Snickers. They taste as good as I knew they would.

"This tattoo was supposed to wear off in a week. It's been a week!"

"Don't worry. You've smeared it so much, no one can tell if it says 'life,' 'turnip,' or 'Go Yankees.'"

"Swear?"

"Swear."

"Just for that, I'll let you use my hula hoop when we get back to the inn."

"Very funny."

"No, you were really good."

I finish off the last bite of the Snickers, and toss the stick in the garbage. "Yeah, I know."

We spend the rest of the day practicing the routine, and most of the next day, too. Lizzy can catch that football with her eyes closed now. Maybe Grandma was right and the talent show won't be so bad.

The announcer clears his throat and booms into the mike, "You will be scored on stage presence, confidence, originality, and entertainment value."

Lizzy leans over to me. "What about my good looks? Don't they count for anything?"

"Shh!" We're sitting in the front row along with the rest of the contestants. I don't want any of the three judges to be annoyed with us before the show has even started. The announcer goes on to introduce the judges — a bald

Broadway producer, a talent agent, and a guy who sings jingles in commercials. While everyone claps, I take a moment to check out our competition. The kid on the other side of me is picking his nose, and the girl next to him is chewing on her hair. At the end of the row, the three girls who pointed out Lizzy's tattoo are dressed in matching leotards and glittery boots. I don't think Lizzy has seen them yet, which is a good thing. She might say she's not nervous, but she's repeatedly pulling the strands of fake grass on her skirt.

"And now, dancing to the classic disco hit 'It's Raining Men,' we have the three Su sisters!"

Everyone claps as the three girls climb up the steps to the stage. Lizzy's eyes narrow, and she sinks a little in her chair. The music comes on, skips a little, and then plays normally. The girls have this whole routine with umbrellas, and they're actually very good. People in the audience start singing along. I turn around to wave at Mom and Grandma in the third row. Mom's all set with her video camera. I can't believe I have to do this. I had made it to nearly thirteen without having to be on a stage. It goes against everything I hold dear. At least it will be over soon, and after all, Lizzy's doing all the hard work.

The girls finish, take a few too many bows if you ask me, and sit back down. Next up is a boy playing the violin, followed by a brother and sister singing a duet. The violin boy was pretty painful, but the singers weren't bad. I nudge Lizzy. "We're next!"

She nods, her cheeks a bit pale.

"And now, allow me to present Lizzy Muldoun, the

best hula hooper in the East. She will be assisted by her friend Jeremy Fink."

The audience applauds politely as we climb up to the stage. I have all Lizzy's props in my duffle bag, and I set it to the side. I look toward the center of the stage, where Lizzy is supposed to be. Except she's not there. I whirl around to find her standing behind me, slightly offstage. She's waving me over. I hold up a one-minute finger to the judges and hurry over to Lizzy. "What are you doing?" I hiss. "We're on!"

Lizzy shakes her head superfast. "Can't go on," she says, clutching her stomach. "Cramps."

"You have *got* to be kidding me!" I say. "How long does this thing *last*?"

"I'm sorry," she says, "I don't know what to do."

The audience is getting restless. I can hear them murmuring. I lean closer. "But you worked so hard. Can't you just push through it?"

She shakes her head again. "You could go on in my place! I can't hula, but I could still toss you the props."

"What? No way!"

The Broadway judge comes up onto the stage. "Is there a problem?"

I don't know how to answer. Lizzy yanks off her grass skirt and shoves it in my hand. "Jeremy's going on in my place. I'll assist him."

The judge lifts one eyebrow, but says, "All right, but we need to get a move on. Ten seconds."

"Please do this for me, Jeremy," Lizzy pleads. "I'll

make it up to you somehow. You know my whole routine. I'll be right there with you."

"Five seconds," the judge calls out.

This is a prime example of why I hate surprises. I look wildly out at the audience to Mom and Grandma. They're standing at their seats with stricken looks on their faces. I point to Lizzy's belly. Grandma looks confused, but Mom whispers to her. Then Grandma starts chanting, "Jer-e-my! Jer-e-my!" To my horror, others in the audience join in. There must be a hundred people stamping their feet and shouting my name. It's like a scene from a bad teen movie where the lovable loser finally runs for a touchdown or approaches the popular girl in school.

Our music starts to play over the loudspeakers. *Someone's* gotta go right round baby right round like a record baby right round, round, round, and apparently that someone is me. I pull the skirt up over my shorts. It barely reaches past my knees. I grab the hula hoop from Lizzy's hand, and move into the center of the stage. I read somewhere that because of the spotlight shining in their eyes, a person onstage can't see the crowd. I guess that doesn't apply in a tent in the middle of the day, because I can clearly see everyone's expectant faces. To my surprise the crowd cheers even before I start moving my hips.

I take a deep breath, put the hula hoop in place around my waist, and get a solid rhythm going. I nod to Lizzy that it's time to toss me the football. I catch it easily and toss it back. I'm only half-aware that I'm actually doing this, because most of my brain is occupied with what Lizzy could possibly do to make this up to me. I'm pretending I'm alone in the living room at the inn rather than doing the hula in a grass skirt in front of a hundred strangers. Otherwise I know I'll freeze up.

A minute later she tosses the banana. I begin to unpeel it and bring it to my lips when I remember that I hate bananas! I force myself to take a bite, then swallow quickly and make a face. I toss the rest of the banana behind me, and it hits the curtain. The crowd roars with laughter. I hadn't meant to be funny.

After what seems like forever, but is actually only one minute and fifty-three seconds, we reach the finale where I pop open a soda, drink some, and then reach down and rest it on the floor next to me, all while hula-ing. The hoop rotates around my knees until the music stops. Then I flip it up around my neck and bow. My head clears long enough for the applause to register. I admit, it feels kinda nice. The last time people applauded for me was when I won the sixth grade spelling bee by correctly spelling the word *neurotic*.

Lizzy scrambles across the stage to pick up the props, and I pull off the skirt and run down the steps. Mom and Grandma rush up to greet us.

I turn to Grandma. "Is this the part where I'm supposed to thank you?"

"You were wonderful," she says. "If you can do that, what *can't* you do?"

Mom pats her video camera. "And I got it all on film." Then to Lizzy she says, "Are you okay, honey?"

Lizzy nods. "I'm really sorry, Jeremy. But you were really, really good. Better than I would have done."

I know that's not true, but the next act is starting, so we sit down to watch. Ten more acts follow. Most do singing or dancing routines, or play some sort of instrument, but one does a stand-up comedy act, and one girl plays the bongos with her feet. While the judges add up their scores, people keep coming up to shake my hand, and to tell me how much guts that took. The whole thing was such a blur. If not for the lingering feel of the hoop around my waist, I could almost believe I'd dreamt it. Never in a million years did I think I could have hula-hooped in a grass skirt in a talent show. I wonder what else I could do that I never thought I could.

I try to convince Mom to let me run out for a fried-dough Twinkie, since there's no way we're going to win. She makes me stay. The judges finally announce they have a winner.

Third place goes to the Su sisters, who don't look thrilled when they go up to receive their twenty-dollar check and small bronze trophy.

"Who's laughing now?" Lizzy whispers.

I'm shocked to hear our names called for second place. "That's us!" Lizzy screams, yanking me up from the chair. The judge hands Lizzy a silver trophy and a check for thirty-five dollars. Lizzy passes them both directly to me. "It's the least I can do," she says. I don't argue.

First place and the fifty-dollar grand prize goes to the girl who played the bongos with her feet.

Chapter 19: Happy Birthday

The sun is shining. The roosters are crowing. I feel older. According to the bathroom mirror though, I don't look it. I thought for a second that I had a chest hair, but it was only a hair from my head that had fallen and gotten stuck there. While I was trying to get back to sleep last night, it dawned on me that this is really the *end* of my thirteenth year, not the beginning. Because if you're a whole twelve months old before your first birthday, then turning thirteen really means I've been on this earth a full thirteen years now. I am officially one day into my fourteenth year. No wonder I feel older!

There's a knock on my door, and I quickly throw on a T-shirt. Mom and Grandma and Lizzy come in, singing the happy birthday song. Grandma has a cake with candles in the shape of the number 13. She sets it down on the little desk, right next to our second-place trophy. Where's the guy who's supposed to give my official welcome to the world of teendom? Where's my secret handshake?

I blow out the candles, and everyone claps.

"Did you make a good wish?" Mom asks.

I slap my hand against my forehead. I had totally forgotten!

"We'll just have to relight them," Grandma says, whipping out the lighter from her apron pocket.

"Do we have to sing happy birthday again?" Lizzy whines.

"Please, no," I say.

This time I close my eyes and concentrate. First, I wish that my family and friends are healthy and safe for another year. But what I really wish for isn't a wish exactly. It's more like a hope. I hope wherever Dad is, if he's watching, that he understands I tried my best to follow the instructions to open his box today. I hope he knows how much it means to me that he gave it to me in the first place. Maybe that's it! Maybe it's the gift itself I'm supposed to learn from, not actually what's inside. I guess I'll never know.

"Okay," Lizzy says, "this has got to be the longest wish in history!"

I open my eyes. "All right, all right, I'm done." I take a deep breath, and blow the candles out on the first try.

As Grandma slices into the cake, Mom says, "We thought we'd go for a picnic at Mosley Lake. What do you think?"

"That's the place Dad used to take me fishing, right?"

Mom nods.

Lizzy looks disgusted. "You guys used to go fishing?"

Mom laughs. "Don't worry, honey. No fish were harmed when the Fink men hit the lake. They used gummy worms instead of real bait."

I grin as Grandma hands me a paper plate with a piece of cake on it. "And Dad would sprinkle Swedish Fish on the water and then pretend to catch them. He had to be fast though, 'cause they sank like rocks!"

"And then the lifeguard told him to stop," Grandma adds, "in case the real fish ate the candy fish and got sick."

"So Dad put on his goggles and swam out and made sure to get every one!"

Lizzy laughs. "That sounds like your dad. Wouldn't it have been funny though, if someone caught a real fish and then cut it open to cook it and found a Swedish Fish inside?"

"A green one!" I shout, after swallowing a big mouthful of cake.

"Or an orange one!" she cries.

"While you two are entertaining yourselves," Grandma says, lifting what's left of the cake back up into her arms, "we'll go pack up the lunches and call you down when we're ready."

Lizzy and I finish off our cake, giggling about the other kinds of candy one might find in a fish. I said that a Reese's Peanut Butter Cup would be the weirdest, just because you never picture a fish eating peanut butter. But Lizzy said she thought Cotton Candy would be the weirdest because it meant the fish was once won at a carnival game at the fair, but had escaped. After we dump our cake plates in the trash can, Lizzy heads for the adjoining door. "I have to finish wrapping your presents. I'll bring them with us to the lake."

She leaves the door open a crack, and I'm tempted to peek at what she's wrapping. But Lizzy and I basically get each other the same thing for our birthdays, so it's not worth spying and getting caught. Each year she gets me an assortment of candy and comics, and I get her a DVD and a book. I try to find a book that she'd like if she gave it a chance. They usually wind up back on my own bookshelf. I already know what I'm going to get her this year — a really nice copy of *Winnie-the-Pooh*. I think she'll like that after the whole Mabel Billingsly thing.

When we pull up to the lake, I'm surprised to see it's not very crowded. Maybe ten people altogether. The old rowboats they keep tied up are empty, and there's no lifeguard. It's one of those perfect summer days. I'd have thought the lake would be swarming with people. When we get out of Grandma's station wagon, I realize why we practically have the whole place to ourselves. I'd forgotten why we stopped coming here.

"What *is* that?" Lizzy says, holding her nose.

Mom and I pinch our noses, too, but Grandma inhales deeply. "Don't you just love it? It reminds me of fishing with my own grandparents. We used real worms, by the way."

Lizzy stares at Grandma. "It smells like the Loch Ness Monster came here to die."

Mom has let go of her nose and is inhaling deeply, too. "This is how you get used to a bad smell," she explains. "Once it gets into your nasal cavities, you'll barely notice it anymore." I hesitantly try her technique. It seems to work. I can only smell the swampyness on every few inhales now.

"Can't we eat in the car?" Lizzy begs.

Mom shakes her head. "Now come on, it's a beautiful day. It'll be better closer to the water."

"Won't it be *worse* closer to the water?" Lizzy asks, grudgingly trailing behind us. I'd have to agree with her, but Mom turns out to be right. We spread out the blanket between a young couple sunbathing and a kid flying a kite in the shape of a dragon. We're still far enough away from both to have privacy though.

Grandma unpacks the cooler. One by one, she pulls out things that smell even worse than the lake. Tuna fish on whole wheat, egg salad on rye, olives, pickles. Lizzy takes the egg salad, and I wait patiently for my peanut butter sandwiches, which I know are coming. Grandma pulls out a Thermos of lemonade, then napkins, paper cups, and forks. "Dig in, everyone."

I tip the cooler toward me. It's empty. "Um, where's my peanut butter?"

"Now don't freak out," Mom says as she pushes the tuna sandwich over to me. "Grandma and I thought since you're thirteen now, it's time to try something else.

My eyes widen. "You're kidding!" How could they do this to me on my birthday? I'm starving. All I had was the birthday cake for breakfast.

Mom smiles. "Yes, we're kidding." She reaches into her beach bag. "Here are your sandwiches."

Grandma chuckles. Lizzy grins, and her teeth have egg salad stuck all in them. Even though she makes me swear to tell her whenever she has food in her teeth, I let it go this time, since she's laughing at my pain.

"Ha ha, very funny," I say, grabbing the sandwiches. "Tease a kid on his birthday. Nice."

"To make it up to you, here's your birthday present." Mom hands me a blue envelope. I'm surprised because she almost never gets me cards. She thinks all the holidays are creations of the Hallmark company.

"Before you open it," she says, "I should explain that it's only a *picture* of your gift, because I didn't want to lug it all the way here."

Intriguing! So the gift is big enough that it would have to be lugged. I tear open the envelope and pull out a Polaroid photograph of a telescope! I can see from the background that Mom had hidden it in the Muldouns' living room.

"Did you know about this?" I ask Lizzy.

She nods. "I'm getting better at keeping secrets."

"Do you like it?" Mom asks.

I throw my arms around her. "I love it!"

"I tested it out on the roof. The view is a bit fuzzy because of all the lights, but it worked better than I expected. I'm sorry we couldn't have brought it out here. You can see the stars much more clearly this far away from the city."

"You can bring it next year," Grandma says. "Turn the picture over."

I flip the picture over in my hand. Stuck to the back is a Post-it note with the words, *The Sky and Telescope Foundation, membership good for one year.*

"That's my contribution," Grandma says. "You can go to their building anytime you like to do research, or to talk to other like-minded folk. It's in Midtown, though, so you'll have to take a subway or bus to get there."

"Is that going to be okay?" Mom asks. "I could make arrangements to take you, if you'd rather."

I pause for a second and then say, "No, that's okay. I can do it now. It's all about the Metrocard."

"Are you ready for my gift now?" Lizzy asks, bouncing up and down on her knees in anticipation.

I nod, taking another quick bite of my sandwich. Lizzy reaches into her beach bag and pulls out a box wrapped in last week's Sunday Comics. I rip it open to discover a smaller lumpy package, four of my favorite comics, and the new *Betty and Veronica* double issue. Lizzy laughs. "I got you that one just to prove to you that people would buy it even without seeing the flyer."

"That's not exactly proving my point. You *did* see the flier!"

"Ah, a tiny detail. Open the rest."

I open the smaller package to find the usual assortment: Twizzlers, Skittles, Fun Dip, Bottle Caps, Runts, and two Peppermint Patties.

"Are you going to eat all that yourself?" Grandma asks. "That will be one big dental bill!"

"I'll space it out," I promise her. "Over the course of a whole day."

Mom shakes her head. "I'm trying, I'm trying."

I turn to Lizzy. "Thanks for everything. It's great." There's something really comforting about knowing exactly what to expect. It's happened so infrequently this summer. I nibble happily on my sandwich. The boy with the kite is eyeing my candy stash, but I pretend not to notice.

"There's one more small thing," she says, reaching into her bag. She pulls out a small red box. It isn't wrapped, so I easily recognize it. It's the box from the wallet I helped her pick out last Christmas for her dad. Is he re-gifting it to me? I really wouldn't mind. It was a nice one, and I could use it. I take the box and open it, expecting to see the thin brown wallet. Instead, on a layer of white cotton, rests a single silver key. I lift it out of the box. At first I don't get it. Is this symbolic of our quest this summer?

Then it hits me. My eyelids stretch so far open they actually hurt. I jerk my head up. "Is this . . . is this the . . . is —"

"Yup," she says, bouncing again. "It's the fourth key."

Mom and Grandma are beaming at me. I have the feeling they knew this was coming. A mixture of disbelief, joy, relief, and anger flood through me. "But how did you, where did you, how —"

"It was in the suitcase. I found it about an hour after we found the second key. You were in the bathroom, so I slipped it in my pocket."

To think that Lizzy kept this from me for a week is almost as hard to believe as the key's appearance itself. "But why would you do that? All this time I've been thinking it was hopeless. But you knew. You *knew*!"

A look of uncertainty flits across her face. "The harder something is to acquire," she says uneasily, "the more satisfying it is when you finally find it. Sound familiar?"

I nod. "Mr. Oswald said that. The last time we saw him."

"Was he right?" she asks, nervously taking a sip of lemonade. "I just wanted to give you a present you'd never forget. Do you hate me now?"

I look down at the key. It catches the sunlight and shimmers. I grip it tightly in my hand. What would it have been like if I'd known a week ago that this key existed? "Just don't do it again."

She draws an X over her heart with her finger. "I won't. I promise. My stealing itch is gone. I think it was all leading up to this."

"Good. By the way, you have egg salad in your teeth."

She immediately runs her tongue over them until I give her the all-clear.

Mom starts gathering up the garbage. "Your Grandma and I could use a walk. Why don't you and Lizzy take one of the rowboats and go out to the big rock." She points into the center of the lake. From here, it looks like one big rock, but up close it's really a cluster of rocks. Dad took me out there once.

"Sounds good," I say, finishing off my sandwich and downing my cup of lemonade. The outline of the key is now engraved in my palm from holding it so tight. I wish I had brought the box with me. Now that I have all the keys, I can feel it calling to me.

Lizzy checks her teeth one last time in the side of the metal Thermos, and stands up. "Should we bring this with us?" She reaches into her bag and pulls out my box, followed by the other three keys.

"You promised no more surprises!" I say, grabbing happily for the box and clutching it to my chest.

"That was the last one, I swear!"

Lizzy chooses the less rickety of the two rowboats tied to the dock, which isn't saying much.

"Odds on us drowning?" she asks.

"Hmmm, I'd say fifty-fifty. But there's no water in the bottom of the boat, so at least there isn't a leak."

I steady it while Lizzy climbs in, and then I unhook the rope from the pole and climb in after her. She has left me the seat with the oars attached next to them. I push one of the tips of the oars into the water, and the boat easily moves away from the shore. We don't talk until we get closer to the rocks. All I keep seeing in my head is the box. Big and looming ahead of me.

"Um, how are we supposed to dock this thing?" Lizzy asks.

"I think my dad just tied the rope around one of the smaller rocks, and it stayed. You'll have to reach out and try to grab onto one of the rocks. Then I'll throw you the rope."

"This should be interesting," Lizzy mutters.

I pull up as close as I can. The boat bangs into the side of the rocks. Lizzy grabs for the nearest one and manages to hold on long enough for me to toss the rope. "You'll have to climb out now, and hold onto the rope so the boat doesn't drift away. Then I'll get out and tie it."

Lizzy mumbles something about being sucked under by the current and dashed against the rocks, but manages to get out just fine. A minute later, I've tied up the boat and have joined her on the largest rock. I place the bag on the towel between us and pull out my box. My legs out-stretched, I rest the box on my thighs. I never thought I'd arrive at this moment. Lizzy has her eyes closed and is tilting her head up to the sun.

I look out over the water and think about everything that led me here. What a bizarre journey it's been. If it weren't for this box, I never would have taken the subway or the bus. We wouldn't have gotten caught breaking into an office and been assigned to work for Mr. Oswald. I never would have ridden in a limo and met people like James and Mrs. Billingsly and Mr. Rudolph and Dr. Grady and Mr. Oswald himself. I'd be a totally different person. No matter what's in this box, I am already grateful to my father for leaving it to me.

Lizzy startles me by yelling "What are you waiting for?" into my ear.

I rub my ear and move the box onto the towel. "One more minute."

She groans and busies herself smoothing on sunblock. Her dad makes her use SPF 40, since she's a redhead.

A thought has crept into my head that I feel guilty for even thinking. But I can't help it. What if I'm disappointed by what's in there? "Maybe we shouldn't open it," I say to Lizzy. "Maybe we weren't supposed to find the keys after all. Let's just toss the box in the water."

She looks like she's going to have a heart attack. Her cheeks turn purple. "Are you SERIOUS?" she shouts.

"Nah. Let's open it!"

She pushes me with all her might, but I had braced myself and manage to stay upright on the rock.

I hand her the two keys for the locks on her side of the box, and she slides them in. Then I put my two in. Neither of us makes a move to turn them. I can tell Lizzy is waiting for my command.

"Okay, turn!"

We hear four simultaneous clicks, and something slides inside. I take a deep breath and lift open the top. It's amazing how easily it swings right up after all the pushing and pulling and jamming of blunt instruments.

On the top is an envelope with my name on it. The rest of the stuff in the box is covered with wrapping paper.

"Hey, I recognize that wrapping paper!" Lizzy says. "That's from your eighth birthday party! I remember because I stole some after you opened your gifts, and it's in my stolen stuff collection!"

Seeing the wrapping paper reminds me again of how long ago Dad put this together. He didn't get to see my ninth birthday party. I don't even remember having one.

I turn the envelope over. It's open, so all I have to do is slide out the letter. Trying, and failing, to keep my hands from trembling, I open it. Dad's handwriting is not the neatest. He always used to joke that he should have been a doctor, because doctors are known to have the worst handwriting. I can tell he worked hard to make it legible. I do my best to read it out loud, but every few lines my throat closes, and I have to pause for a few seconds.

Dear Jeremy,

As I write this, you have just had your eighth birthday party. We took you to the Bronx Zoo, and there was a bear cub who had just lost its mother at only two days old. Do you remember? The zookeepers put the bear cub in with a tiger who had just delivered a litter of her own a few days earlier. The tiger welcomed the cub as one of her own. You stood there for the longest time, tears silently running down your cheeks, watching this tiger nurse her new infant. I asked you what was the matter. You said, "I didn't know anything could be so beautiful." Your mother and I looked at each other and were awed by you. I don't know if you remember this event now, five years is a long time in a child's (excuse me, TEEN-AGER's) life. But it made me feel confident that you'd be ready to receive this box one day. I hope you won't be disappointed.

I want to tell you some things I have learned in the twenty-five years since that fortune-teller in Atlantic City gave me such a dire prediction. Of course I hope I am there beside you on your 13th birthday to tell you all this myself. If I'm not, I hope you can feel that I am always with you. Sorry at how corny that sounds. You'll understand when you have kids one day.

When we got back to Brooklyn from Atlantic City the day of my thirteenth birthday, your grandma made a special dinner for Arthur and me. Arthur had just lost a ball game, and neither of us was feeling very much like celebrating. I asked my father - your grandfather - if someone could really predict another person's future. He said the future changes every day. He said we, not someone else, have the power to create our own lives. Then he told me an old folktale that I asked him to write down afterward. Now I'm going to pass it on to you.

An old man is teaching his grandson about life. "A fight is going on inside me," he said to the boy. "It is a terrible fight, and it is between two wolves. One wolf is evil. He is anger, envy, sorrow, regret, greed, arrogance, self-pity, guilt, resentment, inferiority, lies, false pride, superiority, and ego. The other wolf is good. He is joy, peace, love, hope, serenity, humility, kindness, benevolence, empathy, generosity, truth, compassion, and faith. This same fight is going on inside you — and inside every other person, too."

The grandson thought about it for a minute and then asked his grandfather, "Which wolf will win?"

The old man replied simply, "The one you feed."

Even as children, we have the power to create our own lives. We choose which wolf to feed, and this creates who we become, how we see the world, what we do with the brief amount of time allotted to us. From my 13th birthday forward, I basically grew up with a deadline over my head. I thought, what if this woman was right? If I only had 40 years, how many more times would I eat chocolate cake? (Turned out to be a LOT.) How many more times would I see a sunrise over a beach? Four or five? How many more times will I listen to jazz? Ten times? A hundred? How many more times will I hug my son good night?

I made sure to pay attention to everything I was doing. To be fully in the moment. Because that's all life is, really, a string of moments that you knot together and carry with you. Hopefully most of those moments are wonderful, but of course they won't all be. The trick is to recognize an important one when it happens. Even if you share the moment with someone else, it is still yours. Your string is different from anyone else's. It is something no one can ever take away from you. It will protect you and guide you, because it IS you. What you hold here, in your hand, in this box, this is my string.

Until recently, I thought it was death that gave meaning to life – that having an endpoint is what spurred us on to embrace life while we had it. But I was wrong. It isn't death that gives meaning to life. _Life_ gives meaning to life. The answer to the meaning of life is hidden right there inside the question.

What matters is holding tight to that string, and not letting anyone tell us our goals aren't big enough or our interests are silly. But the voices of others aren't the only ones we need to worry about. We tend to be our own worst critics. Ralph Waldo Emerson wrote: "Most of the shadows in this life are caused by our standing in our own sunshine." I found that quote on a scrap of paper stuck to the back of that mongo grandfather clock. (I wonder if your mother finally got rid of that thing as she always threatened!) Wisdom is found in the least expected places. Always keep your eyes open. Don't block your own sunshine. Be filled with wonder.

I know it wasn't easy for you to open this box. (Don't ask me how I know – parents know everything.) Life is all about the journey. I hope this was one you'll never forget. I love you, Jeremy. I am so proud of you. I hope Lizzy is with you. No doubt she is turning into a beautiful young woman. And I'm sure she's as feisty as ever! Please tell her there's something in here for her, too. Take care of each other. Hug your mom and grandma for me. Have a blast putting your own strings together.

Love,

Dad

When I finish reading, I don't lift my eyes off the page. I run my finger over the ink like I used to do with the writing on the outside of the box. Strange how these squiggles and dots turn into letters and words that can change your life. I look over at Lizzy. Tears are streaming down her face. I heard her give a sharp intake of air when I got to the part in the letter that mentioned her. "Are you okay?" I ask.

She nods through her tears. "Are . . . you?"

I lay the letter in my lap. "I think so."

She wipes her eyes and nose on her sleeve. Through sniffles, she asks, "Should we see what's inside the wrapping paper?"

I rest my hand on it. It's very bulky. "What do you think it is? How could Dad's string of moments be in here?"

"Your dad moves in mysterious ways," Lizzy says.

I reach into the box and feel the outline of the oddly shaped package. It's kind of bumpy. I lift it out of the box and am surprised at how heavy it is. I had thought most of the weight had come from the box itself, but the empty box is very light. I slowly tear into the wrapping paper until I've created enough of a gap to rip it wide open.

"No way!" Lizzy says, then throws back her head and laughs.

Inside the wrapping paper is probably the last thing I would have guessed.

It's not an old book, or a savings bond, or a treasure map. Nope. Staring up at me is a pile of rocks.

Chapter 20: The String

Seriously. It's a pile of rocks. I pick one up, then the other. They range in size from a Mento all the way up to a Reese's Peanut Butter Cup. Some are white, some brown, some smooth, some rough. About twenty of them. A sheet of notebook paper is stuck in the middle. I unfold it. It's Dad's handwriting again.

Rock #1 From the Boardwalk, Atlantic City, 13
Rock #2 From outside the house of the girl I gave my first kiss to, 13½
Rock #3 From the first flea market my parents took me to in Queens, 14
Rock #4 From outside the Tri-State Twin Dance, where I met your mom, 15
Rock #5 From outside Fink's Comics the day my father let me watch it alone, 16
Rock #6 From the courtyard at my high school graduation, 17
Rock #7 From Oregon, the first time I saw the Pacific Ocean, 19
Rock #8 From the cemetery at my father's funeral, 23

I skim ahead a few until I see my name. *Rock #10 From outside the hospital where Jeremy Fink is born, 30.* A lot of the rest of them have to do with me — a rock from the park the first day I walked, and one from this very lake the first time he took me here "fishing." The last one on the list is from a hotel fountain where he and Mom went for their last anniversary.

These are his moments. This is his string. I hand the list to Lizzy.

While she's looking at it, I sift through the rocks. I wonder if he remembered which ones were which. He didn't label them in any way that I can tell. I catch sight of something blue underneath the rocks and push them aside to get at it. "Um, Lizzy, I think this is for you."

I push the pile toward her, and she looks at it quizzically. Then she quickly reaches her hand in and ever-so-carefully pulls out a playing card. At first all we can see is the blue design on the back of the card. Then she flips it over and gasps. It's the jack of diamonds, one of the last two cards missing from her collection. I peer closer. Written across the middle, clearly in my dad's scrawl, are the words *Expect the unexpected.*

"But how . . . how did he . . . ," she stammers, staring down at it.

I'm as freaked out as she is. At the time of the accident, Lizzy had just barely started her collection. Trying to keep my voice from shaking, I reply, "Like you said, my dad moves in mysterious ways." I can't believe I was afraid even for a second that the contents of the box would be disappointing. They are exactly right. They are perfect.

"But you were there," she cries. "I didn't even find the eight of hearts until a few weeks ago!"

"I know."

"So how did he —"

"I don't know."

"But —"

I lift the pile of rocks back into the box. "Maybe some things aren't meant to be known. Maybe they're just meant to be accepted."

"It's like magic," she says, her eyes shining. "Not the kind of magic where you pull a quarter out of a kid's ear, but *real* magic."

I nod, unable to think of any other explanation. Not letting the card out of her hand, Lizzy helps me pack everything back into our bags. I steady the boat so she can climb in, and then I undo the rope and follow. The whole ride back to the beach, Lizzy goes on about how she can't believe it with the card, and how it was really nice of my dad to include her. She's so happy, she's glowing. I'm half-listening and half-thinking about everything, and then it hits me like a ton of bricks. I know how the card got there. I know why Dad knew the box would be hard to open. I'm so shocked by the images pouring through my brain that as soon as the boat grounds on the beach, I scramble out.

Only the boat is nowhere near the beach. This slowly dawns on me when I find myself standing shoulder deep in the lake. Lizzy is leaning over the side of the boat frantically trying to get my attention.

"What just happened?" she cries out. "One second you're sitting there, and the next you turn white as a ghost and keel over the side. It was the most bizarre thing I've ever seen. Well, next to this playing card. Are you all right?"

I nod, which is all I can make myself do at this moment. My head is still busy removing layer after layer of events like those little nesting dolls where every time you take one doll apart, a smaller one is inside.

Mom and Grandma have run to the edge of the water and are waving their arms. I can hear their voices, but can't make out what they're saying. "Do you want me to help you back in?" Lizzy asks. "Take my hand."

I shake my head. "I'll walk," I tell her. "It's not too far. You'll be okay rowing?"

"I can manage," she says, shifting to the middle seat. "Are you sure you're okay? Not ten minutes ago your dad tells us to look out for each other, and the next thing I know, you've fallen overboard. How does that look?"

I want to tell her what I figured out, but I just can't do it. I want to keep the mystery of her card alive for her a little longer. I start walking toward the shore, and Lizzy rows slowly beside me. Every few steps I trip a little and have to swim. I can't believe I fell overboard. At least my bag is still safe in the boat. If Dad's letter and his list had gotten wet, I would never have forgiven myself.

"Explanation?" Mom says as I drag myself, dripping, up onto the beach.

"Can't say that I have one."

"Well, you seem to be in one piece. Did you open the box?"

I nod. "Dad said to give you this." I move closer and give her a really big hug. Even though I'm wet and have no doubt absorbed the smell of the lake, she keeps on hugging me until Lizzy clears her throat and says, "Ahem, can we please all look at my playing card?"

I move on to give Grandma her hug. I always knew how hard it was for me to lose a father, and for my mother to lose a husband, but I hadn't given much thought to how hard it must have been for her to lose a child. I hug her extra tight. I do plan on sharing with them what was in the box, but not yet. I need to sort some things out first. A *lot* of things.

As our train pulls back into Penn Station on Saturday morning, I turn to Mom and ask, "I have to go do something for a few hours, is that okay?"

"Now?" she says. "Don't you want to get settled at home first? Feed the fish?"

I shake my head. "I'm sure Mr. Muldoun didn't let them die. Or replace one without telling me."

She reddens. That's an old joke between us because Hamster died one day while I was at school, and Mom bought another fish that looked like Hamster and tried to pass it off as the real one. She didn't count on my uncanny powers of observation.

One of the conductors helps us bring our suitcases onto the platform. "How are you planning on getting where you're going?" Mom asks.

I've already figured this out. "Bus. I have exact change."

"By yourself?" Lizzy asks, tilting her head at me suspiciously.

I nod.

"You're not going to tell us where you're going?" Mom asks.

"If it's okay, I'd really rather not."

She opens her mouth to say something, but then closes it again. With an odd look that I can't quite decipher, she simply says, "Be home in time for dinner."

"I'll help you put all this stuff in a cab first," I tell them, picking up the handles of both my suitcase and my mom's. The whole time we walk through the station, Lizzy throws me sideways glances. I know she's dying to ask.

I help the driver pile all the bags in the cab, keeping only my backpack. When they're gone, I take a deep breath and walk to the corner. The bus that I need should take me within two blocks. I jingle the quarters in my pocket while I wait. This time when the bus pulls up, I know exactly what to do. I drop my quarters in the slot and take the first available seat. I glance around me. No Garlicman this time. It's a whole different crowd on a Saturday. No briefcases.

As the bus approaches my stop, I reach up to press the tape, but someone beats me to it. I follow a few people out the door, and they all turn in the opposite direction of where I'm going. A woman walks by carrying a poodle. They are wearing matching sunglasses. Lizzy would have liked to see that.

There is only one person who knew what cards Lizzy needed. And there's only one way to have put that card into the box. Without hesitating, I march up to the door and ring the bell.

When the door opens, I ask, "How long have you had the keys?"

Mr. Oswald smiles. "Come in, Jeremy. I've been expecting you."

He leads me through the now empty house and out to the patio. He takes an envelope out of his pocket and rests it in front of him on the table. It has my name printed on it. He doesn't make a move to slide it over to me.

"I've had the keys since your father passed away," he says.

"But how is that possible? My dad left them with my mom, who gave them to Harold Folgard, and he was the one who lost them."

Mr. Oswald shakes his head. "There is no Harold Folgard. Your mother sent the keys and the box to me."

Now *this* I had not expected! "What do you mean there's no Harold Folgard? Of course there is! Lizzy and I were in his office. That's how we wound up working for you!"

"You and Lizzy were in an empty office with a nameplate taped to the door."

"But the security guard . . . the policeman . . ."

"It's amazing how people will play along for a good cause. Your mailman even had a part in making sure the box arrived when your mother wasn't home so you'd take it. Even Larry the Locksmith played his part. Good ol' Larry. He's been chomping at the bit waiting for you to turn thirteen. I think he held off retiring till the day came. This whole thing has been the hardest on your mother, I think."

I stare at him in amazement. "I don't understand. You did all this for me? Why would you do that? You don't even know me. I mean, you didn't even know me before all this."

"I didn't do it," Mr. Oswald explains. "Your father did. He set this all up. He left the details up to me. The jobs you did for me — returning those pawned items — they were all legit, of course."

"But what if I hadn't written in my notebook that Lizzy found that last playing card and mentioned which two were left? How would you have known? What would Dad have left Lizzy in the box?"

"If you hadn't told me, I would have brought the conversation around to your collections. Your dad signed all fifty-two cards of the deck in the hopes that Lizzy hadn't finished the collection yet. And if she had, he asked me to find out what she would want, and to include that instead."

"When did you put it in there?"

"When James suggested you leave your bag in the car one day. I used my keys and slid the card between two edges of the wrapping paper."

I know I'm firing questions at him, but I can't help it. "How long have you known my father? Why didn't he ever mention you?"

"I met your father the same day I met you. Seven years ago."

"But I just met you a few weeks ago!"

He shakes his head. "I looked a little younger then, wore a straw hat and overalls. I'm sure you were too young to remember. Your father approached me at the 26th Street Flea Market. He admired the boxes I was selling. You weren't there with him for too long. He asked your mom to walk away with you so he could buy you a gift."

So *that's* why the first time I saw him on the steps I had that weird idea that he should be wearing a straw hat and overalls!

"Your father and I found we had a lot in common. He began putting this plan together almost as soon as he bought the box. He never told you about me so that when we did meet, you wouldn't suspect anything."

I shake my head in disbelief. "But why would Dad do this? Why wouldn't he just leave me the keys and the box?"

"Don't you know why?" he asks, leaning forward.

I shake my head.

"He did it to give you an adventure. To introduce you to people and experiences you'd never have otherwise. To get you to start thinking about life before hearing what he had to say on the subject. To work for it a little. Okay, a lot!"

I hear what Mr. Oswald is saying, but I have all these "buts" running through my head. "But how did he know we'd go to Larry's Locks or to Harold Folgard's office?"

He smiles. "Your dad took a lot of leaps of faith. He hoped that you and Lizzy would still be friends and that her determination coupled with your natural curiosity would lead you both forward. We had to make certain adjustments based on your actions. If some of the major events hadn't fallen into place, your mother was ready to nudge things in certain directions."

Who knew Mom was such a good actress?

"I hope you can forgive everyone for their role in this."

"I'm just in shock that so many people would do so much for me. And for Lizzy, too. She was in this as much as I was."

"Trust me, everyone involved got something out of 'Operation: Jeremy Fink and the Meaning of Life.'"

I laugh. "That's what you called it?"

He laughs, and nods.

But then something else hits me, and I stop laughing. "If my dad planned this whole elaborate thing, he really must have believed he wouldn't be here."

Mr. Oswald sighs deeply. "I think he did. And he wanted to make your thirteenth birthday unforgettable."

"It was definitely unforgettable. This whole summer has been."

"Good," Mr. Oswald says, pushing back his chair and getting to his feet. "Now that my job is done, I'm supposed to catch the next plane down to Florida."

I jump up. "You're really going? That wasn't just part of the story?"

He smiles. "I'm really going. In fact, you just caught me."

I frown. "But what if you hadn't been here? How would I have known all this?"

He picks up the envelope with my name on it and hands it to me. "It's all in here. Along with a little parting gift from me to you."

That familiar knot forms in my throat again. "I don't know how to thank you for everything you did."

He puts his hand on my shoulder, and we walk inside

and toward the door. "Send me a postcard now and then, will you? Lizzy, too. I wrote my address in there."

"Sure."

I step out onto the front steps, expecting him to follow. He doesn't though. He stays inside, one hand on the door. "And Jeremy?"

"Yes?"

"Thank you."

"You're thanking *me*? What for?"

"For letting me see the world through your eyes for a few weeks. You have great things ahead of you."

I know I'm too old for such things now, but I step back inside and give Mr. Oswald a hug. Then I turn and run down the stairs before I get even mushier. When I hear Mr. Oswald close the door, I turn back. Next to his porch are some small shrubs with white rocks surrounding them. I pick up a rock and shove it deep in my pocket. *Rock #1: From the day I realized that love is stronger than death and that people you barely know can amaze you, 13.*

As I walk to the bus stop, something Mom said right after the box first arrived floats back to me. She said things can only happen the way they happen. It seemed so obvious at the time that I didn't pay much attention to it. But somehow now, after all the twists and turns it took to get me from that day hanging out at my uncle's store until right now, it suddenly makes sense. A sort of peace that I don't think I've felt before washes over me. Also a feeling of control over my life. Each choice I made, or Lizzy made, was based on who we were or what we wanted. That's all I ever have to keep doing, and not be so worried about choosing right or wrong, because there really isn't a right or wrong, there's only what IS. And if I don't like the outcome, I just make another choice.

Anyway, why not start now? The subway would get me home much faster than the bus. There's a station a block away from here; I remember seeing it as the bus drove by. I start to get a little nervous as I get closer, but I keep walking. A few minutes later, I'm checking the subway map on the wall just like we did that first time. I'll have to change trains in the middle, so really this is like *two* subway rides. I use up the rest of my quarters on a MetroCard, and swipe it through like a pro. No need to rely on superstitious Yankees fans today.

As I wait for the train, I decide that when I tell Lizzy the story, I'll leave out the part about Mr. Oswald putting her card in the box. I don't want to take that bit of magic away from her.

When I'm seated and the train starts to move again, I open Mr. Oswald's envelope. I pull out the letter and see at a glance that it's full of the information he just told me. A small yellow envelope is attached to the bottom with a paper clip. Inside the small envelope is a thin piece of cardboard. Stuck in the center, covered in a protective layer of plastic, is a stamp. My heart starts pounding in my ears. It's my dad's stamp! The one he'd been looking for his whole life! I turn the cardboard over. There's a note.

Jeremy,

I came across this last year. I'd always kept an eye out for it in your dad's memory. I'd like you to have it. I've already asked your mother for *permission to give it to you. It should cover the cost of college and maybe even graduate school if invested wisely. Congratulations! You're a philatelist now!*

Your friend,

Mr. O

My eyes burn with tears. I will never have another day like this one.

At that moment, the subway pulls into the station where I'm supposed to switch. I tuck the fragile stamp back in the small envelope and put everything carefully in my backpack. That stamp, that tiny piece of printed paper, is my future. How amazing is that?

When I get out onto the platform, someone is playing a radio. The voice sounds familiar, but I don't think I've heard the song before. A few people clear away, and I realize it's not a radio, it's that guitar player who looks like he should be playing football instead. He sure gets around!

I move closer so I can hear better. When he's done with his song, I drop a dollar in his open guitar case.

"Thanks, kid," he says as he bends over his guitar to tighten a string.

"Um, can I ask you a question?"

He looks up at me. "Sure. What's on your mind?"

"How come you play down here, in the subways? I mean, you're really good."

He smiles. "This is where the best sound is, dude. The acoustics in this place are unreal. It's all about the sound. You know, like that guy from the Grateful Dead said, music is what life sounds like. You know, the music of the spheres and all that."

I shake my head. "I'm not sure what you mean."

A few people have gathered around and are listening.

He explains. "The universe resonates to certain musical vibrations. All the stars and planets revolve in harmony with it. You know, like one big cosmic dance. When I play, I'm a part of that. When you listen, you're a part of it, too." He finishes tightening the string and gives it a twang to test it out. "Any requests?"

One guy yells out, " 'Free Bird'!" A lady yells, " 'Bridge Over Troubled Water'!" I won't get to hear what he decides to play though, because my train is here.

My train is here. I like the sound of that. My train is here, and it's going to take me home. I'm feeling so brave, maybe I'll surprise Mom tonight and have cauliflower or asparagus or — cringe — *beets* at dinner.

Nah. Like Dad said, life is short. I'll keep eating dessert first.

I reach into my backpack and pull out the packet of Fun Dip that Lizzy gave me for my birthday. As I dip the sugar stick into the packet of blue sugar, a little girl sitting next to me pulls on my T-shirt sleeve. She looks about five, and is wearing a yellow dress.

"Can I have some?"

I glance over at her mother, but all her attention is focused on the screaming toddler in her lap. I hold out the sugar packet, and the little girl studies it for a second. Then she licks her finger, sticks it in, and swishes it around. A few weeks ago, I would have thought that was gross, her being a stranger and me not knowing where her hands have been and all. But now I know we're all part of one big cosmic family, so it doesn't bother me.

Oh, who am I kidding? I still think it's gross. She sticks the whole finger in her mouth and slurps off the sugar. When she smiles, her teeth are now blue. She and her mother stand up to get off at the next stop. Before she leaves, I slip the whole packet into her hand.

With four more stops to go, I take out the stamp again. I hope Dad's seeing this right now. If he used to do a little dance in the streets when he found an old record, or a comic, imagine what he'd do over this — his ultimate treasure. I bet it would rival the music of the spheres. I'll just have to do it for him. But not in a grass skirt this time.

The people on the train with me don't know it, but in my head I'm dancing.